TRUTH *or* KILL

TWISTED LEGENDS COLLECTION

A.C. KRAMER

Truth or Kill

Editing by: Outthink Editing, LLC
Proofreading by: Katie Schmahl, Erica Karwoski, & Jean Bachen
Cover Design: Raven Designs
Cover Photography: Regina Wamba
Published by: Ninja Newt Publishing, LLC

Print Edition
ISBN: 978-1-68530-111-8

Dedication

To those who believe in the magic of
unconventional love.

And to Bethany, Katie, Erica, and Jean, without
whom this book wouldn't have been possible.

Welcome...

Ten authors invite you to join us in the
Twisted Legends Collection.

These stories are a dark, twisted reimagining of infamous legends well-known throughout the world. Some are retellings, others are nods to those stories that cause a chill to run down your spine.

Each book may be a standalone, but they're all connected by the lure of a legend.

We invite you to venture into the unknown, and delve into the darkness with us, one book at a time.

TWISTED LEGENDS
AUTHOR SERIES

The COLLECTION

Vengeance of The Fallen - Dani René

Truth or Kill - A.C. Kramer

Departed Whispers - J Rose

The Labyrinth of Savage Shadows - Murphy Wallace

Hell Gate - Veronica Eden

Blood & Vows - Amanda Richardson

Under the Cover of Darkness - Emma Luna

Reckless Covenant - Lilith Roman

Bane & Bound - Crimson Syn

The Ripper - Alexandra Silva

Urban Legend
KILLSWITCH

Welcome to the Twisted Legends Collection.
Where urban legends are reimagined.
And darkness reigns.

Truth or Kill is a unique take on a more recent urban legend—Killswitch. Killswitch is a video game that self-destructs at the end, removing any and all evidence that it ever existed.

Many gamers still question whether or not it actually happened. Because there's no proof that it was ever really played. Some even say it originated with a story, not a true game.

So what happens when you start a game that ends up being real?
Flip the page to find out.
But only if you're ready for a bloody ride.
Because this game is dark. It's twisted. It's riddled with *death*.

There are no heroes here.
Just sharp blades and sadistic worship.
Blood is a currency.
Life is a privilege.
And the stakes have never been higher.

The game is set.
It's time to play…

Prologue
KAGE

Once upon a time, a trio of princes lived in a tower made of glittering diamonds. They were untouchable. Wealthy as sin. The true monarchs of the world.

Until they fell.

Not of their own doing, but from the greed and deceit of others.

They were reduced to nothing but parentless peasants. Forgotten and left to survive on their own in a dark world of politics and lies.

Their legacy has been replaced by a brotherhood of others.

Their memory is no longer discussed.

They've been forgotten and ignored and dismissed from the society they once owned.

But sins are tricky complications. Some provide ample warmth and glorious indulgences. Others have a way of darkening future paths.

Some sins require retribution.

Which brings me to my purpose.

I'm not a man of morals or goodness.

I'm a man seeking revenge for crimes against a bejeweled dynasty.

The elders will pay.

Their children will suffer.

And their societal futures will be dethroned by death.

Consider me the virtual Grim Reaper, for I wear the cloak and carry the scythe.

This game is all about truth.

Lie… and you just might die.

One
SYDNEY

FRESH AIR STREAMS THROUGH THE CAR, QUIETING THE turmoil in my soul. I can almost pretend that I'm outside lying in a forest of solitude, alone with the peaceful quiet of nature.

But then Becca's giggle infiltrates my fantasy, drawing my gaze to the front of the car.

Her lips are moving against Preston's ear while he navigates the single-lane road through the trees. I can only imagine the wicked promises she's giving him right now.

Landon smirks beside me, obviously aware of their little game.

Not that they're being all that discreet.

"What happens on spring break stays on spring break," Becca had announced before we all piled into Preston's four-by-four SUV. It's more of a sports car than a proper off-roading vehicle. Fortunately, we don't appear to be heading toward any dirt roads. Just some pompous estate called *The Lodge* that's located deep inside the woods.

I lost my cellular signal ten minutes ago, something that thrilled me and elicited a deep sigh from Becca. She lives and breathes social media.

Not me.

I prefer escaping reality among the trees and the wilderness, hence the reason I agreed to this trip.

However, her current antics are making me regret my decision to join her on this venture.

Because I'm probably going to end up sharing a room with her and Preston now.

Or worse, Landon.

I'm starting to think Becca only invited me this week to entertain him while she indulged his best friend.

Not. Happening.

I would sooner drag a blanket off into the woods and sleep outside.

Wouldn't be the first time in my life and certainly won't be the last time, either.

Becca giggles again and Preston shakes his head. "Stop distracting me."

"Oh, this isn't me being distracting," she replies in a sultry voice, her plump lips skimming his neck.

"That would require my mouth to be in other areas."

"Feel free to provide a demonstration," Landon drawls. "I won't mind watching."

Charming, I think, just as impressed with him as always.

Landon Matterhorn and Preston Michaels are replicas of each other with their ash-blond hair, pale skin, and light-colored eyes. They're both over six feet tall with aristocratic features and bank accounts containing unfathomable amounts of money, too.

Yet they aren't related in any way, just members of the same elite social circle.

Becca's also part of their world.

All of their fathers operate separate wings of the massive Covington Industries, which is the largest tech company in the world.

Computers. Cell phones. Gaming software and equipment. Television streaming. Securities. They cover it all, and each of their dads manages a unique piece.

Thirteen branches in total.

And I'm sharing a car with three of the company's proverbial heirs.

A unique experience, one that often makes me feel like an outsider looking in, but such is life.

I'm the scholarship kid.

They're the rich kids.

Something that becomes even more apparent—

as though it weren't already—as a sprawling estate unfolds before us.

The Lodge isn't an adequate name.

More like *The Palace.*

It's surrounded by lush green landscape and framed by mountains of trees behind it. There's a large lake off to the side as well, with a dock of fancy-looking boats. No canoes here that I can see, even though that would be far more appropriate for the wilderness.

Maybe I can find one stowed away somewhere.

The Lodge has a row of balconies wrapping around the building, the decorative wood siding the only "cabin-like" thing about it. There's a series of stone steps leading up to the main double doors, all of which are framed by tall windowpanes interspersed with wooden logs. All that glass is what gives the place a palatial vibe more than a lodge appearance.

I'm not surprised at all when two men dressed in suits meet us out front in the large circular drive before the building.

There's a fountain in the middle with three angel-like males dancing with crowns upon their heads in the center. I stare at it for a moment, admiring the somewhat gruesome embrace. Because they're all holding knife-like tools in their hands.

An ominous statue, I think.

Not that anyone else is paying attention. They're too busy dictating to the two valets.

"Bags are in the trunk," Preston says. "Park this in the garage, not outside. I'm not dealing with leaves and shit on my car."

"Of course, sir," the younger of the two men replies. This one appears to be our age. The other is maybe midtwenties. Both with dark hair and matching eyes. Definitely my type more than the twin Ken dolls.

Not that I'm here for that.

I'm here to escape for a few days, breathe some fresh air, and just… relax.

There are only six more weeks of classes, then I'm done with Anton University. If only I knew what to do *after* graduation.

I have a few options.

Options I'll be considering this week.

While enjoying the scenery and calming my mind. Hopefully, I'll have a better direction by the end.

"Ready, babe?" Landon asks as he wraps his arm around my shoulders.

I frown. "Uh, yeah." I take a step forward, trying to dislodge him from my side, but he moves with me and guides me right past the two suit-clad males. One of them smirks as though amused.

Well, that makes one of us, I think sourly.

Fucking Becca.

I should have known that she had ulterior motives for this last-minute invite.

"Oh, hey, do you have spring break plans?" she asked me yesterday after we ran into each other on campus. "Because if not, I'm going with some friends up to this cabin in the woods. My suite has an extra bedroom, if you want to come."

We aren't exactly friends so much as teammates. Well, *former* teammates since we just finished our final season together in November.

We met freshman year, and her straightforward approach to life appealed to me.

She lives with her sorority sisters in a mansion on campus, while I live in the resident apartments reserved for upperclassmen. Two very different worlds.

And yet, here I stand in the center of hers.

Fascinating how that works.

Landon's arm feels heavy on my shoulder as we enter the reception area, his touch a little too familiar for my taste.

The moment Becca enters behind us, I spin away from him to face her. "This place is gorgeous," I tell her without even bothering to look around. But the wood floor and paneling seem to confirm my assessment. "How did you find it?"

"Oh, we were invited," she says with a wave of

her hand. "Covington stuff."

My eyebrows rise. "What?"

She merely smiles. "Don't worry. I ran it by my dad. It's cool that you're here. And as I said, I have the extra room anyway."

"Yep. You're one of us for the week," Landon says, sliding his arm around my waist this time instead of across my shoulders. "And I have some extra space in my bed, if you—"

"You're here!" a high-pitched voice squeals, cutting off the invitation Landon was just issuing against my ear.

I cringe and move away from him again, not just because of his forwardness but also because of the blonde Barbie doll bounding toward us.

Gretchen Walton.

Yet another branch of the Covington empire.

Had I known that this would be a reunion of heirs, I would have passed on the invite.

Becca shrieks in excitement and engulfs the blonde in a hug, their two bodies bouncing in a way that has both Landon and Preston smirking.

I glance around the reception area, searching for an escape.

And meet a pair of striking green irises.

The color of the forest, I marvel, instantly drawn to those gorgeous eyes. The face that goes along with it is rather stunning as well. Sharp cheekbones, a square jaw dusted in a dark five o'clock shadow, and long black lashes.

His full lips curl in welcome.

Or perhaps in amusement at my open staring.

But given this environment and the hell I apparently just entered, I'm not sure that I care about my open admiration.

I much prefer this dark-haired god of a man to Landon.

Not that I'll do anything about it. I'll probably just end up hiding in the woods this whole week while the heirs of Covington Industries all do whatever it is they're planning to do here.

More excitement unfolds in the lobby as two more men arrive, both of whom appear to be good friends with Preston and Landon.

I use the distraction to wander over to the desk. "I don't suppose I can get a key to my friend's room and go hide?" I ask the good-looking male.

"Only if you're on the reservation, I'm afraid," he replies, his deep voice matching the sexy exterior.

I sigh. "No. I'm a last-minute guest."

"Ah, well, then no, I'm sorry Ms....?"

"You can just call me Sydney."

"Well, then I'm sorry, Ms. Sydney. I can't give you a key yet."

"Just Sydney," I correct him. "And I figured that would be the case." I lean against the reception desk, watching as three more people come down the grand staircase leading to the third floor above. I'm guessing all the bedrooms are up there, as the building didn't appear to be larger than four levels from the outside. And the balconies wrapped around the middle, so the bedrooms are likely two stories tall, just like this lobby.

Opulent.

Expensive.

And definitely not the camping experience I anticipated.

"Do you have any canoes?" I wonder aloud, glancing back at the handsome receptionist.

"Canoes?" he echoes.

"Yes. You know, long boats that you use paddles to operate?"

"I know what a canoe is, Sydney."

"Okay," I say slowly, torn between liking the way he said my name and irritated by the condescension in his tone. "Do you have one here that I can borrow?"

"Trying to escape already?" he asks, his tone shifting from patronizing to amusing in a flash.

I frown. "I saw the pond outside and thought it might be fun to explore."

"It's a lake," he replies, his dimples appearing on a soft smile. "And no, we only have motorized boats."

My lips twist to the side. "I see. So this isn't a real lodge at all, just a castle in the woods."

He chuckles. "Yeah, that's accurate."

My excitement for the week deflates in a breath. "Are there at least hiking trails?"

"A few," he admits, his eyes smiling.

"Thank fuck," I mutter. "Can I at least swim in the lake?"

He cocks a brow. "You want to go for a swim? It's, like, forty degrees outside."

I shrug. "Just wondering if it's an option."

He looks me over, intrigue flashing in his features. "You're definitely not like the others here, are you?" While it's phrased as a question, I suspect he's just musing aloud.

I glance at the gathering in the lobby before looking at him again. "I'm taking that as a compliment."

"You should," he murmurs, those dimples flashing again. "What's your last name, Sydney?"

"Seems unfair to give you that when I don't even know your first name," I point out, looking down at his black suit jacket and the dark dress shirt beneath. He isn't wearing a tie like the two men were outside. Instead, his top two buttons are unfastened, giving me a teasing glimpse of a tattoo below his throat. He has another peeking out from beneath his suit jacket along the top of his hand.

He claimed I wasn't like the others behind me, and I could say the same about him. His realness makes him that much more attractive.

I would much prefer his arm around me over Landon's.

"Kage," he murmurs. "You can call me Kage."

"Kage," I repeat, evaluating him again. "I like it." Not just the name, but the man, too.

His smile grows. "Yeah?" His gaze runs over me again. "I think I like *it*, too."

Someone clears their throat behind me, causing me to look back at Preston and Landon. *Great*. Of course they would be the ones to interrupt my fun.

"Aren't you a little underdressed for working here?" a female voice asks, making me frown at Kage. He still has on a jacket, so I'm not sure why—

"Oh, stop it, Gretch," Becca says with a laugh. "That's Syd. We played volleyball together."

"Oh, riiight," the girl replies. "I didn't recognize her in… well… you know. *Sorry*, Syd."

I blink, realizing that her commentary about wardrobe was directed at me, not Kage.

I glance down at my jeans and sweater before turning to look at the blonde bitch beside Becca. "Didn't we take Psych 101 together last year?" I ask her casually, running my gaze up and down her lanky form. I suppose some people would call her model-like. "Oh, no, my bad. You just remind me of a case study. *Sorry,* Gretch." I smile sweetly before looking at Becca, completely ignoring Blonde Bitch's dropped jaw. "Thank you for inviting me. This place is amazing."

A complete and utter lie.

This place is a fucking nightmare.

If my phone worked, I would call a cab for a ride home right now. But something tells me I can't order one this far out in the woods.

Which means I'm stuck here for the next week with all these people.

Awesome.

"Can I have your invitation, please?" Kage asks from behind me, his tone the epitome of formal.

"Yeah, because you don't recognize me," Preston jokes, chuckling with Landon. But he pulls a card from his pocket and slides it across the counter anyway.

Kage doesn't smile, his dark eyes hard as he opens the card, reads whatever is inside, and nods. "Welcome to The Lodge, Mr. Michaels." He turns his focus to Landon. "And your invitation, sir?"

Landon grunts and slides a similar card across. I catch a few words at the top of it. *You're cordially invited to—*

Kage takes the card out of sight before I can finish

reading and slides a pair of keys across the counter. "Welcome to The Lodge, Mr. Matterhorn," he says, reminding me a bit of a robot with his recycled greeting. "You're in room 202, Mr. Michaels. And you're in room 204 across the hall, Mr. Matterhorn."

Landon takes his key. "You hear that, Syd?" he says.

"I'm not deaf," I tell him. "So yes, I heard it. Would you like me to repeat it?"

He chuckles and winks at me. "Love your sarcasm, babe."

Gretchen's eyes—which are a little too blue and likely enhanced by contacts—narrow at me.

"And your invitation, Miss?" Kage prompts, sounding robotic again. I much prefer his deep voice from earlier. But I'm also oddly pleased that he's not using that tone for the others.

Becca pulls it from her purse. Her card isn't folded, allowing me to read more of it than the other one.

Or I can read the final line, anyway. *Assuming you survive.*

"What?" I snatch the card before she can hand it over, and read the contents.

You're cordially invited to attend this year's spring break retreat at The Lodge.

It's a highly exclusive experience guaranteed to

redefine your future.
Assuming you survive.

I blink. "You invited me to some sort of corporate retreat?" I ask her.

She shrugs. "It's not all work, Syd. Just a few bonding exercises."

"You won't have to attend," Gretchen adds. "You know, since you're not a Covington heir."

"Oh, that's too bad," I deadpan.

"Actually, all Lodge guests are required to attend tonight's opening ceremony," Preston says before I can properly celebrate being dismissed from whatever the fuck this is. "Since Becca invited a friend, she gets to play, too."

He smiles at me like he's just given me a gift. "Yay me," I say, handing over the card to a smirking Kage. He seems to be the only one here who understands my actual sarcasm because Becca beams at my response and Landon grins, too.

Why did I agree to this, again? I wonder. *Right. Because I had nowhere else to go.*

Most people went home or on trips with friends for spring break.

My home doesn't exist.

So. Here I am. On a *retreat* with a "friend."

"Here is your key, Ms. Edington," Kage says, breaking up his robotic routine a little. "And here's a key for your guest, too. Room 212 at the end of the hall."

Becca takes them both. "Two-bedroom suite, right?"

"Yes, ma'am," he replies.

"Good." She hands me a key. "Send up our bags."

"Yes, ma'am," Kage repeats.

"Thank you," I say to him.

He smiles, but it's not like his smile from before. "Enjoy your stay, Miss."

Ouch, I think. *That's a clear dismissal.* Not that I can blame him. He's working, after all. And I'm just a guest.

Sighing, I follow the others up the stairs toward the spacious corridor that leads to all the rooms.

I was right—they're all two-story interiors, as evidenced by the wide-open space and glittering glass skylights over my head.

Becca leads the way to our suite after Landon and Preston disappear into their own rooms. The others all stayed downstairs.

She uses her key to open the door and reveals a sprawling living area framed by two floors of windows and a balcony.

A kitchen area sits off to one side, along with a dining table with twelve chairs, and a hallway that I imagine leads to the bedrooms. Only there's another hallway on the opposite side. Maybe there's a study in here, too?

"Perfect," Becca says, her sigh telling me she approves. "And hey, I'm sorry I didn't tell you about the retreat part. But seriously, it's only a minor thing. We're here to have fun and chill. The bonding exercises are just some weird tradition our parents want to create." She rolls her eyes. "I'm sure tonight will be formal. Then it'll be a party from there."

I nod. "I'll just go live on the balcony for a week." I point to the area in question. "So don't worry about me. I'll be fine."

"Oh, I think Landon may try to coax you into venturing over to his own balcony." She waggles her brows. "And his bed."

I snort at that. "I'm not interested."

"Syd, he's Landon Matterhorn. *Everyone* is interested."

I shrug. "Not me."

"He's just going to take that as a challenge."

"It's one he'll lose," I promise her.

"We'll see," she returns, her gray-blue eyes sparkling.

I don't bother commenting. Because we wouldn't be *seeing* anything.

I wander over to the windows to take in the scenery of the mountains outside. I've always loved northern Maine, and this view doesn't disappoint.

It certainly isn't camping.

But it's not a bad way to experience nature, either.

All right, this isn't that bad, I decide, stepping through the glass doors and inhaling the sweet air. *Not bad at all.*

Two
SYDNEY

NOPE. I WAS WRONG. THIS IS FUCKING TERRIBLE.

Every branch of Covington Industries is in this room.

Not the parents, but their heirs.

All thirteen of them.

And then me.

No one else brought a guest, only Becca. It's like attending a family reunion with a new boyfriend, except Becca and I aren't even close to dating. We're teammates. We occasionally shared a hotel room at our travel meets. That's the extent of our relationship, yet I'm sitting next to her now like some sort of stray she picked up off the streets.

I suppose it beats accepting Landon's invitation to share the love seat with him.

But as Becca's focus is entirely on Preston, this isn't much better.

I blow out a breath and listen as they all socialize, catching up on their current academic pursuits and their societal bullshit.

They're not all the same ages, but they're close. From what I've gathered, this retreat is designed for the heirs who are in college. Some of them are the oldest children in their families. Others are the youngest. And a few are middle children.

But this is the first year for *The Lodge* experience.

The excitement in the air is palpable. I'm not sure why Preston said I need to be here. It seems like he's just torturing me for fun.

Or maybe he claimed my presence is needed for Landon.

At least there's wine. I swap my empty glass for a new one and relax into the plush sofa. It's made of soft, beige-colored leather, which I suppose complements the wooden fixtures in the room.

There are no windows in here.

Just a large screen dominating one side of the room, and it's not the type that's pulled down from the ceiling, but a legit screen built into the wall. So we're in a theater of sorts, except it feels more like a lounge with the bar at the back and the arrangement of sofas throughout the wooden-floored space.

But we are all angled toward the screen.

So I suppose that just makes this a posh theater room.

There are little end tables as well, which almost everyone is using for their glasses. However, there's also a remote controller on each surface, which are about the only items in this room that intrigue me—more than the wine, anyway—because I'm wondering what sort of game one would play in here.

"Ladies and gentlemen," a voice booms over the loudspeaker. "Please take your seats. We will begin the opening ceremonies in three minutes."

Opening ceremonies, I repeat with a mental snort. *What is this? The Olympics?*

I drink my wine while I wait. Meanwhile, everyone else seems to be tittering with excitement as they find their seats.

I'm more excited to get this over with so I can run away.

Maybe I'll go on a midnight walk or find a boat to play in. Because it's clear Becca intends to invite Preston to her place. We may be sharing this couch, but she's leaning so far over the edge of it toward him that she's more in his lap than on the cushion.

He chuckles at whatever she whispers in his ear, his blue eyes smoldering with intent as he glances at her. "Later."

"Yes," she agrees.

And that's my cue to either find earplugs for tonight or locate a new bed, I decide, finishing off my wine. I should probably switch to water.

I stand to find some, when the room goes dark. Not just dark, but pitch black, leaving me blind. I fall back onto the couch, blinking from the sudden disruption in my vision.

Music starts to play, the sound eliciting several cheers from the room.

I recognize the tune, but it takes me a minute to place it. *Covington Industries' theme song.*

Because yeah, that's a thing.

They use it on their commercials for all their branding. It's this vivid techno beat that echoes and drums through the air, reminding me a bit of a lion roaring to take command of his pride.

Probably because there's a subtle roar underlining the song.

Fortunately, it only lasts for about twenty seconds.

Then the screen comes to life, displaying the famous CI symbol with a set of three golden crowns swirling around it.

Technology kings, I muse, wishing I had more wine now.

"A little over a century ago, a forward-thinking family developed a concept that would irrevocably change the world." The voice coming through the surround sound is low and soothing, building suspense for a story everyone in this room already knows. Myself included.

"A universe of technology was soon born, the focus on shared programming across concepts. They started small with three primary branches—computers, video games, and cell phones. But they soon grew into so much more. Thirteen concepts arose. Thirteen branches. Thirteen focal points all housed under one umbrella."

Well, this guy certainly possesses a flair for the dramatic. He should have gone into sports commentating.

Maybe that's why they called it the opening ceremonies?

"Founded in technology and led by a brilliant mind, Covington Industries soon became one of the most well-respected companies in history," he continues. "They are the pioneers for technology, the organization everyone wants to be, and the company everyone wants to work for. And you all are their kings and queens, the families that run the empire, the heirs who will redefine this company and push it into a new era."

"Hear, hear!" Preston calls out.

Several of the others reply with similar comments, toasting one another.

Yeah, I really don't need to be here.

"Are you ready to begin your journey? To prove your worth as the company's heirs?" the voice asks. "Because we're about to put your dedication on trial. Take you to your limits. Teach you what true camaraderie is about. You will be pushed to thrive. You will be thoroughly tested. And some of you may not survive."

A few chuckles echo through the room, making the hairs along my arms rise.

Because that sounded ominous to me, not humorous. What kind of company says they're going to test limits in this way?

"Only the loyal will continue. Only those most honorable among you will succeed. And only those who understand the values of trust and mutual respect will be elevated to the next stage."

He pauses, his words making me shiver.

No one says a word, everyone listening intently.

"So we invite you to play a game. One born in truth and discovery. The rules are simple. You'll be asked a question. You can either choose to share your truths among one another, thus embracing the value of trust. Or you can pick a weak link to remove from the game."

Another dramatic halt.

"This weak link should be someone you don't feel is worthy of your trust, someone you worry might not be the team player we require here at Covington Industries." The voice halts again, allowing that to sink in.

Well, at least I'll be removed from this insanity quickly, I think. A good thing because I need a glass of water.

"The game will begin in five minutes. Be ready. Be truthful. Be trusting. And together, you'll pave the way to a future of true greatness."

Silence falls over the room.

Ominous.

Quiet.

Cold.

The lights flicker, but they're dim now, the focus entirely on the icon swirling along that screen.

This is an intermission of sorts, as evidenced by the waiters entering the room with freshly filled trays.

I grab a water this time, my throat dry. It's on the tip of my tongue to ask if I can leave now, but the intensity in the room has me sitting still and sipping my cool drink instead.

Five minutes feels like five hours, the chatter in the room a dull hum that's mostly filled with curious inquisitions regarding the upcoming game.

I just want it to start so I can be removed.

"This is going to be interesting," Becca says, her

words for Preston, not for me. "I wonder what we'll learn about each other."

He glances at her. "A lot, I imagine." His tone doesn't match her flirtatious one, his expression harder than before. It seems the notorious playboy has a serious side.

Perhaps he also picked up on the ominous tone of the game.

Or maybe he's just competitive.

I don't really know Landon or Preston very well. I see them around campus sometimes, but we've only met a handful of times through Becca. Which is what makes Landon's familiarity with me so strange. He clearly thinks I'm the type to just spread my legs for him because of his last name. Becca must assume that, too.

These people live in their own little realm of existence.

Of course, there are a lot of women on campus who would do exactly what Landon expects. So I can't truly fault him for his assumption—it's an accurate one for most of the Anton University population.

The lights go out again, the crowns on the screen spiraling as that damn song begins again.

Except it's a little different now. It's faster, the tempo reminding me of a rave—something the flashing icon on the screen seems to echo.

I close my eyes, willing it to end, and sigh when everything goes black.

"You are about to begin the first sequence. Remember, when you begin the game, there is no going back. You're all in this together. For better or for worse. Choose your moves wisely. And don't forget, the key to success lies in your own truths."

The number three appears on the screen. It dissolves into a two and then into a one. The company logo appears and goes up in flames in the next moment, the graphic so realistic that my lips part. It eats through the screen, burning all the way to the edges until a swirl of darkness takes its place front and center.

Letters begin to spill from the image.

T

R

U

T

H

They fly around the screen, the charging sound of an engine revving as the letters form the word *TRUTH.*

It pulsates once and dissolves into another fire, this one burning brighter to the point of blinding us all.

I shut my eyes, hiding from the screen as an

electrical hum fills the air.

When I look again, the screen is blinking like it's waiting for someone to type a password.

Silence overwhelms us all as we wait.

A minute passes.

Then two.

Which turns into another five.

"Okay..." Becca finally says. "What now?"

Everyone shuffles in their seats, the blinking key the only source of light in the room.

"The controller." Preston speaks as he reaches for the one on the table beside him. "I think we just need to press—"

The screen comes alive with his name in bold letters. *Preston Michaels.* Beneath it is the wing of Covington Industries that he owns, along with his father's name and the expected date of succession.

It doesn't surprise me at all that their lives are fully outlined in this manner.

A series of cards appears next, each of them labeled with a number. There are seven total. Then a script scrawls across the screen, the voice reading it aloud as each word appears.

"Pick your fate, Mr. Michaels. What card would you like?"

Preston relaxes into his chair with the remote in hand. "Do I say it aloud or pick a number?"

"Either," the voice replies, making my eyes

widen. *This is interactive now?*

"Then what's the purpose of the video game controller?" Preston asks.

"Pick a card and you may find out," the voice replies.

"So they can hear us," Becca whispers.

"Indeed we can, Ms. Edington," the voice confirms. "We can see you, too."

Because that's not creepy at all, I think, sipping my water again.

"Let's go with card six," Preston says, confidence underlining his tone.

"Excellent choice, Mr. Michaels." The card begins to spin, and a video of a soccer game starts playing.

I frown. *What?*

A player is running down the field, weaving in and out of the others, showing off his juggling skills, and kicks the ball straight into the net.

Another video starts soon after, showing a similar sequence.

A third follows.

And then a fourth.

Until the whole thing fizzles and burns into a scene showing Preston Michaels's father talking to a man in a suit on the sidelines.

"Mr. Michaels, are you aware of this conversation? Or what they're discussing?" the voice asks.

Preston remains silent for a beat before saying, "Yes."

"Good. Tell us what it was," the voice demands. "Unless... you don't trust us to know the truth. In which case..." The video shifts to reveal all of us in the crowd, making my lips part. *They weren't kidding about being able to see us.* "Use the joystick on your controller, Mr. Michaels."

A target appears on the screen, similar to that of a toy gun.

"If there is anyone you don't want to hear your answer, shoot them, and they'll be removed from the game."

My eyes widen. *Shoot them?*

"The game is called Truth or Kill, and the rules are simple. Either give us a response, or remove the person you don't trust to hear that response."

The silence that follows is deafening.

"This exercise is about sharing all your sins, your history, your secrets, with everyone around you. To tie you all together via an impenetrable bond. To create an air of understanding and trust. If there is someone you don't have faith in, that person needs to be removed."

Well, fuck.

I'm clearly not meant to play this game at all.

"This is hardly a controversial secret," Preston responds. "My father was merely discussing drug testing with the commissioner. He procured an exemption for me."

"Because you were doing drugs yourself?" the voice asks, a new video playing. This one showing Preston scoring another goal. "Did you use performance-enhancing drugs, Mr. Michaels?"

"No," he says. "My father simply disagreed with the invasion of privacy."

"I'll caution you not to lie, Mr. Michaels." The screen appears, and the target is zeroed in on Preston now. "We control this game, not you."

"I'm not lying." Preston doesn't appear fazed at all by the trigger over his face. He doesn't even blink as a red dot forms against his forehead. "If you don't believe me, remove me."

Deathly quiet follows.

The sound of a gunshot fires through the air.

I nearly fall off the couch.

Only to freeze as a flurry of confetti flutters down from the ceiling.

"Well done, Mr. Michaels!" the voice exclaims.

Applause follows, the echo reverberating through the speakers.

"Now that was more of a practice question, but it served as a good introduction," the voice continues. "All right, we can really begin now. Everyone, pick up the controller closest to you."

Becca reaches around me for the one on the table beside me. I don't bother to fight her for it, as my goal is to get the fuck out of this room as soon as possible.

Because why in the ever-loving hell would I want to play a game called Truth or Kill? Especially when I'm clearly the odd woman out in this room.

No fucking thank you.

"Good. Now, Mr. Michaels, spin the crown to decide who goes next."

A golden crown appears, and Preston selects it with his cursor. The crown begins spiraling around the video of the room similar to how the target moved, only this is more erratic and dizzying.

It lands on the couch in front of us, selecting Gretchen.

"Ah, Ms. Walton." A new page opens to display her accolades, similar to Preston's, only she's not noted for succession because apparently she has an older brother.

Nine numbered boxes appear next.

She immediately selects the third one.

Images of her at nightclubs start rolling across the screen. She's dressed scantily in each one, usually with a drink in hand or sitting on a man's lap.

I recognize some of those males as ones in this room.

The photos increase in eroticism, making Landon snicker.

"Is the point to show everyone my tits?" she asks, sounding bored.

"No, Ms. Walton. The point is to share your past. Name everyone in this room that you've fucked." The target appears again. "Unless there's someone you wish to eliminate first?"

I hold my breath, hoping she picks me.

But I'm also slightly terrified by the prospect of being *shot*.

I know she's considering it as she moves the trigger around. Except she starts using it to point out men she's fucked, saying their names as she goes along.

There are only four women in this room—me, Becca, Gretchen, and a girl named Courtney. Gretchen doesn't name any of us.

But she calls out six of the ten males before landing on Preston. She glances over the back of her couch, not at him but at Becca, as she names him as her seventh conquest.

My lips part at the vindictive move.

She could have chosen to remove me from the room and avoided having to answer—or that's my understanding of the rules, anyway.

However, she didn't even consider it.

Because she *wanted* to boast about her

experiences to the room.

And hurt Becca.

The slight gasp beside me tells me it worked.

There's no time for responses, as the crown swirls again, this time landing on Brayden Manchester.

I don't know him, as he doesn't attend Anton University, but I know of him. His father runs the cellular branch.

And apparently, Brayden raped a girl in high school—a new fun fact I learn from this fucked-up game.

The video only shows the smiling girl, a recording I imagine was captured prior to Brayden's crimes.

He admits to the room that his father covered it all up with the private school officials. And he's very unapologetic about it.

Note to self: Stay the fuck away from that asshole.

Another round begins, this one dedicated to Griffin Chastain. He hired someone to take the LSAT for him, and his father bribed officials to accept him into an Ivy League law program for next year.

I idly wonder how he'll pass his classes.

However, I don't care enough to ask.

I actually very much want to leave.

When the next question goes to Becca, I stand up. "I've seen enough."

I don't even bother looking at the others in the room. Nor do I stop when the voice tells me to sit down.

If it wants to target me and throw confetti at my back, so be it.

Because fuck this shit.

I don't even want to know what file they have on me. Assuming one even exists. I was a last-minute invite, after all.

Nothing happens as I leave the room.

No guards jump out to stop me. The gunshot doesn't fire. All I hear is Becca calling out a number in my wake.

"Yeah, have fun with all that," I mutter, walking straight through a side door off the hallway and outside.

It's dark and the stars are out, the reality and calmness of the night immediately putting my nerves at ease.

"Fucking rich kids and their messed-up games," I whisper, tilting my head back to stare up at the sky. "This is so much better."

"I tend to agree," a deep voice replies, making me jump in response.

"Jesus." I press my hand to my chest and glare at the well-dressed male standing only a few feet away from me. "You scared the shit out of me."

"It's Kage," he reminds me. "And sorry. But

you should probably know better than to play in the woods at night."

"I'm not in the woods." I look pointedly at the stone patio beneath my sneakers. "And I remember your name."

He grins. "As I do yours, Sydney."

My blood warms at his sensual tone.

"What are you doing outside?" he asks, his hands in the pockets of his black slacks. He's no longer wearing his suit jacket, just his white button-down shirt. The sleeves are rolled to the elbows, providing a nice view of the tattoos decorating his forearms.

Too bad it's so dark. I would like to see that ink in the sun.

"I was about to go for a walk," I tell him. Not really a lie, as I've wanted to go explore all day. And it sounds better than admitting I just ran away from a fucked-up version of a truth game.

"Right now?" he arches a brow. "Where's your flashlight?"

I show him my phone, then slip it back into the pocket of my jeans. "It doesn't have service, but it still lights up."

He grunts. "Not exactly the best hiking gear, Sydney."

"I would ask to borrow some, but given that you don't have canoes on the property, I'm guessing you also lack proper hiking equipment."

"We have flashlights." He pulls a small one from his pocket as proof. "I never leave the Lodge without one. You never know what kind of killers lurk in the dark."

I laugh. "And you're going to scare them off with some light?"

"Better than a phone without a signal," he returns.

"Hmm. Well." I glance up at the stunning sky again. "I can think of worse places to die." I eye him curiously. "What are you doing out here?"

"Searching for serial killers," he deadpans.

I laugh again and shake my head. "Well, you caught me. Want to go for a walk with me?"

"How very serial killer of you, Sydney," he muses. "Asking an unsuspecting employee to join you for a midnight hike. Tell me, how do you plan to off me?"

I consider him for a moment. "Why don't you walk with me and find out?" I'm not sure how we ventured onto this topic about killers and dying in the woods, but it's amusing me more than scaring me.

It was probably a result of that game, a way to lighten the tension in my limbs by poking fun at an old superstition.

Kage runs his gaze over me, his lips quirking

up at the sides. "What was it you said? I can think of worse ways to die?"

"I said *places*."

"Right." He chuckles. "Well, I can think of worse ways to die than by the hand of a gorgeous woman. So why not?" He gives me the flashlight. "Lead the way, little killer."

Three
KAGE

THIS GORGEOUS GIRL IS GOING TO END UP UNDER MY blade.

But I can't help being intrigued by her. She's stunning in a way many others are not. The type of beauty women pay a lot of money to achieve, yet it's perfectly natural on her.

The moonlight plays off her dark strands as we walk, her creamy skin almost appearing white in the night.

She's wearing a pair of skinny jeans and a sweater, quite the opposite of the other girls here. They're all decked out in designer skirts and flirty tops.

But not this female.

Sydney isn't even wearing makeup. She's simply

herself—all thick lashes, dark eyes, and plump lips.

No plastic. No enhancements.

Just an athletic woman with long legs, a tight ass, and perky tits.

I'm not surprised that Landon Matterhorn wants to fuck her.

However, I am surprised that she doesn't return the desire. He's a notorious ladies' man, taking a different woman home every night. They all want a chance to tame the rich kid's cock.

Sydney hasn't shown any interest in trying. Hell, she hasn't shown interest in any of this.

All she desired was a canoe.

And now a walk.

Who is this beauty? And why did Rebecca Edington pick her as her requisite plus-one? I wonder, my eyes on Sydney's ass as she moves onto the path ahead of me.

The trees are still bare, allowing a speckle of moonlight to filter through. But the evergreens in this area are thick, their needles resilient against the cold.

Sydney pauses to inhale, the movement radiating relaxation and contentment. "It smells amazing out here," she says softly. "Like pine and earth."

I smile. "You enjoy nature?"

"That's the only reason I'm here." She starts

walking again, the flashlight providing a dull glow against the dirt path. "Becca asked me to join at the last minute. I thought we were going to a real cabin. Not a palace in the woods."

I smirk. "You must not know her very well if you expected a camping trip." Which has me wondering again how Rebecca picked this girl.

She shrugs. "We've been teammates for the last four years. She doesn't act like a princess on the court. But I've not really seen her in this, um, *element*."

"Surrounded by entitled dicks and bitchy debutantes?" I ask, defining her *element* for her.

"Uh, yeah." She pauses as we reach a fork in the path. "It's certainly not my world."

"It's certainly not," I agree. She's too pure and beautiful for it.

Which makes it a damn shame that Rebecca brought her here.

Sydney glances at me, her midnight eyes unreadable in the dark. "I can't tell if you're insulting me or complimenting me."

"Definitely complimenting," I assure her. "You very clearly do not belong here. And that is the highest praise I could ever give you."

"You don't seem to like them much."

"Do you?" I counter.

She looks up at the trees before focusing on me

again. "I think they live in a world where my opinion matters little. So to give one would be moot."

"A fair assessment." An intelligent one, too. "So how did you come to be here, Sydney?"

"As I said, it was a last-minute invite." She shrugs. "I didn't have anywhere else to go for the week, and I like the outdoors."

That doesn't really tell me what I want to know. But then, I'm not sure why I voiced the question. It was more of an internal musing. A disappointment of a sort.

Because Sydney shouldn't be here.

And yet, there's nothing I can really do about it. Rebecca recruited her into this mess.

Not me.

I stare at the beautiful girl for a moment, then gesture to the left with my chin. "That way leads to an open field about a mile up. It's a clear night. We'll see a lot of stars."

"And the other way?" she asks.

"Wraps around the rear of the estate and takes you back to the lake, near the docks."

"Where there aren't any canoes," she says.

"Where there aren't any canoes," I echo, amused.

"Hmm." She picks the path on the left. "Stargazing it is."

I smile and follow again, my eyes on her ass more than anything else. She's definitely an athlete, her long strides purposeful as she moves gracefully along the trail.

"You mentioned a court," I say. "What sport?" I assume it's volleyball since I know Rebecca Edington plays for Anton University. But I don't want to reveal all my cards or clue Sydney in to how much I know about her "friend."

"Volleyball," she confirms. "We played the last four years together."

"So that makes you a senior, then?" A guess based on her "four years" comment and the fact that Rebecca is a college senior.

"Yep. Six more weeks of classes and then I graduate." She sounds a bit exasperated by that. Or maybe she's just getting tired since we've started heading uphill.

"What's your degree in?"

"Computer science," she replies, surprising me.

Maybe she had a motive for this trip after all.

"Are you planning to work for the Covington empire after this?" I can't quite hide the edge in my voice. But she doesn't seem to notice because she's too busy scoffing at the question.

"Hell no. Corporate life isn't for me."

I frown. "Then what do you want to do?"

"Isn't that the question everyone asks throughout their twenties?" She tosses me a look over her shoulder, one I don't quite catch because of the shadows. "What about you? How did you end up working at a place like this?"

"Well, I didn't major in computer science," I reply vaguely.

She laughs. "Yeah? What did you major in?"

Revenge. Murder. Blackmail. "Finance." It's not a lie; I do have a finance degree.

As well as one in psychology.

And a legal degree.

All of them are under fake identities.

But that's a topic for another day. *Or not.*

"Finance?" she repeats. "And you're working here?"

"I'm a manager," I tell her. "I run reception." Also not a lie.

She pauses again, this time to really look at me. Of course, I'm as hidden as she is by the night. "How old are you?"

"Twenty-eight," I answer honestly. "You?"

"Twenty-two." Her gaze dances over me. "Why here? Why The Lodge?"

"Why not The Lodge?" I counter.

"It's a bit rich for my taste."

"Not necessarily a bad thing when working in hospitality. Working with the rich typically equates to higher tips."

"At what expense? Your pride? Your dignity?" She falls silent for a moment. "I don't think I would enjoy working here. You must have the patience of a saint."

I chuckle. "I wouldn't go that far."

"Hmm," she hums and resumes her hike.

We continue for a while in silence, allowing the forest to swallow us whole.

If Sydney is nervous to have me at her back, she doesn't show it. She appears to be too lost to nature's sounds and scents to concern herself with my presence.

A dangerous assumption.

But something tells me this girl enjoys taking risks. Almost as though she doesn't have much to lose.

Her steps are fluid, her instincts seeming to guide her naturally over the tree roots and around branches that may snag her sweater.

It's sort of hot to observe, her confidence a beacon that calls to my inner deviant. I want to play with her. See how deep that self-assurance really goes.

I want to know her.

Taste her.

Hear her scream.

All dark inclinations that will undoubtedly end badly for her.

Yet there's something beautiful about a woman who trusts as easily as this one seems to.

It's a sweet sort of innocence that's astutely uncommon in this world. Her honesty is refreshing as well.

Of course, we've barely skimmed the surface. It's easy to be truthful about superficial details.

"Oh, wow," she says as she steps through the woods into the clearing. "*Wow.*" Her gaze is on the stars as she moves forward, her face fully illuminated by the moon. "This is beautiful."

Yes, I think. *It is.*

A foolish thought, given that we've just met. But she really is gorgeous.

And out here, surrounded by trees while walking beneath the stars, she's positively alluring.

A forest nymph with a smile that takes my breath away.

How cliché, I think. Although, it has been a while since I last fucked a woman. These last few months have been quite busy. And I certainly wasn't expecting a woman like this to step through The Lodge doors today.

Brats like Rebecca Edington? Yes.

An adventurous female with a flair for sarcasm? No.

Sydney's gaze is still on the stars as she moves to the center of the field.

Where she proceeds to lie down among the

overgrown grass, not at all caring about her clothes or her hair or anything else. She's purely captivated by the sky above.

And as I'm equally charmed by her, I join her in the grass.

She says nothing for a long time, seemingly unaware of me watching her.

Then she slowly looks at me and smiles. "Thank you for the recommendation. I think I'll sleep out here."

I laugh. "On the ground? Without a sleeping bag or anything at all?"

She shrugs. "I've stayed in worse places. At least it's peaceful here." She returns her focus to the glittering night above and closes her eyes. "I won't have to listen to Preston and Becca fucking out here either. Double win."

Another laugh leaves me. "You have no filter, do you, Sydney?"

"It's a waste of effort to sugarcoat everything, Kage. And I learned a long time ago that life is short. People spend all this time trying to placate others with lies and bullshit phrases when the truth is usually a much faster route to happiness."

"Very philosophical." Accurate, too. "So you prefer nature to people."

"Always," she replies with a sigh. "Nature doesn't talk back."

"Am I bothering you by being here?" I wonder.

She rotates her face toward mine again, her gaze roaming over my features. "No. You're not bothering me." Rather than look away, she holds my gaze.

It's bold.

It's hot.

It has me wanting to inch toward her and introduce her to a new game in this field.

But Judge will kill me if I mess up tonight's theatrics.

Perhaps that's the true draw here—the off-limits nature of this woman. She's not mine to play with.

Not yet, anyway.

Still, I feel a strange urge to give her something. An explanation of sorts. A truth. One I shouldn't utter aloud, yet that notion of *forbidden* only makes me want to voice the secret more. To give her a piece of myself as an apology for the horror to come.

She's an innocent.

One who shouldn't be here.

But in addition to life being short, it also isn't fair.

"You asked why I work here," I say softly. "It's because my family used to live around here. So I'm partial to the trees and the lake. Reminds me of a previous life."

She stares at me for a beat. "It reminds me of a previous life, too." Her expression seems to change, some of that confident flair leaving her features. "My mom loved going on hikes. I used to go with her. But then one day, she went on one and never came home."

Ah, I think. *And there's the reason Rebecca chose you.*

"Nature is where she used to go to think," Sydney continues. "And I guess I inherited that from her."

"My mother loved nature, too," I say, recalling the lavish gardens she used to manage back at our manor. "Flowers, specifically. Roses of all colors."

Sydney doesn't reply, probably because she knows that nothing she can say will fix the situation.

We both used past tense in our statements. The implication that our mothers are dead is clear. And as two people who mutually understand loss, we know there's nothing to say.

"I never knew my father," she admits after several minutes of quiet. "He donated his sperm and fucked off to God only knows where. My mom was all I had."

I know better than to apologize for her loss. Instead, I say, "I was fortunate to know my father. He was a good man who didn't deserve his fate. Similar to your mom, I suppose."

She nods a little. "People are cruel."

"Which again is why you prefer nature, I

assume."

She smiles, but it's not exactly happy this time. "Yes. Yet another reason why I prefer nature."

Silence engulfs us again, the minutes quickly turning into an hour. I start to wonder, though, if she was serious about staying out here all night.

But just as I'm about to say something, she slowly sits up with a shiver. There are leaves in her hair and debris on her sweater. She doesn't bother brushing it off, just looks back at me. "I don't suppose you have any sleeping bags? Or a tent?"

I chuckle. "Just a lodge full of elegant bedrooms, I'm afraid." I go up onto my elbows, not yet ready to leave our little haven.

She releases a sigh as a chilling breeze sweeps through the night. "I didn't dress right for this. The air is going right through my sweater."

"It's only going to get colder," I warn her. "It may even snow."

Her lips curl down. "So much for that swim."

"Unless you're into that sort of thing."

"Maybe I like warming up afterward." She frowns. "Except I haven't seen a single fireplace. What kind of lodge doesn't have a fireplace?"

One built by the three boys who nearly burned to death two decades ago, I think. Instead, I force an easy smile and say, "I think we've established that The Lodge isn't your typical cabin."

She grunts. "It's a palace in the woods."

"Yes, you've mentioned that." I study her profile, tracing my gaze along her delicate jaw to her slender neck. It would bleed so prettily beneath my blade.

She swallows as though she can sense my violent thoughts.

And I imagine a thin red line there, bleeding as her throat works.

I would trace it with my tongue, then feed her blood to her.

Before kissing her deeply.

A morbid desire, perhaps. But something tells me this girl may just be into it enough to play with my dark side.

Or maybe I wouldn't want to hurt her at all.

Alas, that debate may not survive the night.

I release a breath and sit up beside her. She appraises me, her gaze curious rather than fearful.

I hold her gaze while I reach over to remove a leaf from her hair. She watches as it falls between us, my fingers already heading toward the debris along her back. I brush it from her with a few gentle strokes, the touch more tender than I remember ever being with a woman.

She surprises me by returning the favor, silently sweeping her palm along my spine and shoulders.

It feels intimate. Warm. An invitation for more.

Which, unfortunately, can't happen.

Not tonight.

But if she survives... maybe.

We stare at each other for a moment longer.

Then I stand and hold out a hand for her. She accepts it without question, allowing me to pull her up from the ground. I don't immediately release her, the feel of her skin too tempting to resist. She's warm, too.

Despite the cold air.

Despite the ice drizzling through my veins.

She's more like the sun than the moon, and I find myself wanting to lose myself within her. To kiss her. Take her. *Taste* her.

Who is this sweet little enchantress? I wonder. *This darling nymph?*

She smiles as though she can hear my thoughts. "Thanks for not being a serial killer, Kage," she tells me, startling a laugh from me.

Oh, little dove, if you only knew. "Don't thank me yet, Sydney. The night is still young, and we have to make the hike back to The Lodge."

Her lips curl. "Then it's a good thing I have the flashlight."

"I don't need a flashlight to stalk you through the woods, darling," I tell her. "I grew up here, remember?"

"That almost sounds like a challenge," she says, narrowing her gaze. "Should I race you back?"

"Would you enjoy that?" I ask her seriously, wanting to give her this final gift of excitement. An evening to remember. Something she can dream about in death.

"I do like to run," she hedges. "What do I get if I beat you back to The Lodge?"

"What do you want?" I ask her. She won't win, but I am curious about her desire to play with me. Especially after her clear disinterest in the game inside.

She considers for a long moment. "A canoe."

I grin. "I don't have a canoe."

"But you grew up around here, right? Surely you know where to find one."

This woman's tenacity is admirable. "You're probably not wrong."

"Then that's what I want." She folds her arms. "What do you want if you win?"

Oh, is that what this is about? I muse, my gaze falling to her mouth as her tongue darts out to dampen her lower lip. *Are you goading me into a chase that you know I'll win? Or do you want me to admit that I desire you?*

She was forward before.

Voicing her desires.

Telling me she didn't believe in wasting time.

But now she's clearly coaxing me into a delicious game of cat and mouse. The flare of her nostrils tells me she knows I'm onto her. However, her gaze holds a challenge I can't resist.

Come and get me, that look says.

"Is this the part where I ask for a kiss when I win?"

She's still holding my hand, her grip squeezing a little. "If you want to kiss me, Kage, you don't have to ask."

"But what would be the fun in that?" I inquire. "Isn't foreplay all about the chase?"

"Then we should race." She releases me, taking a step back. "Maybe I'll let you kiss me in that canoe."

"You won't let me do anything, Sydney. You'll beg me."

She smiles. "Prove it." She takes off through the field, heading straight for the path.

I grin.

It would be so easy to best her, especially as that path is a scenic route.

But I can't afford to play chase with her tonight.

Not with everything else on the agenda.

So I let her go and maintain a safe distance behind her, mostly to ensure she doesn't injure herself.

She fist-pumps when she makes it back to

The Lodge before me, causing my lips to curl in amusement. I debate going around the other side and leaving her there.

But it may be the last time I see her alive.

Which is why I wander toward her and say, "I'll figure out that canoe."

"Good." She hands me my flashlight. "Thanks for not trying to kill me in the dark, Kage."

I laugh again and shake my head. "We'll see what tomorrow brings."

"I look forward to it," she replies. "Because I plan to go canoeing."

"We'll see," I say, opening the side door for her. "Try to get some sleep, Sydney."

My brother Judge is waiting for us in the hallway, still wearing his suit from earlier.

Sydney clears her throat upon seeing him, her smile fading. "Thanks for showing me the stars, Kage."

"You're welcome, Ms. Evans," I reply, falling into formal mode.

She pauses and glances at me. "How do you know my last name?"

"Ms. Edington provided it," I lie. "Do you know how to make it back to your room?"

"Up the stairs and down the hall," she deadpans.

My lips twitch. "Have a good night, Sydney Evans." A cruel statement, considering what I know is coming.

Because this poor girl just entered a game she likely won't survive.

Unless I help her, I think, meeting Judge's stormy gaze.

He doesn't say a word as he leads me away from Sydney. Away from our one evening of fun. Away from a path I would have enjoyed exploring just a little bit more.

But family comes first.

Always.

Which means I can't help Sydney.

I almost glance back at her to say goodbye with my eyes.

However, I know better than to allow my emotions any ounce of control.

This is a game of life and death.

A reunion of the families.

The foundation of a new future.

One where the fallen princes rise to become kings.

Maybe we'll find each other again, I think at Sydney. *In another life.*

Four
SYDNEY

KAGE LEAVES WITHOUT A BACKWARD GLANCE.

Which is fine.

It allows me a moment to check out his fine ass in those dress pants. He still has the sleeves of his dress shirt rolled to the elbows, the cool air outside having clearly not bothered him at all.

Tomorrow night, I'll wear layers, I decide, sighing as I head toward the main staircase.

The guy who met us at the door didn't appear very pleased to find me with Kage. I recognized him as one of the two valets from earlier but now suspect that he might be some sort of manager. His grayish-green eyes held a note of censure in their depths, one Kage responded to immediately by dismissing me and walking off with the other man.

Hopefully, Kage won't get into trouble, I think as I make my way up the steps.

If he does, I'll just tell that guy I asked Kage to accompany me outside in the dark. Or something.

A problem to consider tomorrow.

As I have another one to ponder now—*Becca and Preston.*

Something that becomes increasingly obvious as I near my room. Because I can hear them talking.

No. Not talking. Yelling, I realize as I open the door to Becca screaming, "I can't believe you removed me from the game!"

"What the fuck was I supposed to do? You were getting hysterical."

I debate walking right back out the door, as neither of them has seen me yet.

"Because you chose Gretchen!" she shouts at him. "When were you going to tell me?"

"Tonight, apparently," he mutters, glancing at me before I can make an escape.

"I can't believe you did this to me," she says, sounding broken. "You… you chose her."

"My father chose her," Preston tells her. "Your guest is back."

"I… I can go…?" I offer.

Becca spins toward me, her eyes wild. "No! Preston was just leaving. You stay."

I suddenly feel like a pet again with that command, but seeing the tears trailing down her face makes me pity her a little.

Something clearly set her off during the game.

I can't imagine why that would happen. It's not like the questions were designed to hurt each other or anything.

It was clearly a way to display all the skeletons in their closets, to force them to confide in each other.

Nothing brings a clique closer together than an endless array of blackmail, right?

Preston clears his throat. "We'll talk more about this tomorrow, Rebecca."

"Oh, go fuck yourself, *Mr. Michaels,*" Becca snaps. "No, wait. Go fuck Gretchen instead. Since bottle-blonde seems to be your thing now."

He sighs and just shakes his head as he walks by me.

I move out of the way in the foyer to let him leave, and jump as the door slams in his wake.

Well. This isn't awkward.

Becca starts to cry, her sobs echoing through the suite.

Do I hug her? I've never been big on affection or knowing the right thing to say. I suppose that's a consequence of losing my mother at the age of eight and being raised in the foster system. I just don't connect to people easily.

Although, I connected to Kage pretty well tonight.

Except he didn't kiss me. Or even try.

So maybe not.

Becca releases another sob, drawing my focus to her.

I move toward her slowly and put my arms around her, something that must be the right move because she clings to me as she continues to cry.

Freezing in the woods would have been a better plan, I think after several minutes of patting her back.

When she eventually calms down, I find her a glass of water. She mumbles a "Thank you" and sips it while making her way to the couch. "He's marrying Gretchen."

"Oh." I'm not sure what else to say to that.

"His father gave him a choice—me or her. It'll bring the branches together and allow for more collaboration between our two specialties. But… but he chose her."

Okay, so we're apparently going to discuss this, then.

That's fine.

Except I have no idea how to reply, so I just sit on the couch adjacent to her and say, "He made the wrong choice." It's the truth. I would pick Becca over Gretchen any day.

Well, I would actually pick neither of them.

But something tells me Preston wasn't offered that alternative.

"I know," she says emphatically. "It's the wrong choice! And he didn't even tell me. That stupid game did when it asked him about a recent contract. With *Mr. Walton*." She snarls the name and slams the water glass on the table.

Fortunately, it doesn't break.

"He let me date him, too. He let me think I had a chance. All because he wanted to fuck me—another thing he admitted. And when I reacted, he used that damn trigger on me!" She's yelling now. "Can you believe that?"

Yes. I can absolutely believe it. But I don't say that aloud. "He's a dick."

"He is a dick," she agrees. "A lying asshole."

So, a typical guy, then, I think.

"God, how could I be so stupid? I let him play me, and if it weren't for the game, I would be sucking him off right now."

That's a bit more information that I want right now, but I don't comment. She obviously needs to vent, so I let her continue.

Which she does.

For what feels like hours.

It's really only minutes, though. And all she's doing is talking about how she planned to seduce him this week, to convince him of their compatibility.

Something he clearly intended to allow.

Until the game called him out on it.

And then he "killed" her by shooting her in the game.

"What kind of game makes you kill your friends and colleagues?" I wonder aloud.

Becca blinks as though she forgot I was here. "It's just some stupid virtual reality thing. A Covington Industries game meant to pit us all against each other as some sort of fucked-up team-building exercise."

I'm not sure she understands that virtual reality is a little more in-depth than a video game with a trigger controller.

But that part of her statement isn't what I focus on.

It's the "team-building exercise" comment that has me gaping at her.

"By having you kill each other?" I ask skeptically.

"Yeah, I know," she sighs, seeming to sober a bit from her weeping fest. "But it's definitely something our parents would orchestrate. They love finding out-of-the-box ways to prepare us for the future."

"I see." A complete lie. Because I absolutely do not see how any of this is okay or normal or even remotely acceptable. I get that it's a game. But it's a seriously fucked-up one.

"You'll understand more tomorrow when we enter round two," she tells me before grabbing a tissue and blowing her nose.

"It's continuing?"

"Yeah, it's the point of this entire trip." She trades the tissue for her water and finishes the glass.

"Oh." I'm not sure what else to say. Although, I'm very tempted to ask her why she invited me into this mess. A corporate chess match involving blackmail and dark secrets isn't really my thing.

It also seems like the sort of activity that may get me in trouble for knowing too much.

"And I'm expected to play?" I ask her incredulously.

She shrugs. "I mean, they let you leave tonight. So I don't really know." She looks at me then, her gray-blue eyes narrowing. "Hey, where did you go tonight?"

"Hiking," I admit. "Just out to a clearing to see the stars."

Her eyebrows rise. "Alone?"

I shrug. "Nature doesn't scare me." It's not a real answer, just a dismissive one. I don't really feel like telling her about Kage. She's not my best friend or anything of the sort. And my hike with him feels too private to share.

"You're braver than me," she says, sighing again. "I suppose we should go to bed."

An invitation to leave this uncomfortable bonding session? Yes, please.

"Sleep sounds good." I stand, not wanting anything to keep me from accepting her offer for escape. "I'll see you in the morning, then."

I start down the hallway she assigned me earlier. Both bedrooms are the same size, so she took the one with a view of the lake, while mine is all trees.

"Hey, Syd?" she calls just as I reach the corridor.

So close. "Yeah?" I ask, forcing myself to stay in place and not run.

"Thanks for being here. I know it's strange, but I couldn't do this without you."

My brow furrows. *What?*

I turn around to ask what she means by that, but she's already heading in the opposite direction.

Her door opens and closes, leaving me staring after her in confusion.

Have I completely misunderstood our friendship? I thought we were acquaintances, not close friends. But she just made it sound like she needed me here for emotional support or something.

I purse my lips and head to my room while thinking through every encounter between me and Becca.

We get along just fine.

But beyond that, nothing.

It must have been her emotions talking. Our hug just knocked a screw loose and made her spout nonsense.

Everything will be better tomorrow.

I force all thoughts of Becca and her world from my mind as I ready myself for bed.

Then I fall asleep with Kage's image in my mind.

An image of him lying in a canoe.

With me astride him.

As we rock, back and forth, in the middle of the pond.

All night long.

Five
SYDNEY

It's freezing.

My eyes feel heavy as I force them open, the world around me resembling ice. For half a beat, I wonder if I sleepwalked last night and ended up outside again.

But no.

I'm snuggled into the blankets and shivering.

A floral scent in the air draws my attention to the balcony doors. My brow furrows. *When did I open that?*

It's not wide open, just cracked. However, it's enough to frost over the room.

Which explains my frozen state.

Ugh.

My teeth chatter. There's only one way to fix it. And it's not going to be fun.

I count to ten before forcing myself from the bed. The door slams from me hitting it so hard.

My heart pumps wildly in my chest, ensuring that I'm officially awake. The rising sun outside helps, the beautiful glow casting ripples of red and orange across the trees.

I admire the view for a beat, ignoring the chilly air.

My bathroom has a window, I think, smiling as a new plan forms.

I bypass the bed, my feet moving across the wood floor and onto the marble of the bathroom. It's even colder, shooting ice up my spine, but I ignore it in favor of the walk-in shower. I turn it on to max heat, strip out of my flannel pants and tank top, and step inside as soon as the water warms up.

There's a window across from me, over the sink, allowing me to look outside while I shower. So I spend a little more time than is necessary beneath the lava-like spray.

It's relaxing and peaceful.

And it heats me right up.

I eventually dry off and find warm clothes for the day—jeans, a long-sleeved shirt, a sweater, some thick socks, and my favorite boots.

Normally, I wouldn't fuss with my hair and just

throw it up into a wet bun. But that won't work in this weather. So I dry it before tossing it up into a ponytail.

Next up: coffee.

I hope the kitchen has a coffee maker.

Yawning, I leave the scenery of my bedroom and trade it for the windows of the living room. It's a beautiful morning with the sun cascading light across the mountains in the distance.

I start toward the doors, momentarily ignoring my need for coffee, only for a blur in my peripheral vision to distract me from both goals.

My brow furrows. *What is that? Water?*

It looks like a coffee spill in the shadows of the room because the sun isn't high enough to cast proper light yet.

I glance up, curious as to if there's a roof leak. But all I find are wooden beams. No sign of water damage.

Maybe Becca dropped something last night and just left it there for the maids to clean up?

Seems like something she might do.

Sighing, I walk over to evaluate the mess. There are towels in the kitchen, so I'll just grab a few and…

"Becca?" Her name falls from my lips as I realize that she's lying beside the pool of liquid.

No.

In the pool of liquid.

And it's not really a pool so much as a smear.

Of blood. "Oh, shit!" I fall to my knees beside her. "Becca? Becca!" I… I don't know what to do. My hands flounder above her uselessly as I try to determine our next move. "I…"

I can't see her face. And I'm afraid to move her. Isn't that the worst thing to do in a situation like this?

Or is that when someone has a head injury?

"Becca?" I try again, hoping she'll magically respond.

She doesn't.

I crawl around to her other side, trying to find her face. But it's covered by waves of brown hair, the edges of which seem to be stuck in the… in the *blood.*

"Oh God…" I press the back of my hand to my mouth. "Help!" I scream. "Please help!"

Except this palace is too fucking big!

No one is going to hear me. I need a phone. Something to reach someone.

I stand, my knees weak, my heart beating a mile a minute in my chest. My stomach twists with warning, but I swallow the bile rising in my throat.

Help. We need help. We need a phone. Where the fuck is the phone?

I spin around the living room, careful not to step in the blood on the floor.

There are no phones.

I have no cellular service either.

"Fuck!"

I run toward the door, then double back to the bedroom. Because phones are usually on the nightstand, right?

Yes.

There's one right there.

I grab the phone and dial the police.

Only, a male voice says, "How can I help you, Ms. Edington?"

"The police." I sound breathless. *Hoarse*. Barely understandable.

"I'm sorry. I didn't quite catch that."

It's Kage. I recognize his deep tones. That sensual voice. "Help," I whisper. "I… I need help."

"Sydney?" He utters my name in a way that makes my knees feel weak.

"Police," I repeat. "P-please."

Jesus, I'm losing it. I sound hysterical. I… I don't know how to process anything. And I feel so fucking dizzy.

He says something back to me, but I don't catch it.

The phone slips from my hand as the world

shifts, my balance off-center and sending me to the floor.

Get it together, I tell myself. *Fucking stand up and go out there to check her pulse.*

Yes.

Yes, I should do that.

Somehow, I find my footing.

Except I can't figure out how to check her pulse without moving her.

"God, I'm so sorry, Becca." I feel utterly useless.

Swallowing, I crouch before her again and try to move her hair away from her neck to find her pulse.

But a bang at the door has me shooting back up to my feet. I run toward the foyer just as the door opens to reveal Kage. He takes one look at me and pulls me into his arms. "What's wrong?" he says against my ear. "Are you all right?"

"N-no," I stammer, pointing at the living room. "Becca..."

He releases me and darts forward, his movements triggering some part of my brain to follow.

I gasp as he rolls Becca to her back.

Her glassy gray-blue eyes stare at nothing.

And her forehead...

Fuck.

It's... it's the source of the blood.

"Jesus," Kage breathes. He pulls something from his back pocket. Not a phone. But some sort of communication device. Because he speaks into it, calling for assistance up to our room.

I stand in the living room, lost in a daze as people start coming and going.

I can't seem to process the scene.

Becca's dead.

Is that a bullet wound?

Did someone just say something about murder?

No one speaks to me. No one seems to notice I'm even here.

And it takes me far too long to realize that no one has called the cops. "Is… is someone going to call the police?" I finally ask.

"No." Preston's voice comes from beside me, making me jump.

I didn't even realize he was here.

Hell, it seems like everyone has arrived now.

Griffin. Gretchen. Courtney. That guy who raped the girl and got away with it. Whatever his name is.

I can't think clearly about any of them right now, the shock of watching Becca's body being strapped to a gurney consuming all my mental power.

"I mean, obviously she did it," Gretchen says, somewhat drawing me into the conversation.

"Is that why she's asking for the police?" the rapist drawls. *Brayden. Yeah, that's his name.*

"Maybe she wants to confess," Gretchen suggests.

"Sydney didn't do this," Griffin says, clueing me in to their discussion. "It's just too obvious."

"I didn't do this," I echo, slightly mortified that they would even accuse me of it.

"Well, I did leave you here alone with her last night," Preston points out.

I gape at him. "Yeah, after you both fought over the fact that you chose to remove her from that fucked-up game by... by *shooting* her."

"So you're saying I did it?" He laughs heartily. "That's rich, Syd."

"And what motive do I have for killing her?" I demand, my voice less raspy than before.

This line of questioning seems to be bringing me back to reality, yanking me from the nightmarish images of the morning and making me realize the full ramifications of what the fuck just happened.

My roommate is dead. And these assholes think I did it.

"Jealousy?" Courtney suggests. "I mean, she has everything that you don't."

My eyebrows lift. "So being supposedly jealous is a motive now?" I ask, nearly hysterical. "I can't fucking believe this." I spin toward the foyer, needing to escape. "This… this is insane. We need to call the cops. Someone. *Anyone.*"

"I've already notified my father," Landon says as he steps through the door and blocks my path. "We don't need to involve anyone else." His blue eyes capture and hold mine. "He says his people will handle it."

"Handle it," I echo. "Handle it how? And how did you call him? Our phones don't work out here."

"I used the landline at the front desk." He leans against the door frame. "He says we need to gather downstairs and wait for further instruction."

"I… I don't want to leave Becca." A lie. I want to get the fuck out of this room. But I don't want to go with these people either.

"It wasn't a request, Sydney." He gives me a look that warns me not to fight him. "We're going downstairs." He glances over my head. "The staff will handle the cleanup."

"I…" This feels wrong. Leaving Becca up here. *Staff cleaning up*. What does that even mean? This is a crime scene, right?

Landon steps forward, his hand going to my elbow. "Let's go, Syd."

I don't want to go. I want to fight him. To tell him *no*. Run into the woods and find a place where my cell works. Call the cops. Do something other than let this asshole manhandle me.

Yet I find my feet moving as though he's controlling me with a string, dragging me through the hallway and down the stairs to the room everyone gathered in last night.

Where more staff are serving breakfast.

Everyone sits down and starts to eat like we didn't just witness a murder scene.

No one is crying.

No one is demanding answers.

They're all just eerily calm like this shit happens every day.

Maybe this is all a nightmare? I muse. *That or I've fallen into a Stepford reality where no one has feelings.*

Landon and Preston start discussing some stocks. *Finances*. Like… like it's a regular breakfast. Like Becca is actually sitting here enjoying it with us.

I gape at them all, not understanding how they can be so calm and collected.

"Eat your breakfast," Landon tells me, the command in his tone reminding me of the look he gave me earlier. He's no longer flirting or trying to fuck me. He's somehow become the boss of this situation, dictating to everyone around him.

His father is considered the alpha member of

Covington Industries.

It seems that's a trait he's passed on to his son.

But all these assholes are just too content. "Becca's dead," I whisper.

"Yes, and the situation is being handled. So eat your breakfast," Landon says. "*Now.*"

I wince. Part of me wants to argue and fight back. But my preservation instincts kick in, and I force myself to comply.

These people are dangerous, I realize. *And royally fucked up in the head.*

I need to get the hell out of here.

But I can't do that on an empty stomach. Or without a car. Or without a damn phone.

I continue eating while trying to figure out what to do.

Everyone continues socializing like it's a normal day. Nothing's wrong. No one *died.*

It's surreal.

The morning bleeds into the afternoon, all of us imprisoned in this fucking room.

They're just waiting for someone to provide an update.

Is this how they live? Just letting others clean up their messes? Waiting for Mommy and Daddy to tell them that everything is all right?

Preston and Landon turn on the screen, each of

them picking up a set of controllers as they find a game to play.

A *shooting* game.

Are you for fucking real right now? I want to demand.

Courtney and Gretchen giggle as they observe the guys.

Several of them get in on the game, causing the screen to divide into quadrants as four of them begin firing at each other. Or maybe those are drones. Whatever the hell it is, it's *wrong*.

I can't do this.

I start walking backward toward the doors.

I can't fucking do this.

I reach the door without anyone noticing because they're all too consumed with themselves to care. It's… it's *insane*.

They're all fucking insane.

They're monsters.

I… I need to call someone. The police! Landon mentioned a landline at the reception desk. *Yes.*

Except it's surrounded by men in suits when I arrive.

Shit.

I dart off to the side, my head spinning.

I… I just need some air. Some fresh air. To breathe. To run. To… to do something other than allow all this crap to happen.

My feet are moving before my mind reaches a decision, my instincts taking over and sending me down a hall toward another building exit.

Only for a man to step in front of me, wearing one of those dark suits.

A curse taunts my tongue until I meet a pair of familiar forest-green eyes. "Kage," I breathe, almost falling into him.

He wraps his arms around me and pulls me into the room he just stepped out from. His lips are at my ear as he whispers, "Shh. It's okay, Sydney. You're okay."

It's only then that I realize I'm trembling, on the verge of falling apart.

I didn't even really like Becca. I mean, I did. We were teammates. But… but this… I can't seem to wrap my head around any of it.

"They're acting like nothing is wrong," I tell him. "They're playing video games!"

"I know," he says. "I know, Syd."

"We have to do something. We have to call the police."

"We can't." His voice is soft. "Sydney, these people… You can't call anyone."

"B-but it's wrong," I stammer. "Landon said his dad is handling it. But what does that even mean?" God, I feel like I'm losing my mind. Like I've landed in some sort of universe where I'm weak and sobbing and falling apart every five minutes.

But this is crazy.

It's fucking insane!

"They're powerful people," Kage assures me. "Just breathe for me, okay?"

"But—"

"No, Syd. I need you to take a deep breath. Right now. Inhale." His words wrap around me like a whip, forcing me to pay attention to him. To *obey*.

I do what he says.

"Good girl," he praises me. "Now slowly exhale."

I do.

"Beautiful. Okay, now do it again. Inhale. That's it. Now exhale. Very good, sweetheart. One more time." His voice swathes me in a warm blanket of serenity, calming my racing heart and making me *breathe*. I close my eyes as he continues to coach me, my body complying on instinct.

It feels so good to let someone else be in charge.

To submit to another's care.

To rely on someone other than myself.

I almost feel dazed from the feeling, my hips swaying a little.

Kage pulls me onto a couch, his arms strong around me as he continues to tell me how to breathe.

I lay my head on his shoulder and just let him be in charge.

Some integral part of me trusts him. I have no idea why. Maybe because we seem to share a similar history. Maybe because I'm so desperate for someone to help right now that I'm willing to accept that assistance from a stranger.

It doesn't matter.

I finally feel safe, and that's all that counts right now.

"They're going to notice soon that you're missing," he says after what feels like hours of lying in his arms. "You'll need to be there when Mr. Matterhorn provides an update. I know you didn't kill her, but you're at risk of being framed for it."

A chill sweeps over me at his words. "I didn't do it." He just told me that, but I feel the need to make sure he believes it.

"I know, sweetheart," he says. "One of them did. But their families will clean it up. They always do."

I lift my head away from his shoulder to look at him. "They cover up murders?"

He gives me a soft smile, his green eyes holding a touch of sadness. "They cover up everything, Sydney. That's why they're here this week—to reveal all their sins."

"Blackmail," I echo, recalling my thoughts from

last night. "The game is all about having blackmail on each other." I frown. "And you were watching?"

He nods.

My eyebrows lift. "Won't they...? Won't they hurt you?"

He shrugs. "No more than they already have," he says cryptically. "And you should be more worried about yourself."

"Because they're going to frame me."

"Likely," he says.

"I..." I sit up straight. "Fuck. I need to get out of here, Kage."

He studies me for a moment. "I can't help you. Not right now. Not while everyone is here. But later... tonight..." He swallows, then clears his throat. "I can try tonight. In the dark."

"You'll try to help me?"

He nods. "But only after it's dark. So I need you to go back in there and pretend like everything is fine. If they lock you up, I can't help you."

"They might lock me up?" I gape at him. "*Jesus.*"

"Kage," he corrects with a twitch of his lips. "Sydney, you need to go back to that room and act like you're okay. Just play along. It's what they're all doing anyway—*playing*. So join their game, and later tonight, we'll figure this out. All right?"

I start to nod, but then a thought occurs to me. "Why would you help me?"

"Maybe I like you."

I stare at him. "At the expense of your own life?"

"I risked it last night in the dark with you, didn't I?" He tucks a strand of hair behind my ear, my ponytail having come undone at some point. "Syd, I know you don't have any reason to trust me. But you need to go back into the room for now. We'll talk afterward tonight. Okay?"

I'm not sure what choice I have. "If I say no, will you take me back there anyway?"

"If you say no, I may be forced to lock you up, and I really don't want to do that. So please don't make me."

My throat works as I try to swallow, my insides suddenly reminding me of a boulder. *Dry. Heavy. Harsh.* I see the truth of what he's saying in his eyes.

If I fight him on this, he'll put me in a cage somewhere.

Which means I really don't have any other option here but to obey and pray that he's going to help me.

Fuck.

Six
KAGE

I CATCH THE MOMENT SYDNEY DECIDES TO FOLLOW MY advice and trust me.

It's a heady feeling, that sense of ownership and possession that comes along with a woman putting her faith in a man.

This woman wants to believe in me.

A foolish notion on her part.

But that doesn't stop me from wanting to smile in triumph.

Instead, I focus on the shadow lurking in the corner and give him a look that tells him not to interfere. I sensed his presence a few minutes ago, his darkness naturally calling to my own.

He's my brother, after all.

Sydney doesn't notice him, her focus on me and

the situation at hand. She hasn't properly looked at the room around her either, not caring at all that I pulled her into a staff lounging room.

That's how much faith she has in me right now—she's trusting me to lead her blindly through the woods at night and into rooms where I could so easily harm her.

It's an intoxicating sensation to be in charge of what I know is a strong woman. She's feisty underneath. A survivor.

And I find myself abundantly thankful that she lived through the night.

Because it means I can play with her now. I can get to know her. I can possibly even keep her.

"Are you ready to go back?" I ask before I do something impulsive like chain her to my bed. My brother shuffles in the corner, ducking behind one of the curtains hanging from the ceiling. They cover the wall of windows behind it, providing a dark ambience in the room, similar to that of the theater hall.

Which happens to bump up against this area, something Sydney has failed to notice. A good thing, considering how much tech lurks in here. Including recording equipment and other various items we're using to play this deadly game.

That's why Judge is lurking.

If Sydney notices any of it, he'll have her head.

Maybe I shouldn't have pulled her in here, but it was that or head outside, which would also lead to dangerous consequences.

At least in here, I could calm her down and take control.

Something she's beautifully allowed me to do. "Where can I find you later?"

"Don't worry about that, Sydney. I'll find you." I kiss her forehead and help her up, then stand to block her view of the room.

She's so focused on me that she doesn't notice. "We'll meet outside?"

"If that's what you want, then yes," I tell her. "But don't bring anything with you." The last thing I need is for someone to think she's actually leaving.

She won't be.

Especially not after the next stage in the game is revealed.

"Okay," she says, nodding.

I cup her cheek, my instinct to soothe her overriding the reason in my mind. "It's going to be okay, Sydney."

It really won't be.

But maybe it will be for her.

Maybe she'll turn the villain of this story into a hero.

Not likely, I think. *But I could be her villain, perhaps.*

An easy thought, considering the way she's looking up at me now. All that trust. All that earnest innocence.

It makes me wonder if I would have been able to complete the alternative plan for last night.

"Thank you," she whispers.

Don't thank me, I want to say. Instead, I just press my forehead to hers for a moment and breathe her in. *Vanilla. Sugar cookies.* So fucking sweet that I want to taste her.

But I don't.

Instead, I walk her to the door and back into the hallway.

"See you soon," I promise her.

She nods and leaves while I watch her go from the doorway, my shoulder propped up against the wooden frame.

Her pretty, near-black eyes meet mine once more as she glances back at me. I encourage her with a nod, and she ducks back around the corner.

I wait a beat, just to make sure she doesn't head this way again, before stepping back into the room and walking over to the row of monitors along the wall. It's set up like a business center, which is what I would call it if she ever asked me about it.

But it's not a business center at all.

It's a security room with access to every camera on-site, including the one in the theater hall.

I flick it on now and count to ten before I see her step through the door. "Thank fuck," I breathe. That was a little too close for comfort.

Fortunately, no one seems to notice her.

It's like she's invisible, something I really don't understand. She's the most beautiful woman I've ever seen. I suppose Landon recognized that, as he clearly seemed into her yesterday. But he's too busy shooting Preston on the screen to give a fuck about getting pussy right now.

Priorities, I think, shaking my head.

"Is she going to be a problem, K?" Judge asks as he steps out from behind the curtain and joins me at the monitors. We always call each other by the first letter of our names, mostly to disguise whatever aliases we're going by now.

I'm currently Kage.

He's currently Judge.

And our other brother has aptly chosen Loki.

However, among each other, we're just K, J, and L.

"No, she won't be a problem." I glance at him. "But I may keep her."

He arches a brow. "As a pet?"

I shrug. "Undecided. She's feisty."

"She's trouble."

My lips twitch. "I like trouble."

He gives me a warning look. "We've planned

this for far too long to be led by our dicks, brother."

"My dick isn't leading me anywhere except for her bed, J. And I haven't decided if I want to fuck her or kill her yet. Maybe both." Not a lie. If she proves to be a problem, I won't have a choice. And he's right to assume she may be an issue. She's smart and intuitive. If she figures out what we're doing here, I'll have to kill her.

But I will absolutely fuck her before that happens.

Judge sighs, shaking his head. "Just don't fuck this up."

"Says the man who let Landon make that call."

"I knew Loki would catch it," he murmurs. "And he played it off beautifully."

"Just as I'll play this off beautifully," I promise, thinking of all the ways I would *play* with Ms. Evans.

Judge snorts. "You and your games."

"I'm not the one who created Truth or Kill."

"No, we have our dear little brother to thank for that," Judge says as the male in question enters.

He takes one look at us and laughs. "And here I thought I would have to corral you two away from the blood to come play with me."

"It was a boring scene," I drawl. "One bullet to the brain."

"Who would have thought he'd be so on point?" Loki taunts, glancing at the screen. "I guess video games are good practice after all."

"You would know," I tell him, folding my arms. "How long until the next phase."

"Sixty minutes." His fingers start flying over the keyboard. "And I have an idea for later tonight."

I arch a brow. "Oh?"

He doesn't elaborate, too busy pulling up footage from across The Lodge.

Loki is the brains of our operation, his skill with computers putting mine and Judge's to shame.

We all have our talents, though. And I'm not bad with hacking at all. Neither is Judge. But Loki is just a natural on the keyboard, his ability to program a gift that rivals our father's old skill.

I pull up a chair and flip it to straddle it, my arms wrapping around the upper back as I rest my chin on my forearms.

Judge mimics my position.

We both know better than to interrupt our brother at work.

"Cleanup crew says they're almost done," Judge says after a few minutes of silence, his focus on his watch. "Do you want to keep the girl in the same bedroom or move her?"

I consider it for a moment. "I'll decide later tonight." She may end up in my bed. Or in a ditch. It remains to be seen.

Judge nods. "I'll have another room made up,

just in case."

"Good." I watch as Sydney fidgets on the couch, her nerves showing in the way she clenches and moves her fingers. But her face is otherwise devoid of emotion, something I find fascinating, given how upset she is right now.

Perhaps she's a better actress than I thought.

I study her as Loki works in silence. Judge excuses himself to go handle some employee business. We own all of them, and everyone is aware of the stakes in this game.

This has been a long time coming.

Only those loyal to our family are working in The Lodge.

And all the guests are our enemies.

Except for her, the beautiful brunette with midnight eyes.

What side will you fall on? I wonder, admiring her once more. *How long will you last in this game?*

I suppose I'll soon find out just how resilient she is.

Because the next phase is about to begin.

Seven
SYDNEY

MORE FOOD.

More wine.

More bullshit.

Everyone is laughing and socializing and having a grand old fucking time, while I'm sitting here trying to figure out how to escape again.

How long will they keep us in this damn room?

I left once. No one noticed. Can I do it again?

The questions roll through my mind on repeat as I force myself to eat the steak dinner in front of me. They've made a family-style table, just like they did for breakfast, where all of us are seated. I'm sandwiched between Griffin and Landon, and I could not be more uncomfortable.

Their world is just so fucked up.

But I cut my steak like I don't care at all. Because that's what Kage told me to do. Then tonight, he'll help me escape.

I'm not sure why I believe him. I probably shouldn't. But there's just something about him that makes me feel so secure that I can't help but hope he's telling me the truth.

He's the only one who seems real to me.

He understands that this situation is messed up.

He didn't fault me for wanting to leave.

But he also told me not to call the cops, saying this world doesn't work that way.

Which tells me he's very familiar with how this society is run, something that doesn't particularly shock me since he works here.

Because his family used to live nearby. *Where?* I wonder, deciding to ask him later.

Assuming I'm ever allowed to leave this room again, anyway.

Dessert arrives.

I barely taste it.

More alcohol—the theme for this week, apparently—is offered after the dishes are cleared.

And Preston suggests we all find our seats from last night. It seems like a cruel reminder to have to sit on the couch Becca occupied with me just yesterday, but I do it anyway. Mostly because I'm hoping this means we're finally going to hear from someone in charge.

Not that I expect anything to improve. But I'll do pretty much anything to make this day end so I can meet Kage and hopefully leave.

Unless he decides to lock me in a cage, like he threatened earlier.

Or perhaps Landon and Preston will do it for him.

God, why did I agree to come here this week?

Deciding my future feels so insignificant now. I'm too busy trying to survive this current hell.

What if they won't let me go? What if I know too much?

This whole week is the definition of a nightmare.

Landon settles onto the cushion beside me rather than taking the seat from last night.

"Don't, Preston," he says as his friend starts to speak. "I can sit wherever the fuck I want to sit, and right now, it's next to Syd." He looks at me, and for the first time, he doesn't have that smarmy playboy air about him. He actually appears to be concerned. "Are you all right?"

"No," I answer honestly. "No, I'm not fucking all right, Landon."

He nods. "I didn't think so." He reaches around me to grab the controller on the table, then relaxes into the cushions again.

"How can you all be so calm about this?" I ask him, pitching my voice low. "Becca's dead."

He lifts a shoulder. "People die every day, Sydney. It's usually best not to fret about accidents outside our control."

"Accidents?" I repeat. "You think her death was an *accident*?"

"I don't know what to think yet. But I'm sure we'll have answers soon."

"From your father."

He nods.

"Because Daddy cleans up all your messes, right?"

He glances at me, his blue eyes flashing with warning. "I didn't kill Becca, Syd. So it's not *my* mess he's cleaning up."

"Are you saying I did?"

"I'm saying that maybe you should consider shutting the fuck up until we know more." The edge in his voice has my jaw tightening.

I've never been a fan of authority.

And I certainly am not a fan of *his* authority.

Yet I had no problem accepting commands from Kage earlier, a realization that makes me frown now. *Why is that?*

"That's much better," Landon praises me, his

knuckles brushing along my cheek. "Keep being a good girl and maybe I'll let you share my room tonight."

My lips part. "Oh, that will—"

Darkness falls over the room, sending a chill down my spine. *Why do they do that?* I think, nearly cursing out loud.

Instead, I clasp my hands tightly in my lap. Otherwise, I may reach over and strangle Landon for talking to me like I'm twelve.

And also insinuating that I would behave for him just to fuck him.

That will absolutely not be happening, I was about to say before the theater hall went black. Now I'm waiting for the stupid ceremony to begin, to finally tell us *something* about—

A giggle echoes through the speakers.

It's soft at first but grows almost into a maniacal laugh.

Oh, what the fuck?

The sound swirls and booms, making me jump as Becca's face appears on the screen. "Gotcha," she says, and my lips part.

"What?" I breathe. *How? How is that possible?* I saw her dead body. I saw her head with a fucking bullet in it. I saw her glassy eyes. *What is this? Some morbid joke? Some sick and twisted…?*

"Game," I whisper to myself. *It's all a game...*

"Stop talking," Landon hisses under his breath.

My fingers curl into fists, the urge to punch him and hurt everyone in this room slamming into me like a freight train. These people are fucking sick.

"Well, I can't say I'm pleased about being the first to die," Becca says with a dramatic sigh. "But that's the purpose of the game."

To fake your death? I want to demand. But I don't want to catch Landon's attention again. It's bad enough that he's sitting beside me and offering me rewards for "good behavior." I really don't want to know what he'll do if I "disobey" him.

"Think of this like one of those murder mystery parties," Becca continues, her brown hair perfectly styled as always. She's wearing a cornflower-blue dress and pearls, resembling the perfect housewife. "You have to work together to hide my death and discover my killer."

Hide my death, I repeat to myself, frowning. *Why? You're obviously alive.*

Unless she means hypothetically.

In which case, sigh.

This is such a ridiculous team-building activity.

"It's all about answering truthfully, something I didn't do. I was hiding a secret, one I chose not to divulge. And that's why I died." She grimaces on that last part. "Well, not really. But you get what I mean."

I really, truly do not "get" what she means at all.

She clears her throat. "Anyway, the reason the game is called Truth or Kill is because those who lie will die. Those who tell the truth will remain. And together, you have to discover who the killer is. Because it's someone among you."

Silence falls on that pronouncement, causing several of the men in the room to look at each other.

Courtney and Gretchen immediately stare at me.

Because yeah. I'm the killer. I almost roll my eyes. *Idiots.*

"The culprit is someone who already knows all your secrets," she says. "The person is already on the inside, being granted with internal knowledge to help govern this game. So when you lie, the killer knows. And you will be removed from the game." She points to herself. "Like me."

"What did you lie about?" Gretchen asks her. "You were only asked about some stupid sorority thing."

"And about who she wanted to marry," Courtney adds.

Gretchen snorts. "Yeah, but that wasn't even a fair question. Everyone knows she wants Preston."

I glance at the male in question, just in time to

see his resulting smirk.

Landon doesn't seem to share his amusement, his narrowed gaze on the screen. He almost appears angry.

"You don't want to end up like me," Becca says, drawing my focus back to her. She doesn't give anything away on her face—no sadness or remorse—just a blank stare, as though she's reading a cue card. Which she probably is, given how well scripted this is.

But she's holding a newspaper with today's date on it.

Almost to serve as proof of life.

Which is a bit strange. Wouldn't these people just believe her anyway?

Hell, never mind. They wouldn't care either way.

"So tell the truth," she says. "Work together to determine who the killer is. Remember what I said about the killer's knowledge of your secrets. And try to survive the game."

The screen goes black again, making me blink.

What the actual fuck?

The Covington Industries tune begins to play as the crowns start to spin on the screen, just like yesterday.

And everyone starts looking at each other, wondering who the killer is among them.

Gretchen, of course, looks at me. "Well, obviously it's Sydney."

My eyebrows lift. "Yeah, except I wasn't even here last night. I haven't been playing. And I couldn't give two shits about your secrets."

"Uh-huh. That's so believable, isn't it, Court?"

"No, she's too obvious," Landon cuts in before her friend can chime in with her agreement. "Syd's the only one who wasn't originally invited, so she's probably not even on the roster. And if she is, again, it's too obvious. Our parents are smarter than that."

"They also wouldn't trust an outsider with our secrets," Preston adds.

"Does that mean I'm excused?" I ask. "Because I really don't want to be here."

"Stop talking," Landon tells me again.

I glare at him. "Make me." Okay, yeah, I'm going to see what happens when I disobey. Because fuck this. Fuck him. Fuck *everyone* in this room.

He raises both eyebrows. "Oh, darling, if you want something to do with your mouth—"

"Sydney Evans," the voice says from the screen, making my blood run cold.

Oh, hell no…

"I think it's time for you to play Truth or Kill," it continues, my face appearing on the screen along with all my details.

Twenty-two-year-old female.

Born: Athens, Ohio.

Father unknown.

Mother deceased.

Foster child.

Academic Scholarship.

3.95 GPA.

Computer Science major.

It's all right there, clear as day. Nothing about being an heir. No skeletons in the closet to showcase with a video. Just my picture and a bunch of facts.

"Ask me anything," I dare the voice. Because what the hell do I have to hide?

The screen melts into a series of numbers.

Ten to be precise.

I take the controller from Landon—who seems to be frozen beside me—and I randomly click the first box.

"Excellent choice, Ms. Evans," the voice says. "Tell us, who would you rather fuck—Preston or Landon?"

"That's easy." I don't even give him a chance to pull up the image of the room or form a trigger. "Neither."

Gretchen and Courtney gasp.

"You're supposed to tell the truth," Landon reminds me.

"I am," I reply, setting the controller down.

"Ah, ah," the voice says. "You missed last night's fun. You'll pick a second box now to make up for missed truths."

I roll my eyes and select box two.

"Not very original," the voice chides me.

"I could say the same about this fucked-up game," I tell it, eliciting more gasps from the peanut gallery. But this is between me and whoever is running this twisted retreat.

"I see." Silence falls for a deadly beat, the video turning into the room as the trigger appears right over my face. "Would you prefer to die, Ms. Evans?"

"Is that my truth?" I counter, my heart racing in my chest. "Because no, I don't want to die."

"Then tell Landon why you don't want to fuck him. Or…" The trigger moves to him. "You can choose to remove him."

I consider it for a moment, only because something about his offer sticks with me. Some sort of hidden suggestion. A way to really play this game.

As Becca said, it's like a live version of Clue.

Except in this case, the killer knows everyone's secrets.

What happens if you remove that person? Is it Landon? He does seem to be in charge. But wouldn't that be too obvious?

Why am I even thinking about this? I wonder.

I don't want to be here. And this isn't my game to play.

I shake my head, clearing it.

And look at Landon. "I don't want to fuck you because I just don't want to fuck you." I shrug. "You're not my type. And I didn't agree to come on this trip with Becca just to be a piece of meat for a billionaire heir to play with while bored." I refocus on the screen. "Is that good enough for you?"

"Your truth is appreciated, Ms. Evans," the male replies.

Of course, it could also be a female.

I thought it was a real voice last night. Now I suspect it's some sort of advanced computer-generated voice, similar to the ones in smart homes. An artificial intelligence that displays emotion and inflection just as well as a human.

I would be impressed if it wasn't narrating this insane game.

"Spin the crown," the voice tells me. "Pick our next target."

I hate that it's forcing me to play, but I do as it asks.

It's obvious that I won't be allowed to leave tonight.

So I make myself at home and listen as these idiots share all their deepest and darkest secrets with each other. It feels like I'm essentially being buried alive with information.

Information that's likely going to get me killed.

Becca may be alive now—a fact that still baffles my mind. *Because who does that?* These people, apparently.

But something tells me I won't be as lucky as Becca by the end of the week.

Which means I need to find a way out of here. Or find out why she chose me to attend this retreat.

It's starting to feel less random and more… planned.

I just don't know why.

"Mr. Matterhorn, tell us all where you were last night," the voice says, causing me to glance at him.

Silence falls as Landon runs the trigger across the room, obviously considering what he wants to divulge. I half hope he shoots me so I can leave.

But he seems to think better of it.

"Can you be specific on timing?"

"Of course," the voice replies. "Between the hours of one and three a.m."

That would have been after I went to sleep.

Is the voice implying that Landon may be the killer? Do we know what time Becca supposedly died?

"I was in the living area of my suite, on a conference call with my father and Mr. Michaels."

How? I want to demand. We don't have cell

service. And as far as I know, there isn't any internet here either.

"What?" Preston asks.

Landon ignores him and says, "My laptop is upstairs if anyone wants to check the browser history and timestamps."

"What was the conference call about?" the voice presses.

"The realignment of the Edington Branch," he says. "Or rather, the acquisition of it under the Matterhorn part of the enterprise."

"What the fuck are you talking about?" Preston demands.

"You'll need to speak to your father about it," Landon tells him calmly.

"No, Mr. Matterhorn. There are no secrets here, remember? Answer Preston's question. Unless you wish to remove him?" The trigger appears again.

Landon sets the controller down and faces Preston, ignoring the screen. "The Edington part of the business lost one point five billion dollars in assets last year due to that hack on the CovCell tech. The board voted to privately dismantle their part of the business and disperse it to the other areas. I will be inheriting most of the responsibilities upon graduation."

"Does Mr. Edington know?"

"He will in two weeks when it's announced,"

Landon replies.

Preston considers it for a moment. "And what happens to Mr. Edington?"

"He'll be removed," Landon says.

"And his stock?"

"My father is working on the sales of it right now."

"Without his knowledge, I assume."

"Of course."

"I see." Preston no longer sounds angry, but thoughtful. "Then I guess Rebecca's death, or whatever you want to call it, is more symbolic than we all realized. Hell, it's downright *expected*."

"Indeed," Landon agrees, my stomach twisting with how easily they just accepted Becca's *death*.

Sure, she may be alive now, but to speak about her with such carelessness after being part of their clique for all these years? It just seems heartless.

"Why wasn't I included in this discussion?" Preston asks.

"Because you're not going straight into the company like I am," Landon tells him. "You chose law school like Griffin."

Preston nods. "That's fair."

And just like that, he's calm again.

Which prompts the game to continue.

Whereby I lose another two hours of my life before we're finally excused.

There doesn't appear to be any drama tonight, with no one forcing anyone to leave the room. I think because they're all suspicious of each other. Something that becomes increasingly evident after we're dismissed and silence descends upon the room.

No more laughter.

No more jokes.

No more *video games.*

Just a serious atmosphere of evaluation as they all study one another.

I swallow when Landon focuses on me. "You don't want to fuck me? Fine. You can sleep outside."

My eyebrows lift. "Excuse me?"

"Rebecca Edington is no longer a guest of the hotel," he tells me as he stands. "You were her plus-one. That means you're without a bed. Have a good night, Sydney."

Wow, I guess his ego's a bit bruised from my denial.

That's fine.

I don't have any intention of staying here another night anyway.

Assuming Kage stays true to his word and helps me.

Landon leaves the room with Preston on his tail.

The others start to follow, none of them bothering to offer me so much as a couch to rest on.

Not that I'm surprised.

I would like to know where my bags are, though.

Probably at reception.

Sighing, I stand and shake my head. "Fucking rich kids," I mutter under my breath.

I'll face my fate in a bit. First, I need some air. And maybe the stars.

A hike will help calm my mind, help me think, help me *breathe*.

Then I'll figure out what to do.

I consider looking for Kage, but then I recall what he said about finding me later.

Well, let's see if you really meant it, I think as I leave the theater hall. *Catch me if you can, Kage. And maybe we'll play our own version of a game.*

Eight
KAGE

SYDNEY EVANS IS MAGNIFICENT.

She even impressed my brothers, something not many people have ever achieved.

"All right. I'm starting to see the allure," Judge admitted after she bluntly told Landon why she wouldn't fuck him.

"She's fucking hot," Loki echoed, amused by her feisty side during the game.

"She's mine," I told them both.

A fact I'm currently proving as I follow her through the woods. If she knows I'm here, she doesn't show it. Which makes me feel like a predator hunting my prey.

Accurate, I suppose.

Because I intend to ensnare her very soon.

Landon didn't want to offer her a bed to sleep in? That's fine. I have one.

Or maybe I'll put her in the room that Judge arranged for her earlier.

I never told him my decision, so he prepared it just in case.

Landon Matterhorn does not dictate who stays in The Lodge—I do.

If he doesn't want her to be his guest, then she'll be mine instead.

End of discussion.

He doesn't own this land. My brothers and I do, something he'll learn soon enough.

"Shit," Sydney curses up ahead. I can't see her well beneath the canopy of trees, but I'm guessing her sweater snagged on a branch.

"You know, a flashlight may prove useful," I say as I casually walk up behind her.

She jumps, making me grin. She scares beautifully.

"Jesus," she breathes.

"Kage," I correct. "Unless you're trying to change my name? I mean, you seem to mistake me for *Jesus* a lot."

Hmm, perhaps she'll refer to me as *God* later.

"Maybe because you keep sneaking up on me," she snaps.

"Am I doing that?" I ask innocently.

She snorts and turns to continue along the path toward the field. "If I have to be truthful in this place, then so do you."

"Ah, but I'm not playing the game."

She spins on me, causing me to walk right into her. I grab her hips on instinct, startled by her sudden halt. "So you do know about the game?"

"Of course I know about the game." *My brother created it.*

"Don't you think it's fucked up?"

"Yes. But the same can be said about most of high society."

Her palms go to my chest, but she doesn't push me away. She just rests her hands there and stares up at me in the dark. "Becca isn't dead."

I don't reply. Because I can't.

"The whole thing was staged. Did you know?" she demands.

That it was staged? "Yes."

"And you didn't tell me?"

"I told you to remain calm and wait for tonight," I remind her. "Now you know why."

She says nothing for a long moment. "You knew I would find out that it was all a setup. That I would no longer see a reason to go to the authorities."

Not exactly. But I can't say that. "I knew you would feel more at peace after tonight, yes."

"More at peace," she repeats. "Except now I'm stuck playing a game with a bunch of rich imbeciles who don't give a flying fuck about anyone other than themselves. And they're sharing all their secrets in front of me. Which means I'm probably going to die after all this is done."

Smart girl, I think. Because yes, she will know far too much after this week ends.

So she'll likely need to be killed as a result.

Unless I can make her understand the purpose of all this.

Unless she lets me keep her.

Unless a lot of things, really.

"The future isn't always as clear as we believe," I tell her cryptically. "Maybe the powers that be will let you live."

"Or maybe you can help me escape," she suggests, but there's a note of incredulity in her tone.

Because she already knows that I won't help her.

Not in that manner, anyway.

She sighs, long and hard, her nails curling into my sweater. "Why me, Kage? Why did Becca bring me here?"

Because you're expendable, I nearly admit. *Because she's a horrible person who never cared about you. Never saw your potential. Merely made you a pawn in this dangerous game.*

I lift my hand away from her hip and bring it up to her face. "I'm not sorry about meeting you, Sydney. Even if the circumstances are… unique."

"Unique," she echoes with a sardonic twist in her voice. "That's one way to describe it." She leans into my palm, her face too shadowed for me to read her expression. "You can't help me at all, can you?"

"Depends on your definition of *help,* little dove." I draw my thumb along her lower lip. "I may not be able to aid in your physical escape, but I could provide a mental one."

"Sex," she says. "You can give me sex."

I nearly laugh. Her bluntness is a fucking turn-on. "Sex, yes."

"So you'll fuck me into oblivion, then watch them kill me." She almost sounds amused. "How romantic."

"I've never claimed to be romantic, Sydney. Merely practical and straightforward. And occasionally honest."

"Right. Because you don't have to play the truth game."

"No. I wasn't invited to play." Just to observe. And to clean up the mess afterward.

"Do you want to fuck me, Kage?" she asks.

I'm not going to lie to her. Nor am I going to waste time, something she's already told me she refuses to do. "Yes, Sydney. I want to fuck you."

"I should demand that you help me get the hell out of here in exchange for sex," she says, sounding tired. "But nothing is what it seems in this place, including you."

"You're not wrong."

She sighs again and nods. Then she takes a step away from me, but her hand falls to mine at her hip. She removes it but doesn't drop it, instead linking our fingers together before starting down the path again.

I move along behind her, letting her lead.

She doesn't pause until we reach the clearing. And all she does then is glance around before finding the place she wants to lie down.

I join her and watch as she observes the night.

After several minutes of peaceful quiet, she says, "According to Landon, I no longer have a room at The Lodge. So do you know where my things are?"

"In your new room," I tell her.

She rotates her face toward me. "What new room? He told me to sleep outside."

And something tells me she intended to do exactly that. *However...* "Mr. Matterhorn isn't in charge of reception, nor does he own The Lodge." *My family does.* "You have a room, Sydney. Rebecca's family prepaid for her stay. I'll just apply her overpayment to your new room."

A bit of a white lie—I didn't intend to charge for the room at all.

But Sydney doesn't need to know that.

"Or you could give me keys to a car and let me drive off," she suggests.

"I don't have a car here for you to borrow," I say, choosing my words carefully. "And as you've already inferred, I can't help you escape in that way."

"Can't or won't?" she asks.

I consider the distinction for a moment and decide not to lie. She deserves at least that much from me. "Won't."

"I see." She returns her gaze to the sky. "You work for them."

"No. I work for myself. But I'm a selfish man, Sydney. And I don't want you to leave." All true.

I half expect her to get angry and yell at me.

But she merely closes her eyes and releases a long breath.

I'm not sure if she's waiting for me to explain more or if she's just done with the conversation. I don't have anything else to say, so I remain quiet, and a comfortable silence befalls us.

Her breathing evens out, and I begin to wonder if she's asleep. But then she says, "Landon had a conference call. Via the internet, I assume?"

"He has a special pass, yes." However, it's not what Landon thinks at all, something I don't elaborate on now.

"I don't suppose I can have one, too?"

"You don't need one." Nor does she deserve one. Those passes are meant for darker versions of this game. And I don't want to rope her into one of those.

"Maybe I want one."

"Maybe I want you," I counter.

She frowns. "Sex for a Wi-Fi pass?" She opens her eyes to stare at me. "Really?"

I laugh. "That's not what I meant. I don't care how good a fuck you are, sweetheart. I'll never give you one of those passes." Because they're a punishment more than a gift.

"So you won't really help me at all? Not even if I blow your mind?"

"The internet pass won't help you," I promise as I roll to my side. I lift up onto my elbow and prop my head on my hand so I can stare down at her. "And you're already blowing my mind, Sydney. Most women would be losing their shit right now."

"I'm not most women."

"I've noticed." I study her mouth, the luscious curves and alluring texture. "I'm going to be blunt with you, Sydney. There's no escaping this. You're in the game now, and you have Rebecca Edington to thank for that. Running isn't an option. Hiding isn't an option. Embracing destiny is the only way forward. No one can save you except yourself."

"I'm clearly not doing a good job of that, considering I'm lying in a field instead of hunting for car keys."

"You won't find any. The people in charge here thought through every angle." I was certain of it, as I was one of those people. "You can either embrace it or live in a state of perpetual fear. What's it going to be?"

She gazes up at me. "Is that what you tell yourself? That you only have two options—embrace it or fear it?"

"Yes," I answer honestly. "I learned long ago that the only one who can change my fate is me. But to do that, I had to accept the path I was already on. Only then could I reconstruct the future destination."

I'm revealing a lot without elaborating. And she seems to know this because she's studying me intently. "I see."

"Do you?" I wonder. "Do you really?"

"Not all the details, no. But you're telling me to take charge of this opportunity and use it to craft my end point."

Not exactly what I said, but an admirable interpretation. "There's nothing you can do to change your present. But there is still plenty to be done about your future."

"Assuming they don't kill me for knowing too

much."

"Maybe you should focus on being worth too much to kill," I counter as I cup her face with my free hand. I'm still balancing on my elbow and looking down at her, the position now blocking her view of the stars.

But she's not focused on the sky anymore anyway.

She's focused on me.

Her gaze is on my mouth. Her desire is written plainly in her expression.

I don't say anything cheesy like, *What if this is your last night to live? Don't you want to make the best of it?*

I've never been that man. I'll never be that man. Because I'm not a hero. I'm not her white knight. I'm simply Kage. And I take what I want.

Which, in this moment, is her.

So I don't ask permission. I don't spout poetry about her beauty or seduce her with words.

I simply kiss her.

It's not soft or tentative, but an unspoken desire to claim.

And this beautiful girl accepts it openly, her lips automatically parting to receive my damning possession.

Fuck. She's going to destroy everything.

She's going to tempt me into a dance with fate.

She's going to end up owning me as much as I intend to own her.

I'm not sure what it is about her. I'm not sure I even really care. I just want her. And I've never been the type to deny my cravings.

Her fingers graze my wrist, my hand still against her face. Then she trails her touch up my bare forearm to where my sleeves are rolled against my elbow. Upward she climbs to my shoulder and my neck and eventually to my hair.

She doesn't just thread her fingers through the strands; she tugs on them.

And it's not in a way that says she wants me to back off.

It's in a way that tells me she wants *more.*

But I'm patient. I enjoy delaying the inevitable. And I show her that by slowing our kiss, my tongue setting the pace and dominating her with each stroke.

She pulls harder on my hair, making me smile. "You want something from me, you take it," I tell her.

Her dark eyes flash as they open, her thick lashes grazing her cheek. "Anything?"

"Anything," I tell her. *Except for your freedom.* Because that's something I can't give her. Not yet.

But I know that's not why she asked.

She wants to know my limits just as badly as I want to know hers.

We gaze at each other for another beat, her pupils and irises blending into a perfect ring of midnight.

"Do you have a condom?" she asks softly.

"Yes."

"Good." Her grip tightens in my hair, almost painfully so. And I fucking love it. "Then take me to that oblivion you mentioned, Kage. Help me escape my mind. At least for a little while."

Fuck, I may just marry this girl. An insane notion, considering we just met. But she's so goddamn perfect that I can barely see straight.

So I do what any immoral man in my position would do.

I kiss her.

Deeply. Thoroughly. Completely.

Telling her without words that she's about to become mine. Even if just for the night. *Or maybe for the week.*

Nine

SYDNEY

GOD, THIS IS SO FUCKING WRONG. I SHOULD BE screaming and begging him to help me.

But I know he can't.

This world isn't like the one I've known all my life. It's some sort of alternate reality where typical formalities and laws don't apply. These people live in their own bubble, creating rules on a whim that they mutually understand.

I'm the outsider.

Yet Kage is different. He's like me. I can sense it in my bones, feel it in my spirit, that he just gets me. Maybe because of similar life experiences. Maybe because we both choose to live in the moment. Maybe because we both see through the bullshit and right to the heart of this insanity.

We're in it together, just by a different set of circumstances.

Becca invited me under false pretenses—something that is astutely clear to me now.

Meanwhile, Kage chooses to be here. Or I assume he does, anyway.

However, perhaps there's no choice in it for him at all. He told me his parents used to live near here. Did they have some sort of slave-type agreement with the Covington Industries elite?

Or is he truly here because he wants to be here?

I don't have the mental capacity to ponder it anymore. I'm all out of fucks to give. This morning drained me. Becca's death unnerved me. And her coming back from the grave thoroughly pissed me off.

I don't want to think anymore. I don't want to give in to the chaos of my emotions. I just want to *feel,* to exist in a temporary state of bliss, to lose myself to the man hovering over me.

Somehow, this is about more than his looks and physical appeal. It… it simply feels *good.* Even though I know we shouldn't be doing this, and even though I know it's probably not the healthiest reaction, I give in to the sensations anyway.

It's an escape.

A way to feel alive in a forest tainted by deadly desires.

Kage's tongue is masterful, taming mine and teaching me his preferences with every stroke. I moan, falling into his kiss completely, giving him every piece of me and not caring at all if he breaks me.

This isn't about trust. This is simply about truth.

I want him. Why wait? Why engage in a game of cat and mouse when we already know he's going to win?

That's not my brand of foreplay. I prefer to take advantage of the moment and live in the present because the future isn't guaranteed.

Especially my current future.

Fuck everything, I think, my palm wrapping around Kage's neck. *Fuck everything except this.*

God, this man can kiss.

It's like he's seducing me with his tongue alone.

He's not hungry or violent or even overpowering, just beautifully sensual with an underlying hint of dominance. He's in charge and he knows it. But he's giving me time to enjoy it, too. Ensuring my pleasure rivals his.

I feel cherished. Which is exactly what I need. And somehow he knows it.

He doesn't rush. He doesn't immediately grab me or start ripping off clothes. He takes his time.

I melt beneath him, loving this approach. It's skilled. It's patient. It's perfect.

And it draws out the moment.

Making me want him to move. To take charge. To *touch* me.

He told me to take what I want. So I do. I draw my nails down his back to his hip and around to his belt. I unbuckle it slowly and feel him grin against my mouth.

But he doesn't speak.

Nor does he stop kissing me.

Not even as I unfasten the top button.

I draw the zipper down, then trace the outline of his cock. I can't see his boxers in the dark, but I'm guessing they're black. Just like his pants.

Just like our souls.

He catches my wrist and pushes my hand over my head as he rolls onto me, his mouth still dominating mine. I groan at the feel of his weight, loving the way he pushes me into the earth.

It leaves me breathless.

Heady.

Intoxicated by him.

I want more. I want him. I want… *Oh, yes…*

His lips move across my cheek to my ear, nibbling the lobe. "Remember my name, sweetheart," he whispers. "*Kage*. Not Jesus or God, just Kage."

I still don't know his last name.

And I'm not sure I care. Not right now. Not like

this. Not with his mouth kissing a path down my neck.

Goose bumps fly up and down my arms, the sensation of having him at my throat making my toes curl. He grabs my free hand and pulls it over my head to join the other, his palm ensnaring both my wrists to keep me captive beneath him.

While his opposite hand trails along my arm to my side and down to my hip. Then back up again beneath my sweater and undershirt.

Grazing. Skimming. Touching me softly.

I shiver as the frigid air kisses my exposed skin. Oh, but his fingers quickly chase away the chill as he ignites a fire along my belly. A fire that soon spreads to my chest.

Fuck.

I bow up off the ground into him as he palms my breast, his mouth still against my throat. It's like he's testing my pulse with his tongue, seeing how fast my heart can race from his mere touch alone.

My entire body goes up in flames, my mind no longer processing anything beyond *Kage.*

Kage is kissing me.

Kage is touching me.

Kage is burning *me.*

His name leaves my mouth, the plea for more evident in the breathless quality of my voice. "Kage,"

I say again, arching into him.

"Mmm," he hums, his mouth returning to my ear. "Such a good girl saying my name like that." He kisses my temple, his gaze holding a devious promise as he lifts his head to look down at me. "Are you okay with the cold?"

"Yes."

"Good. Because I want to take off your clothes." He straddles my waist and sits up while pulling me with him with his hand around my nape. His lips are still near mine, his breath warm and minty as he drops his hands to my waist. "Lift your arms for me, gorgeous."

I feel as though I'm under a spell as I comply, my gaze holding his as he starts lifting my sweater and shirt. His eyes only disappear for a second as the fabric moves over my head. He kisses me then, his mouth distracting me while he reaches around me to deposit my clothes.

My bra joins the pile.

Then he lays me back on top of it and shifts to undo my jeans.

My shoes disappear.

My pants follow.

My socks and thong, too.

I'm so hot for him that I barely feel the cold. His hands and mouth stoke my inner flame as he begins to explore me openly with his tongue and palms.

Stroking up my sides, kissing a path down my neck to my torso.

Sucking. Biting. *Licking.*

"*Kage,*" I breathe, squirming.

"Shh," he hushes. "I'm exploring."

He has me sprawled out on my clothes, cushioning me against the cold earth. Between that and the heat emanating from him, I feel protected from the elements. Warm, yet still sensing the biting chill at the same time. It's an incredible mix.

It's perfect.

It's exactly what I need to chase the chaos from my mind.

His forest-green eyes appear black in the night as he looks up at me with my nipple between his teeth. He doesn't bite down harshly, just enough to sting. Then he soothes the pain with his tongue, leaving me quaking beneath him.

I feel like I'm already on the edge, teetering between this reality and a dream.

But he's not done.

He moves to my other breast to repeat his actions while his hands continue to roam along my sides.

"G-ah…" I almost say *God.* "Kage."

His gaze smolders because he knows that I nearly slipped up. But he's pleased that I caught myself. I can see it in his expression, all male arrogance and pride.

"You're beautiful," he tells me softly, surprising me with his praise. "Like a little nymph illuminated by the moon."

"This nymph wants to fuck," I say, not bothering with the flattering words or romance. That's not what this is about.

"And she will be fucked," he agrees, his lips going south. "Just as soon as I'm done making you come with my tongue."

Oh God…

He's going to kill me with his mouth and hands, his mastery of my body uncanny and unfounded. No one should be this good at foreplay.

Yet Kage is.

He's… he's…

Fuck.

He finds my clit with the first flick of his tongue, and I nearly explode for him on the spot, something he must know because he chuckles in response. Which only vibrates my sensitive flesh that much more. "Spread your legs for me," he says. They're already spread, but I move them a little to accommodate him better. "Wider, Sydney."

He demonstrates by grabbing my thighs and testing the limits of my flexibility.

Which he must find pleasing because he rumbles

in approval and stares up at me with stark desire in his gaze. Then he licks me deep while I watch, making my insides combust with renewed need.

His name leaves me on a pant, so he does it again.

And again.

God, I'm ready to explode. I can feel the heat building inside me, edging me closer and closer to oblivion. His tongue coaxes me onward, his eyes beckoning me to shatter for him.

He slides a finger inside me.

Then a second.

And curls them in a way that has me seeing stars. "Oh, *Kage…*" His name is replacing the Almighty's on my tongue, his domination overwhelming my mind and forcing me to think of him as the higher power and no one else.

With his tongue and fingers driving me to the brink of insanity, it almost seems right to consider him as my god.

Except it feels like he's worshipping me, not the other way around.

I groan as he sucks my swollen nub deep into his mouth. It's so intense that it almost hurts. I'm balancing on a cliff, the threat of a fall making me breathless.

He knows.

I can see it in his eyes that *he knows*.

A wicked smile.

One full of masculine expectation and approval.

He releases my clit and swirls his tongue around it, then applies just the right amount of pressure to send me to the stars.

My body locks.

My limbs shake.

Either my eyes close or I go blind.

This is what I needed, what I desired. This sensation of bliss. Of euphoric madness. Lost to the sensations. Lost to Kage. Lost to this single moment in time.

My throat hurts from screaming, but it's just so powerful that I can't hold back my reaction. I don't even try. Why not let the forest know that Kage is between my legs? It only seems appropriate. He's a deity to me now, a god of a man, an *addiction*.

I'm only vaguely aware of him moving, the sound of his pants a rustling noise that barely reaches my ears. Something rips. *A condom wrapper,* I think drowsily.

I blink and suddenly he's there, kissing me, feeding me my own pleasure with his tongue.

I moan, the taste of my arousal on his tongue doing things to me.

"You're exquisite," he whispers. "So fucking exquisite."

I open my mouth to reply—though, I'm not sure what to say—only to be silenced by his mouth again.

He's more aggressive now. Savage. *Commanding.*

It proves that everything until this moment was for me, his own way of seducing me into comfort and ensuring my pleasure.

And now, this is for him.

Or maybe for us.

I'm really not sure. I can't think much beyond him settling between my thighs. His cock is a brand against my damp heat, his arousal so thick and potent that it makes my head spin.

"Wrap your arms around me," he says.

I do, my fingers automatically going into his thick hair. "Don't stop kissing me."

"I won't," he promises, his hips aligning with mine. "Legs around my waist, gorgeous. Now."

He doesn't wait for me to agree, or ask permission, just thrusts into me as my thighs cradle him. I arch on a hiss, his girth unexpected and hurting just enough to give me pause.

He's long.

Thick.

Strong.

"Fuck," I whisper.

"Yes," he replies, his tongue tracing my lower lip as he stills above me. It's a beautiful pause that allows me to acclimate to his size and just... *exist*. "Tell me when you're ready, Sydney," he whispers against my mouth. "And be prepared to hold on because I won't be holding back."

No, he doesn't strike me as the type to go slow and easy. That's why his earlier kiss surprised me. But it seems he isn't the kind of man who fucks the same way that he kisses.

It's a discovery that burns me up inside.

Nothing about him is anticipatory. He runs on impulse, taking what he wants, however he wants it.

Knowing it's me he wants now is an exhilarating notion.

"Fuck me, Kage," I tell him. "Fuck me."

His mouth captures mine, his tongue thrusting inside to claim me with the same force as his cock. I groan in response, his possession making me dizzy.

This feels like so much more than a passionate embrace.

It feels like a dark promise. An intense meeting of bodies and mouths underlined in some foreign enchantment. One I can't understand. One that makes my pulse race and my heart sing.

What is this? I marvel. *Why do I feel so light?*

I'm hot, too.

Combusting from the inside out.

I can still feel the aftershocks of my orgasm, but

another one is mounting, growing, pulsating in my lower belly. Moans spill from my mouth, only to be swallowed by his own.

My hips move, my body demanding I keep up with his bruising pace.

His hands roam, gripping my hips and angling me to receive him even deeper.

And then one palm slides between us, his thumb finding my clit as he pounds into me.

I'm absolutely drunk on him. Lost to his domination. Floating somewhere between despair and incredible pleasure.

He's owning me entirely.

His tongue is speaking some language I don't fully understand, yet I'm kissing him back as though I comprehend every word.

Oh, and that inferno, it's roaring inside my lower abdomen, shredding me apart and putting me back together with every pump of his hips against mine.

He's destroying me.

Irrevocably.

And I can't even be sad about it.

Not when death feels this good. "Harder," I tell him. "Please, Ka—"

He grips my throat, silencing me.

My eyes fly open to see the dark depths of his, the devious intent flickering down at me. I try to inhale and can't, his grasp too strong.

Fuck, he's going to leave a bruise.

On my hip, too.

Because he's holding me so tightly I feel like my bones are going to shatter.

Yet it's my insides that pulsate in response, my blood heating from the very real threat on top of me. Some rational part of me knows I should be fighting for my life right now.

But I'm too lost to the flames consuming my insides to do anything other than tremble beneath him.

So much power.

So much danger.

So much *Kage.*

He lessens his grip just enough for me to breathe, then clamps down again. "I'm going to make you come like this," he tells me. "You'll try to scream, but you won't be able to. Because I won't let you."

Why is that so hot? I wonder, shaking now. *Why is this making me burn? What is wrong with me?*

I'm clearly damaged. Perhaps from my life. Maybe from the last twenty-four hours. However, I can't deny how intense this sensation is between us.

"You're close," he whispers, his gaze holding mine as he continues to torture me with his cock. "You don't even need me to stroke your clit. You're going to explode without it, aren't you?"

Yes, I think. *Yes, I am.*

"Inhale, baby," he says, relaxing his grasp again. "Right now."

I comply, stealing as deep a breath as he'll allow.

Then he clamps down again, his touch even harsher than before. *This is fucked up. This is so wrong. He may kill me like this.*

The thoughts consume me, causing my heart to sing in my chest.

I may just die like this, right here, with his cock lodged deep inside me.

Perhaps that was the plan all along.

It should bother me.

It doesn't.

I'm too lost in his darkening stare to care. Too overwhelmed by his touch, his thrusts, his strength.

"Come for me, Sydney," he demands, his lips brushing mine. "I want to see you cry as you fight to breathe. Watch you dwindle in despair as pleasure swallows you whole. Observe your mouth as you try to beg me for your life, silently saying my name over and over again."

This is so fucking crazy.

Yet I feel the maelstrom of sensation coming undone in my core as he slams into me, touching that place deep inside.

Fuck. Fuck. Fuck!

I succumb to the flames, allow it to drag me to hell, as my life spirals around in a sea of black fire.

"That's it, gorgeous," he says, nuzzling my cheek and spreading the dampness there.

Because I've started to cry.

It's all so intense and overwhelming. I'm not sure I can distinguish the pleasure from the pain now. It's… it's… a mixture of both.

"So fucking beautiful," he continues, his tongue tracing my quivering lips.

This man is the devil.

And he's just seduced me to the underworld.

Drawn me down to his lair to become his plaything, his fuck doll, and I'm his to command. Utterly and completely.

"Scream," he says as a rapturous wave swallows me whole.

The stars are no more. Only Kage. Only his dark, wicked eyes. His sinful mouth. The air he's breathing into my lungs.

Literally.

Oh God…

He's pushing air from his mouth to mine, his hand still on my throat as he forces me to breathe.

I'm not sure when I stopped, the orgasm so intense that I can't do much more than feel. Survive. *Pulse.*

He's fucking me. *Hard.*

While I cry in some convoluted mixture of delight and terror.

And then he follows me into the oblivion with a growl against my mouth, my name rumbling through him like some morbid benediction.

I think I come again.

Or maybe I never really stopped.

All I feel is immense euphoria pumping through my body, exploding over and over again as I shake and weep beneath this beast of a man.

So savage and cruel.

Yet attentive and angelic, too.

Who are you? I want to ask him, my gaze searching and seeing nothing but darkness. *Who are you, Kage?*

"I could ask you the same question," I hear him say against my ear. "What are you doing to me, sweet girl?"

I think I smile. But it feels too stretched, too exhausting to truly do. Just as I want to throw his words back at him.

And maybe I do.

Because I seem to be confusing thoughts with voiced words.

Nothing is right in this warped reality. Everything's wrong.

But Kage makes that oddly okay.

He… he makes me feel free.

For a moment.

Giving me my mental escape as I fall down, down, down into a swirl of blissful darkness.

I fall asleep. Or I assume I do, anyway. Because a floating sensation comes to me next, the kind of fantasy that reminds me of swimming in the clouds.

And when I wake again, it's morning.

I'm no longer in the field, but in a bed and staring at a single black rose.

For half a beat, I wonder if it was all a dream.

But one shift of my body tells me it wasn't. Because I'm sore. I'm bruised. I've been thoroughly used.

Yet I don't feel an ounce of remorse about it.

Instead… I smile.

And drift back to sleep, where I dream of a tattooed god of a man strangling me while I come.

Again.

And again.

And again.

Ten
KAGE

SYDNEY IS DREAMING OF ME.

Her mouth moves while she sleeps, her lips revealing my name. I smile and gently trace the mark I left against her throat.

Next time, I may bring out one of my knives. Assuming she trusts me enough to play again.

I surprised her earlier. Her shock was evident in the widening of her eyes. Just as her acceptance and resulting arousal were unmistakable in the way she came for me.

Fuck, it was beautiful.

Just thinking about her tears makes me hard again.

She came so damn hard that she passed out. Or maybe that was a result of her forgetting how to breathe. I released her in plenty of time, but the rapture took her under and so thoroughly drowned her in pleasure that she didn't even think to inhale.

I brought her back with a puff of air, and her resulting tremble took me right into oblivion with her.

The whole experience was so damn *hot.* I only wish I wasn't wearing a condom.

Next time, I want to take her bare.

She's on birth control, something I know because I packed her bags for her earlier.

I also unpacked them after carrying her here.

I didn't dress her in any pajamas, though. I left her naked because I prefer her this way.

If it was my choice, she would remain in this state indefinitely.

Alas, I don't want anyone else to see her like this. She's mine now. Perhaps just for the week. Perhaps for longer. That remains to be seen.

I'll have to wait and see how she reacts when she wakes up.

She stirred for a few minutes at one point, just long enough to see the rose I set on the pillow. Then she fell back asleep again, losing herself to dreams of me.

"Kage," she mouths without sound, her body trembling.

I wonder if it's a nightmare or a dream. Maybe

a mixture of both.

I brush my lips against her temple and continue combing her hair. She's so sweet and delicate like this. Fragile, too.

This girl doesn't play games the way most women do.

I like that about her.

My entire life has been one big chess match. I need someone in it who doesn't fuck around. Maybe that someone can be her.

A rash proclamation.

But like her, I don't believe in delaying the inevitable. I seize the moment when it's available and own it.

Just like I seized her. But will I own her, too?

Perhaps.

I relax beside her and watch the sun playing over the horizon. I've been by her all night, resting only a little.

My brothers will come for me soon.

It's a new day, and I'll be needed for the upcoming task.

Just a few more minutes, I decide, stroking Sydney's hair and arm. *So pretty.*

She hums in her sleep, her eyes moving behind her closed lids.

Do you see me right now? I wonder. *Am I staring*

down at you while I fuck you? Or am I licking you between your thighs?

I glance down her body to the spot in question and grin when I see her legs tense.

I'm absolutely devouring you in your dreams, aren't I, little dove?

Maybe I'll make that dream a reality for her later.

"You're incredible," I whisper to her, my lips near her ear. "I wish I could lie here all day with you, gorgeous." Because I would.

Except my brothers will absolutely kill me if I don't show up for my job soon.

I brush my knuckles along her cheek and throat, then lean in to gently kiss her mouth. She sighs in her sleep, her body rolling toward mine, seeking my warmth.

"Later," I murmur, pulling the sheets and blankets up around her.

I decide to borrow her shower, mostly because I'm hoping she'll wake up and join me. She doesn't. When I walk back out into the bedroom, it's to find her curled into a ball around a pillow—the same one I used for my quick nap.

My lips quirk at the clear desire to be closer to me.

Maybe I'll keep you after all, I think at her as

I pull on a new pair of pants and a dress shirt. I grabbed some after initially dropping Sydney off in this room. I almost didn't return, but leaving her felt wrong.

Which is strange—I typically can't escape a conquest fast enough.

But this one is different.

This one… is Sydney.

I stand by the bed and observe her for another long moment, then fix the blankets around her again. As beautiful as her tits are, I really want to keep that view all to myself.

My wrist buzzes, telling me it's time. But I don't immediately depart.

Instead, I kiss her again, this time on the throat. "See you soon, little dove," I say against her ear.

It takes effort to back away from her, but I eventually manage it.

She has everything she needs in here. It's smaller than the double-bedroom suite Rebecca originally booked, but there's a small living area and a kitchen.

And the balcony is close enough to mine that I can easily hop over here if needed.

Of course, I have a key. So I'll sooner use that than perform an acrobatic act.

I don't bother leaving her a note. The rose will do.

Judge is waiting for me outside her room,

holding a suit jacket. I take it from him, as well as the tie, and wander toward the stairs in silence.

Loki is already in the makeshift business center, seated before all the monitors. "You can turn the camera back on in her room," I say.

He doesn't need to ask who I'm talking about.

His fingers fly over the keyboard as he pulls up Sydney's room and turns on the security cams.

She's still curled around the pillow, her dark hair fanned around her. *Gorgeous,* I think, my lips curving upward.

"Not a problem, hmm?" Judge asks.

"If she is one, she's my problem," I tell him.

"You realize we may still have to kill her," he reminds me.

I lift a shoulder. "If that happens, it happens. But for now, I'm going to keep having fun."

"Just don't go falling in love, baby brother."

I give him a look. Because I *hate* when he calls me that. Loki is the youngest, not me. But we're both younger than thirty-year-old Judge. "I've known the girl, like, three days." *If that,* I think. "She's a good fuck. That doesn't mean I love her."

"Tell that to your expression," he says, gesturing at my face. "You went all lovey-dovey eyes when Loki pulled her up on the screen."

"Because she's beautiful and naked and in a bed

we just shared," I say.

"You did a number on her throat," Loki comments, making me realize that he's zoomed in on her while she's sleeping.

"Hey, cut that shit out," I demand. "Seriously, stop zooming." Thank fuck I covered her with the blankets before coming in here.

"Just admiring," he replies.

"Careful, L. She may just become your future sister-in-law," Judge jokes.

I roll my eyes. "Oh, fuck both of you. And seriously, L. *Stop*. She's sleeping. Have some decency."

Both my brothers laugh and look at me.

"Decency?" Loki repeats. "That's rich coming from you."

"She's mine to be indecent with," I tell him. "Not yours."

That makes Judge laugh even harder.

Apparently, I've become a regular old comedian.

"Seriously, she's off-limits." I take control of the mouse so I can zoom out of the image on the screen. "Go find Chastain. I need to know where he is so I can grab him."

"And he says he's not in love," Judge says, wiping fake tears from his eyes.

"You find a girl who screams like that for you, and we'll see how you feel about sharing her," I tell him.

He just shakes his head. "You're so fucked."

I am. Probably. But I don't want to think or talk about that right now. "Griffin Chastain, brother. Where is he?"

"Passed out in his bed like all the other fake Prince Charmings," Loki drawls. "Want me to neutralize him?" His cursor hovers over the sleeping-gas icon.

I shake my head. "I'll do this the old-fashioned way."

It'll be fun.

And it'll help me take my mind off Sydney Evans.

"Want any help?" Judge offers, arching a brow.

I evaluate Chastain on the camera and shake my head. "He'll be easy enough."

Judge doesn't seem disappointed. He knows I prefer to work alone. "We'll watch from here, then."

I nod and focus on the comms, slipping one into my ear. "Test." My voice comes through just fine. "Good."

Loki ignores me, his attention still on Sydney's screen.

I narrow my gaze at him. "When she wakes up, give her privacy."

He heaves a long, dramatic sigh. "Taking the fun out of everything, K."

"She's mine." Which I've already said, but it's worth repeating.

Judge is laughing again.

I ignore him and give Loki a challenging look. "I mean it, L."

"Yeah, yeah." He waves me off. "Go play, K. We'll be here."

I consider him for a moment, then head over to the weapons locker to pick out my blades of choice. By the time I return, Sydney is no longer on the monitor. *Good. It had better stay that way.*

Judge isn't laughing anymore, his focus on Landon.

"He's up early," I say, frowning. "What's he doing?"

"I don't know, but I'll handle it," Judge replies, taking a seat beside Loki. "Go initiate the next phase. We'll reach out with any issues."

Loki is already pulling up all the hallways and screens near Griffin's room. "All clear," he tells me.

I consider the monitors for a moment, then nod and leave.

If something goes wrong, they'll get me out.

But I don't anticipate this being a problem. Griffin Chastain is a pampered child.

And he's about to find out what happens when a prince falls off his throne.

He becomes a killer.

Eleven
SYDNEY

I'M GOING TO NEED A TURTLENECK TODAY, I DECIDE AS I stare at myself in the mirror.

Kage did a number on my neck. However, I'm not mad about it. If anything, the reminder of our night together just turns me on again.

Which suggests I have a head injury.

Or that I'm losing my mind.

Because I should be pissed. I should be trying to escape. To run. To get the fuck out of this place.

Instead, I inhale the aroma from the black rose and then calmly take a shower. It's obvious that Kage spent the night here because the marble floor is still wet and one of the towels has been used.

Something about that makes me giddy inside.

Kage doesn't strike me as the type to stay the

night with a woman. And to be fair, I'm not exactly the sort of person who enjoys post-sex cuddling sessions either.

But Kage feels unique to me. Perhaps because of this whole fucked-up situation we're in. He's the only "normal" part of any of this.

Which is pretty telling, considering he's not normal at all.

He's my kind of normal, though. He gets me. And on some level, I understand him, too.

I dress in a pair of dark jeans and a matching turtleneck sweater. It's a tribute to the rose—all-black, including my boots and my undergarments.

After drying my hair, I toss it up into a messy bun and head out in search of coffee and breakfast.

Which, of course, is being served in the theater room again.

I half expect Landon to tell me to go eat outside, but he's nowhere to be seen when I arrive.

Good, I think, ordering coffee—black, no sugar or cream—and a plate of eggs.

Things feel a little more normal today, probably because there wasn't a dead body this morning. Or none that I'm aware of, anyway.

Landon still hasn't arrived by the time I finish eating. Neither have four of the other guys.

It seems a bit strange.

Maybe they went out this morning to actually

enjoy the scenery?

I decide to do exactly that and go hunting for Kage. He still owes me a canoe.

"Syd." Landon's voice whips down the hallway, the snap of a command underlining his tone making me freeze. "Where were you last night?"

I slowly turn. "Excuse me?"

"Where did you sleep?" The question is spoken through his teeth, his demeanor all alpha male.

Preston steps out from the room, his expression curious as he glances between us. "What's going on?"

"I want to know where Syd slept last night." Landon's gaze is still on me. "Tell me. Right now."

"Why?" I ask. "Are you trying to make sure I slept outside?"

"I want to know where you were last night."

I fold my arms across my chest and repeat, "Why?"

"Stop fucking playing with me and tell me where you were," he snaps.

"Why don't you ask reception?" I suggest.

Landon steps forward and grabs my throat so quickly I don't even have a second to react. He slams me back against the wall in the next second, stealing the air from my lungs.

"Jesus Christ!" Preston snaps. "What the fuck?"

"Where were you?" Landon demands, ignoring

Preston and everyone else that just entered the hallway. "Tell me right fucking now."

I grab his wrist, but his dress shirt covers his skin, making it difficult to dig my nails in. "Let me go." I use my other hand to push against his chest, but he doesn't budge.

Instead, he squeezes harder, his opposite palm going to my hip.

Which is just fucking great because that's also bruised from last night.

"Answer my fucking question." Landon isn't yelling or vibrating with anger. He's actually eerily calm. And something about that scares me more than a raving lunatic would.

Because this man is dangerous. More dangerous than anyone else seems to realize.

That flirtatious playboy act he puts on is clearly for show.

This is the real Landon Matterhorn.

A leader who isn't afraid to assert his power over others. Because he's above the law and he knows it.

I swallow, and my throat burns in response. Jesus, at least Kage made this enjoyable last night.

Landon? Not so much.

"I'm not going to ask again," he says, his tone telling me he means it.

"With Kage," I grit out, unable to speak much beyond that. Not with the way he's squeezing my already bruised neck.

"Who the fuck is Kage?" Landon asks.

"Reception." I choke on the word, my airway aching.

"Dude, let her go," Preston says, grabbing Landon's shoulder.

"Griffin's missing," Landon hisses. "She's the odd one out. And I want answers. Now who the fuck is Kage?"

"Landon, you're the one who said she wasn't even on the roster. Remember?" Preston's voice is soft, almost coaxing. "She doesn't even really know Griffin."

He's right. I don't. But I would like to know what he means by "missing."

"They still had questions for her last night," Landon says, his grip unrelenting. "They had a profile on her, too."

"Yeah, with a bunch of superficial bullshit, and the questions were about who she wants to fuck," Preston points out. "She's a red herring. Let her go."

Well, that's an interesting shift. Just yesterday Preston commented on how I was alone with Becca when she died.

Now he's saying I have nothing to do with this.

Which was Landon's stand yesterday.

But apparently, now I'm the bad guy. Because I didn't sleep with him?

Because I denied him?

"Come on, man," Preston continues. "Let her go."

Landon's blue eyes flicker with furious flames. "Who is Kage?"

"The reception manager," a deep voice says.

It's not Kage but the man who was waiting for us the other night.

"Is there a problem?" the man presses, arching a dark brow.

Landon looks him over. "And who are you?"

"The Lodge's general manager," he replies. "Kage works for me."

"And is it typical for the help to sleep with a guest?" Landon demands as he releases me.

So now I'm a guest again? I want to ask. But I'm too busy coughing.

"No. But it is typical for my staff to accompany guests on midnight hikes to ensure they remain safe. Which is what happened last night. Apparently, she was looking for a suitable place to sleep outside." He stares at Landon, making me think he knows exactly why I thought that last night.

Landon's jaw ticks.

"It's my understanding that she didn't realize we moved her things to a new room." The manager's grayish-green eyes meet mine. "My sincerest apologies, Ms. Evans. I trust that Kage rectified the situation?"

"He did." My voice is scratchy, thanks to Landon's manhandling.

"Excellent. Is there anything else?" His attention returns to Landon.

"Have you seen Mr. Chastain?" Landon asks.

"Yes. I believe he's waiting for you in the theater." The manager waves toward the room I just vacated. "May I suggest finding a seat? There's a game to play, yes?"

Holy shit. He's in on it, too?

What is this place? A retreat haven for the wealthy and the insane?

Landon storms off into the room with Preston hot on his tail. The others all follow.

I don't.

I much prefer my earlier plan to go find a canoe.

"Ms. Evans," the manager says, his tone polite. "You're expected to join them."

Of fucking course I am.

"Where's Kage?" I ask, ignoring his comment entirely, as well as the full rasp in my voice. "He owes me a canoe."

And maybe a painkiller, I think, wincing at the rawness of my throat.

Note to self: No more strangling Sydney today.

The manager's dark brow arches again. "A

canoe?"

"We raced. I won. I want a canoe." End of story. Mostly because I really don't want to talk anymore.

He stares at me for a moment, and I swear he wants to laugh. But he doesn't. "You need to go in the theater, Ms. Evans."

"It's Sydney. And no, thank you." I try to infuse a hint of firmness in my tone, but it doesn't work with how damaged my voice is from Landon's not-so-affectionate touch.

"It wasn't a request," the manager tells me, a warning in his tone. "You don't want to test the limits of this game. Trust me."

This strikes me as one of those battles I don't want to enter. Because the steel in his gaze tells me I won't win.

There's an edge to him, an edge that reminds me a bit of Kage.

Maybe they're related.

He did say his family lives nearby. Perhaps they are all employees here at The Lodge.

Maybe they're slaves to the rich and the elite.

At this point, there's not much that would surprise me.

"All right," I concede. "But inform Kage that I still want my canoe."

"Of course, Ms. Evans." His lips twitch just a little. But in a blink, he's stern again and gesturing to the room.

I sigh and go back to the dreaded theater.

Everyone has found their seats, with Landon on my couch again. I almost select a new seat, but I don't want him to mistake me for a coward.

His gaze goes to my neck when I sit down, and he immediately hands me a bottle of water.

It's not exactly an apology, but I accept it anyway. Because my throat still hurts and a drink seems like a pleasant way to relieve some of the ache.

With my luck, it's probably drugged.

But I'm beyond the point of caring right now.

I'm trapped here. I don't know where they park the cars, something I can't even try to find because everyone keeps insisting I join this fucked-up training retreat.

Maybe tonight I can search for a vehicle.

Preston drove here.

He gave the keys to the valets—one of which I'm pretty sure was the manager I just spoke with.

I frown. *Nothing about this place is adding up at all.*

And as though the powers that be heard my thoughts, the room goes dark.

Why do they always start this way? For dramatic effect? As some sort of ominous warning? What?

I sigh and settle into the sofa for another game of Truth or Kill.

Except it isn't a series of spinning crowns on the screen this time.

It's a man tied to a chair with a black helmet over his head.

Griffin Chastain, I assume. *Shit.*

"The rules of the game are evolving," the voice informs us. "To find the killer among you, you must ask the right questions. And it will be up to you to decide the truth of each response."

A subtle buzzing sound comes from the table beside me, drawing my attention to the shifting glass top. My lips part as it reveals a compartment inside. It's a small nook that's maybe one foot by one foot.

And inside it are two tablets.

I didn't even notice that the controllers were gone until now. It seems they've been collected and replaced by the tablets hidden inside this compartment.

Have they always been there? Or were they put there specifically for today's game?

"Each of you will be allowed to ask him one inquiry," the voice continues. "An inquiry that Mr. Chastain must answer truthfully or he'll suffer the consequences by your hands."

There's a pause to let that settle among the crowd.

No one asks about the consequences.

Or what he means by it being done by our own hands.

"You'll use the tablets to ask your questions. Then we will compile the answers into a video when this activity is done. For all of you."

I shiver. *Does that mean we will all take turns in that chair? Because no, thank you.*

"But there's one minor detail to add—Mr. Chastain won't know who is asking the questions," he adds. "None of you will. Everything is conducted in a virtual reality of sorts. So what he's seeing right now isn't real. And the same will apply to the rest of you, too."

Great. That means we all get to play. How not fun. So what will we be seeing, then?

Of course, the voice doesn't tell us that.

Instead, an image of the room appears, and the three crowns begin to spin.

"Choose your questions wisely," the voice warns. "For you only get one per candidate. Please begin writing them on your tablets now."

Preston takes a tablet from the table between him and Landon, which causes Landon to look expectantly at me.

I swallow, screw the plastic top back onto my water bottle, and place it on the cushion between us before leaning over to grab a tablet for him. "Thank you," he says, glancing at my neck again. Still no apology, but I don't exactly expect one from a man like him.

I retrieve the other tablet for myself and press a button to turn it on. A screen appears asking for my thumbprint.

My lips pinch to the side as I consider not doing it and leaving the room. But something tells me I'll be noticed immediately and brought back here by the staff.

A thrill runs down my spine at the notion that maybe Kage would be the one to find me.

But I really don't want to put him in that position.

Sighing, I give in and press my thumb to the place indicated on the tablet.

The screen whirs to life with an image of the room and a single gold crown. Instructions are written at the top.

Drag the crown to each person and begin asking your questions. Choose wisely, as you won't be able to erase or change your questions after submitting.

So we have to write all our questions down now.

And the point, I imagine, is to try to draw out

the supposed killer among us. Like a fucked-up game of Clue.

I debate writing a few questions like, *Do you own a candlestick? Were you in the library? Do you like rope?*

But something Kage said last night sticks in my mind, something about proving my worth.

Maybe if I solve this puzzle, they won't kill me for learning all their secrets.

It's a wild consideration. One that I really shouldn't ponder at all. Because why would they care if I figure this out or not?

Yet the challenge of it nags at me.

I've always liked a good riddle. So maybe if I play detective and determine the answer, I can use it to my advantage.

What do I have to lose? I'm already on thin ice just by being here.

So why not play? Why not catch the killer?

I shrug. *All right.* I consider the thirteen people in the room—which is when I realize this image is from last night because Griffin is on a couch. Becca isn't there. And I'm the thirteenth person, seated right beside Landon.

Is that a clue or just for the ease of selecting everyone for questions? I wonder.

I keep that question in the back of my mind as I

consider each person and their expressions through last night's game.

No one appears guilty. I look positively uncomfortable, though. Maybe I need to hide my expressions better.

Okay, who should I start with?

Or maybe I should ask them all the same question.

It's hard to say because I have no idea what inquiries everyone else will make. We may have duplicate ones, which spoils the opportunity. Perhaps that's the point.

So asking the same one to every single individual may be the right way to go.

Well, to me, there's an obvious question to voice: *Did you bring a gun to the retreat?*

Of course, that assumes that Becca's death scene was staged purposefully. And that the killer will admit to bringing a weapon.

But the whole point is to tell the truth, right?

Can the killer lie?

Probably.

So perhaps I need to make it less obvious.

Perhaps I should ask for an opinion instead, something no one minds answering.

If the killer used a gun, and the scene was staged with that in mind, maybe I can determine the potential candidates by finding out how the others in this room feel about gun policy. Surely whoever "shot" Becca isn't averse to firearms.

And the question is innocuous enough to not be seen as directly related to that incident.

Maybe.

I tap my fingers along the edge of the tablet.

I'm not sure what else to ask. It seems obvious that the first step would be to find out who likes guns and who doesn't.

Hmm, what about gun range or shooting-practice questions? No. That seems too related to skill, which could be interpreted as, *Do you have experience that would allow you to hit your target with one shot?*

Asking about policy feels less clear. It's more of a question that asks, "How do you plan to vote in the future?"

All right, then, I decide, selecting the first person on the top left of the screen.

Gaylord Pompkins. He's been pretty quiet this week, his questions all technology related. I've gathered he's the smartest one in the room, something evidenced by his profile appearing on the screen.

MIT Senior.

3.97 GPA.

Major: Computer Science.

He's the eldest in his family, so he has a succession date marked. His family oversees the laser tech wing.

I imagine he'll be dealing with government contracts a lot in the future.

He seems like my type of guy. Except for the whole Covington Industries bullshit and the fact that he didn't seem to care about Becca's death.

Whatever.

I click the box that asks for my question and type the one I intend to use for everyone. *How do you feel about gun control policy?*

After I click Done, his image is grayed out, making it impossible to edit, just like the device warned.

I click the male beside him and repeat the question.

Then I do it for everyone else in the room, including myself.

The golden crowns spin on my device when I'm done, so I set it down and wait.

This is going to be a long day.

Twelve
KAGE

"YOUR GIRL ASKED EVERYONE ABOUT THEIR THOUGHTS on gun control," Loki informs me when I enter the room.

I arch a brow. "Gun control?" It takes me less than a second to realize why, and I nearly smile. "She's trying to find out who would use a gun. Because she knows Becca was shot by one."

"So she's trying to solve the game?" Loki glances at the screen. "Why would she care?"

"She's proving her worth." Which is exactly what I told her to do.

"Are you going to let her solve it?" Judge asks from the corner.

Am I? "Maybe."

He gives me a look. "That's a dangerous plan,

brother."

"So was fucking her," I tell him. "And I quite enjoyed that." So why not continue playing?

"About that," Judge says, pushing away from the wall. "There was an incident earlier while you were busy with Griffin."

I frown. "What kind of incident?"

Loki and Judge exchange a look, and Judge nods at him.

A video of the hallway appears, showing Sydney leaving the room. I fold my arms, already amused. I bet she gave my brother hell about having to stay.

Except no, it's not my brother talking to her. It's Landon. His voice comes through the speakers as Loki turns up the volume, allowing me to hear him question Sydney about where she slept last night.

I snort. "That asshole tells her to sleep outside and has the audacity to demand to know what—"

My lips part as he slams Sydney against the wall with his hand around her throat. I immediately look at the screen showing their current situation, where she's sitting beside him.

"He's still fucking alive?" I'm ready to fix that problem, my feet already moving.

But Judge catches me by the arm and whirls me back toward the screen. "Keep watching."

"Who the fuck is Kage?" Landon demands, making my eyebrows fly upward.

"Reception," Sydney chokes out, making me grimace.

That motherfucker, I think. *I'm going to fucking kill him.*

Preston seems to be trying to talk him down, but Landon isn't listening. He's upset that Griffin is missing and has apparently decided to blame Sydney. Or perhaps he's just using it as an excuse to push her around.

"Who is Kage?" Landon demands again.

"The reception manager," my brother answers as he steps into view.

All calm, cool, and collected. Typical Judge. "You should have punched him," I mutter.

"It was easier to defuse the situation by speaking with my mouth rather than my fists."

"He doesn't deserve that kind of respect," I argue.

"No, he doesn't," my brother agrees. "But there will be time for that later."

I nod, my jaw tight as Landon finally moves off the screen. The amusement I anticipated regarding Sydney's refusal to cooperate no longer exists even as I hear her question my brother.

"She wants a canoe," he tells me before she reaches that part of the discussion.

My blood is boiling too hot for me to properly

react to that statement. *Landon put his hands on her. That motherfucker choked my female.*

And her wince told me it hurt.

As did the rasp in her voice.

Because she's sore from last night.

Fuck.

It makes me want to go to her, to make sure she's all right. Which is the exact opposite of what I can do right now. We have a very important game to play today, one I started this morning via the interrogation with Griffin.

He gave me everything, something my brothers already know because of the videotapes.

Which means Landon's "conference call" the other day proved just as useful as my brothers and I had hoped.

Same with the internet passes we gave to certain guests upon arrival. Each one has been used to log in to the Covington Industries systems, which has granted us access to several pertinent files.

And those internet login codes have provided us with plenty of personal details, too.

Because using those passes gave Loki backdoor access into each of their laptops.

All of this has added another layer to the game by adding to our blackmail files against the heirs.

And now we also have access to all the financial accounts, thus allowing me to really play.

But there's still a lot of work to be done, including today's and tomorrow's virtual reality simulators.

Griffin will be up first. Then he'll get a tablet to ask his own questions, which I imagine will be quite vicious after the experience he's about to undergo.

"You good?" Judge asks me, noting my lack of a reply to his comment about the canoe.

"Are you asking if Landon may live until the end of the week?" I counter. "Because that remains to be seen."

"I can set it up," Loki offers.

But Judge shakes his head. "He's too important to the endgame."

I grit my teeth, hating that he's right. I've always put family first. And this will be no exception.

However, that won't stop me from perhaps facilitating an accident in Landon's future.

Maybe a few weeks from now.

Anything could happen between now and then.

"Leave him for now," I say, my hands flexing as I fight the urge to curl my fingers into fists. "Has everyone written down their questions?"

"They have," Loki says.

"Good. Then Griffin's ready to roll." He's exhausted from our morning session, which is what makes him the perfect candidate to initiate this sequence. And after the others see his reaction to today's events, they'll be too terrified to lie.

Or that's the hope, anyway.

"Which simulation do you want to use?" Loki asks.

Judge glances at me and I shrug. "He was useful this morning. Easy to crack." Of course, it helped that he thought he was talking to his father. Which he'll later assume was a dream. Because his morning is about to end in a nightmare, one that will overshadow everything else in his mind.

"So you don't feel like punishing him," Judge translates.

"They all deserve to be punished," I return. "But it's their parents who deserve it most."

Judge nods in agreement. "He's already been in a virtual state for a few hours. I don't want to give him a heart attack, so let's just go with the water simulation."

It's the least violent of all the virtual realities, so I agree with a nod.

Rather than watch what comes next, I head over to my laptop and pull up the interrogation from earlier today. I already took notes on all the accounts, and verified several, but there's a lot of movement that needs to happen in the next five days.

Stock exchange fun.

My favorite.

But it has to be delicate. If I'm too obvious, someone will notice. Which is why I needed all that backdoor information from Griffin. He's the heir to the finance branch of the organization. His law school admittance is more of a formality than anything else. He needs a law degree to be a proper estate attorney. Given how our morning went, I question his ability to do well. He's far too gullible to be a lawyer.

However, his name matters more than his brains, thus he's being groomed to take over for his father.

Which is how Griffin was able to provide me with several important company details.

Details I am now using without his knowledge.

Because he thought he was talking to his dad earlier today.

I can't wait for the moment when these assholes realize we used their own technology against them. Although, technically, it's not *their* technology. It's *ours*.

Because our father created it.

Our family is the rightful heir to the Covington Industries throne.

And after this week, we'll take it all back.

With one giant grand finale of a performance that will put the original takeover to shame.

"Holy fuck!" Griffin shouts from the screen, causing me to glance up.

"What feed is going to the theater?" I ask Loki.

"Just him sitting in the chair. They can't hear anything. And obviously they don't know about the electrodes or the hallucinogens, so it looks like he's calm because, outwardly, he is. Unless you want me to change that?" He pulls the sensory indicators up on another computer monitor, as well as a panel for the restraint controls.

One shock to Griffin's system, and he'll be in a traditional virtual reality mode where he can move around again. Right now, he just thinks he's moving because of the electronic stimulators overwhelming his mental receptors and senses. It's pretty advanced shit, but it's going to change the landscape of gaming everywhere.

Just as soon as my brilliant brother introduces it to the world, anyway.

Well, and after the sensory technology gets passed through all the official channels, too. The hallucinogenic injections we're using for this week's experiments won't be part of the final product.

"No," Judge says, taking over the chair beside him. "It'll be more fun to let him loose in the room afterward so they can see how shaken up he is."

I nod, agreeing, and go back to my finance work.

The simulation only lasts thirty minutes, but I imagine it feels like hours to Griffin. Which explains all the information he's giving on the screen.

Loki's fingers are flying over the keyboard as he

captures certain parts of his statements, preparing the script for his future video.

He has three employees working in the other room, all of whom are aware of the end goal. "Yeah, that one," I hear Loki saying. "It'll pair well, yeah. Can you grab the minute marker? Yeah. Thanks, Sabrina."

My heart skips a beat with the name. *Our mother's best friend*. When we pitched our idea to her, she immediately volunteered to help.

Everyone here did.

My parents might have been overthrown from their empire, but they still had friends.

As evidenced by the fact that my brothers and I survived.

"I think he's ready to be released," Loki says as the simulation completes. Griffin is slumped over in his chair, something everyone in the theater should be able to see.

"I agree," Judge says, glancing at me.

I merely nod in agreement. "I have what I need from him."

"Cut the feed," Judge says, and Loki ignites the company logo for the theater hall.

Judge leaves the room to handle the turnover.

The room goes dark, but Loki has night vision on the camera feed, allowing us to see what's happening.

Three men with eye gear enter to begin removing the sensory equipment from Griffin's body. We told him it was for a polygraph since it's similar tech. But it's so much more than a lie detector.

Which is why Judge's men handle the equipment carefully.

When they're done, they step out of the room, leaving him strapped to the chair with the head covering still in place.

"He looks pissed," Loki says as the helmet opens around Griffin's head. It's pulled back up into the ceiling in the next instant, but Griffin doesn't seem to see it. He doesn't seem to see anything other than his own anger.

"He just spent thirty minutes watching his life be ripped apart by everyone he's supposed to trust," I say. "He should be pissed."

Pissed enough to kill, I think.

When a prince falls from his throne, he resorts to revenge and violence. That's the point of today's exercise.

And it seems Mr. Chastain fully understands that now.

How far does he need to be pushed to become a killer?

Given the rage emanating from him right now, I would say it's not very far.

His arms and legs are released from their

straps. It's all automated, the chair moving on its own, thanks to our access to Covington Industries' robotics tech.

He immediately leaps off the chair and glares at it.

Then the voice starts speaking, telling him the point of this exercise. It's similar to what everyone else would have heard in the theater, but also slightly different.

"You were chosen to go first to set the stage for everyone else. They asked their questions. It's time for you to return the favor," the voice tells him. "There's a tablet by the door. Choose your questions wisely."

"Oh, I'll fucking choose my questions," he snarls, walking unsteadily over to the tablet.

"Did he reveal anything of use?" I ask Loki while Griffin starts furiously typing on the screen.

"Nothing we didn't already know, but at least we have him admitting a few more things out loud. It'll help with his montage later." Loki's dark brown eyes grin back at me. "His father is going to love it."

"I bet," I say. "Almost as much as he's going to love the surprise I'm leaving in his accounts right now."

Loki chuckles but returns his focus to Griffin while I busy myself with the array of accounts before me. Thirteen, to be precise.

Thirteen branches.

Thirteen families.

Thirteen thrones to destroy.

I fall into my work, barely paying attention to Griffin's return to the theater. There's a lot of male posturing and snarling going on. The only one I bother glancing at is Sydney. She's gaping at everyone like they've lost their damn minds, Griffin especially.

You're not wrong, sweetheart, I think at her.

Then I go back to the Covington Industries performance portfolios. They're mostly what I anticipated, given my thorough knowledge of the company and its assets.

I only find a few surprises waiting for me, none of them providing much of a challenge.

But it takes me several hours to go through them all.

Which is fine because this virtual reality game with the "heirs" is time-intensive as well. There's a lot more than just enduring the thirty-minute game inside their minds. There's prep required in between as well, which is part of what Loki's team is helping him with. They have to organize the questions in a way that fully impacts the individual they're assigned to.

It's all a mental mindfuck.

One Loki designed.

And seems to be very much enjoying carrying out right now.

Yet he calls me psychotic. Perhaps we all are.

It's not until Gretchen is up that I start to pay attention again. Because that means Sydney is next.

She's squirming on the couch beside a bored-looking Landon. He's putting on a good show. And I can't wait to watch him break.

Alas, he's on the docket for tomorrow—something he doesn't know, so this cocky show right now is simply him pretending to not give a fuck. But he'll care tomorrow.

Sydney is the last on today's schedule, as we had to split the "heirs" into two sessions. Seven today, six tomorrow.

"What simulation do you want me to prep for her?" Loki asks without looking at me.

I don't need him to tell me who he means by "her." The only one he would possibly give me a choice on is Sydney.

"The fire simulation," I tell him, already prepared to answer that question.

He gapes at me, clearly having not expected that. "Are you insane?"

"Probably. But I need her to understand."

"By setting her world on fire?" he counters, whistling. "You really are a sadist."

"It's a good way to test her." Perhaps *cruel* is

the better adjective to use. However, I need to know what she can handle. I also want her to get it. To finally see the light. To figure out what's really happening here.

A dangerous aspiration, one that may culminate in her death.

Or maybe she'll appreciate it all in the end.

We'll find out soon.

I close the lid on my laptop. "Give me a minute with her first," I tell both him and Judge as he reenters the room. "It may be the last time she lets me kiss her."

Loki shakes his head. "Fucking psycho," he mutters.

But Judge gives me a look that says he understands. "Five minutes," he says.

I nod, accepting the time limit, and leave the room to wait for her.

The voice will tell her where to go soon, and I'll grab her before Judge's men do.

She doesn't leave through the main theater doors, but through the side ones that go into the back hall, which is what everyone has been told to do so far. When they're done, they reenter through the main doors again. But when they head into the "interrogation" room, it's via this path.

All dark and murky with low lighting.

It's meant to be ominous.

To give everyone a sense of dread as they wander along this corridor.

But it works beautifully for me now, as it provides ample shadows for me to hide within.

I pick one by the corridor exit, knowing she's going to head straight for that door. Because her expression says she plans to tell everyone to fuck right off.

Fuck, that feisty air about her makes me instantly hard.

She really is perfect.

Her turtleneck is hiding her throat, though. A disappointing choice, as I want to see my marks on her. They tell the world she's mine.

Perhaps I'll bite her lip, make her bleed, just to ensure everyone sees that claim later.

A strange desire, as I don't typically like to leave my imprint on anyone.

But there's nothing normal about this female.

She almost moves past me and jumps when she realizes I'm leaning against the shadowy corner. "Kage," she breathes, her hand at her chest.

"Look at that—you remembered my name," I marvel in a whisper. I grab her hips and pull her into me before sidestepping through another door into a dark room.

I don't give her a minute to ask questions or speak. I merely push her back up against the now closed door and take her mouth with mine.

Claiming.

Punishing.

Consuming.

I'm not even sure what truly describes my desire here. Perhaps all of the above. I want her, and I need her to know just how much I crave her.

She's been in that theater all damn day.

And we can't see each other tonight.

So all we have are these five precious minutes. I'm not wasting any of them by speaking.

I palm her breast, memorizing it with my fingers as my opposite hand goes to her ass to press her up against my groin. She gasps, those luscious lips providing me with entry to destroy her with my tongue.

I do.

I fucking plunder her until she's panting against me in what is likely an aroused, dazed cloud of confusion.

It's cruel. I know it's cruel. I should be helping her. Saving her. Assisting in her escape.

But instead, I'm condemning her with this game, forcing her to play, to see it through to the end.

I need to know, I think at her, fully aware that she's not supernatural or a mind reader. *I need to know if you're truly different from them. If I can trust you. If it's safe… to keep you.*

This obsession is intoxicating.

This desire is overwhelming.

This need to possess her is *damning*.

I'm already going to hell, sweetheart. Won't you join me? I'm saying with my tongue. *Will you be mine?*

She's kissing me back like she's already agreed to spend eternity with me in the underworld, like she's agreeing to be my eternal mate.

But sex can be deceiving.

That's the point of this trial. That's the point of continuing this game. That's the point of seeing how clever she really is.

If she fails, I'll determine what to do with her then.

But in the interim, I'll be cheering for her. Silently from the sidelines. Praying to whatever god exists that she makes it out on the other side.

Perhaps she'll convince me to believe in a higher power after all.

Or maybe she'll confirm that life is solely run by the devil.

It's a lot to place on one woman's shoulders, but as her nails bite into my neck, as she drags me that much closer, I decide that she can handle it.

Because this girl gives back just as good as she

gets.

She's trying to make me bleed with those claws while she devours the fuck out of my tongue, and it makes me fall just a little harder for her.

I wrap my palm around her throat, but I don't squeeze. It's just enough to assert my dominance, and she responds by biting down on my lower lip.

"So violent," I muse.

"Get me the fuck out of here."

"No," I tell her.

"Kage."

"Sydney," I return, kissing her again. "You can do this, gorgeous. You're resilient. I have faith in you." One final brush of my lips, and then I step away from her.

Our time is up.

I can sense Judge's men closing in on us. They were already in this room, waiting for her. The exit sign she was heading toward was a false lead.

This room was her fate.

And now I need to leave her. "Show the powers that be how worthy you are of survival, gorgeous."

I don't wait for her reply.

I merely slip away and allow Judge's men to take over. They have on night-vision goggles that allow them to see. I don't need a pair, as I know this room exceptionally well from all the test runs.

Sydney shouts my name as one of them grabs

her.

Then she begins cursing at them as I slip out through another door near the back of the room.

This isn't my battle to fight. It's hers. But I'll absolutely be watching to see if she wins.

Thirteen
SYDNEY

I'M GOING TO FUCKING KILL HIM, I DECIDE AS I'M strapped into a chair.

When Kage grabbed me, I thought he was saving me.

But no.

He was just kissing me goodbye before delivering me to the two silent men currently manhandling me. I can't see them. It's too dark. However, I can *feel* them. There's at least two. Maybe even three.

I growl, wanting to fight. It's futile and I know it, but it's just instinctual to try to get away in the dark.

Alas, my wrists are cuffed to the arms of the chair in what feels like a handful of seconds, and that fucking voice is talking to me.

"Calm down, please," it says. "We need to ensure the sensors are adhered appropriately."

"Sensors?" I repeat.

"Yes. To properly measure your heart rhythm and bodily reactions, and to make sure that they are accurately recorded."

"I'm sorry, what? My heart rhythm?"

"This is a polygraph, Ms. Evans," the voice informs me. "The most accurate way to determine your truth is to measure your bodily reactions. Now please relax and let the men assemble the instruments around you."

"A polygraph?" No one mentioned that in the room. "Am I the only one taking one?"

"No, everyone is undergoing the same procedure," the voice replies. "But you are subject to secrecy until it's done. This is a lesson on truth and when not to speak."

"I thought the point was for all of us to share all our dirty secrets and blackmail each other for eternity," I say, not bothering to hold back. "Now you're telling me that we're supposed to keep some secrets from each other? Seems like you're going back on your training principles."

I swear I hear someone laugh.

Maybe one of the guys in the room.

Maybe the voice himself. But that can't be right. He seems to be some sort of lifelike artificial intelligence. Unless he really is a person? One of the fathers? A psychologist who specializes in fucking people up?

"Truth is one of the primary principles of this organization, Ms. Evans. But sometimes, secrets are necessary. And it's how we proceed with those secrets that counts."

"I don't work for your organization," I remind him. "So can I be exempt from this exercise?"

"Perhaps you'll work for us in the future, if you prove yourself worthy enough. As was just suggested minutes ago, yes?"

I blink. "You mean Kage luring me in here just to leave me?"

"I have nothing to do with that, Ms. Evans. But the young man had a point, did he not? You're a skilled programmer. Perhaps you'll be of better use to us alive. However, that can only happen if we trust you. So can we trust you, Ms. Evans? Are you capable of speaking the truth as required and knowing when it's appropriate to maintain a secret?"

I'm not even sure who to gape at, so I'm just sitting here with wide eyes, staring at the darkness in front of me. Did he just imply that they want to hire me? Inferring that this is just some sort of intensive interview process? "This is so fucked up."

"Be that as it may, this is happening, Ms. Evans. I suggest you start thinking about your future and what you want to make of it."

Something clamps down on my finger, making me flinch. The sleeves of my turtleneck have been pulled up as well, some sort of sensor sticking to my skin.

And I'm sitting on some kind of pad.

It's not a normal seat. Not by a long shot.

One of the men skims the area under my breasts, making me snarl. But he's just adhering some type of cord. *The heart rate monitor thingy?* I wonder. Because another goes along my back.

I'm somewhat glad Becca's alive right now. It means I can kill her later for all this shit.

Because *fuck*.

"I want it noted for the record that I'm not consenting to any of this," I inform the voice.

"Consider it noted, Ms. Evans."

I roll my eyes. Of course they don't care. Why would they? I'm a pawn in whatever this is. A game. Truth or Kill. A retreat. Company bonding. Training. Elite fuckery.

I'm not sure what to call it.

"Close your eyes and sit very still, Ms. Evans," the voice instructs me.

I almost tell him to fuck off, but the whirring sound over my head makes me comply. My neck is already in a fragile state. I don't need whatever this is to worsen my pain.

Kage must have known because he was surprisingly gentle when he wrapped his hand around my throat.

Although, that kiss wasn't gentle at all. It was borderline savage.

And hot as fuck.

Which makes me royally messed up in the head because he fully distracted me from my intent to run. *Asshole,* I think. He did it on purpose. I'm sure of it.

What exactly is your role in this game? I wonder at him. *Why are you really here?*

I'm missing something. Some clear connection. Some obvious sign.

Because I can't imagine anyone would willingly work for an organization that plays these sorts of games with their kids. Unless the endgame isn't as horrible as I think it will be.

Something touches my head, making me freeze.

The helmet, I realize as it continues its descent. *Shit.*

I really don't want to be part of this exercise at all. A series of questions set in a virtual reality scenario sounds ominous, especially after seeing the impact it had on the others. They all looked like they'd just run several marathons when they returned, yet all we saw on the screen was each person sitting there calmly.

There was no sound, either.

But clearly, they were—

"Ow," I mutter as something pricks my arm from one of the sensors. Another prick touches my fingertip from the clamp. And a third pinches my other arm.

What did they just inject into my system? I wonder, feeling dizzy. *Shit. What the fuck is going on?*

This is starting to feel more like a torture chamber than a polygraph. Not that I really know the difference, but—

My helmet clicks on, and suddenly I can see everything in the room. It's all illuminated in shades of yellow and black, like the mask covering my eyes just gave me night vision or something.

Weird. Is that supposed to happen?

The chair hums beneath me, some sort of motor starting. "Uh…" This definitely did not happen on the theater videos. "Hello?" I call as I begin to move backward. "Is this normal?"

My stomach twists as I pick up speed, the chair moving backward toward an unknown fate.

Doors open and I'm suddenly in the hallway. Except it's not the hallway I entered from, nor is it a hallway I recognize from The Lodge. It's… it's brighter. Less woodsy. With marble floors, white walls, and a high ceiling littered with skylights.

It's actually rather pretty. Palatial, too.

Where am I?

The virtual reality part of this tour has obviously started, and I have to admit that it feels real. I can feel the cool air coming from a nearby door, smell the sweet scent of roses prickling my nose, and sense the warmth of the sun shining in from above.

It's peaceful here.

Beautiful.

I feel… relaxed. At peace. *Sleepy.*

But that can't be right.

Where are the questions? Why isn't the voice talking to me?

"Hello?" I call into the pristine hallway.

Nothing. Just the sound of my chair humming along the stone floor. It looks so real. I almost reach down to touch it, but the cuffs prevent me from moving.

I can see them now. Metal bands across my wrists. I lean over to see that my ankles are held down by similar restraints.

There are no sensors, though.

No cord around my middle.

I'm also not wearing jeans or a turtleneck anymore, but a summery white dress. "You know, if you're going to force someone into a virtual reality situation, you may want to consider giving that person an outfit she would actually wear."

The voice says nothing, making me sigh.

"Fine." I'll just bask in the fake sunshine while this chair wheels me along.

It reminds me of one of those roller-coaster climbs, where it just keeps going up and up and up with no end in sight. Mostly because I'm still going backward, not forward.

But I eventually halt near the front hall, the three-story foyer reminding me a bit of the reception area of The Lodge. Except the wooden interior is all white columns and the windows are stained with color. There's a chandelier above and a grand staircase that leads to the third level—and that is almost identical to the one I've climbed a few times now.

It's clear this building has similar bones, the architectural layout almost exactly the same.

Except all the furnishings are different.

And there's no reception desk here, just a foyer with fancy chairs and a living area off to the side.

My chair pauses in the center of them, almost as though it wants to give me a full tour of the grand foyer. Then it rotates to face the door.

Where a crowd of people are standing.

I frown, not really recognizing any of them. A few of their faces are somewhat familiar, but not really. One of them looks a bit like Landon. However, it's not him. Their parents, maybe?

Are these the people behind all this bullshit? The branch owners of Covington Industries?

They don't speak. They just stare at me like they're evaluating who and what I am.

I stare right back at them, waiting to be grilled, waiting for whatever stupid questions these people want me to answer.

"This is what you deserve," one of them finally says. A woman with dark hair and spray-tanned arms. She looks a bit plasticky, making me wonder about the quality of this virtual reality picture because everything else is incredibly realistic.

Maybe she looks like this in real life.

"You're a disgrace," she continues.

"Okay," I reply. "I could say the same about your skin toner, but you don't hear me being a bitch."

"You should have listened to us," another says. This time a male with slicked-back gray hair and spectacles on his button nose. Given the way he's wearing those glasses, I suspect he doesn't actually need them and just thinks it's fashionable. "We gave you a chance."

"Gave me a chance to do what, exactly?" I ask him. "Because as I said at the beginning of this fuckery, I don't consent to any of this."

"Now we have to take it all away. And for what?

A few moral issues?" This comes from a redheaded male near the back of the group.

"I'm pretty sure nothing about this could be considered *moral*," I reply. "And what kind of questions are these?"

"I would say we're sorry, but you brought this on yourself," the redheaded one continues. "You knew what would happen if you made the decision to go public, and here we are."

I frown. "I didn't go public with anything. How could I? I've been trapped here."

"Your rule has come to an end. And now you'll get to watch your kingdom burn." This comes from the bottle-tan lady.

"I'm sorry, what?" I really don't understand what she's saying to me or why.

"But don't worry. We'll take up the mantle for you," the redheaded male says. "Your company will be safe with us."

My frown deepens. It… it's like I'm in someone else's dream.

No. Someone else's *body*.

I glance down at my dress again and realize the white fabric is now covered in blood. "Oh, what the fuck?" My eyes widen.

Because it's not just me.

There's a dark-haired man beside me in a similar state. Dressed in a suit. Bleeding from his chest. With a gag in his mouth. He's alive. And he's furious, his dark green eyes blazing with a need for retribution.

I blink, startled, because I recognize him. *Mister Covington.*

He's the godfather to Covington Industries.

He and his family died in a tragic fire roughly two decades ago.

"I don't understand," I whisper, staring at him and then down at myself. We're both tied to chairs and being mocked by the crowd before us.

The branch families.

"What is this?" I demand as I struggle against the binds.

But the people are suddenly gone.

Leaving only one faceless male in their place. Faceless because he's in a suit and wearing a black mask.

"Hello, Sydney," he greets, his voice the one I've heard far too much these last few days. He's *the* voice. The artificial intelligence come to life in masculine form. "Are you ready to begin?"

Fourteen
SYDNEY

I GAPE AT HIM. "YOU MEAN THAT MACABRE SCENE WASN'T the beginning?" I glance at the bound man beside me again.

Except he's gone.

And when I look down, I'm no longer in the white dress, but in my jeans and turtleneck.

What the hell is happening? I'm still in the same palatial surroundings, but the moon has replaced the sun.

And there's a strange scent brewing around me.

The roses… are gone.

Replaced by a putrid stench.

My nose crinkles in response. "What's going on?"

"It's time for your questions," the voice tells me.

"But you need to understand that lying will only secure you to that chair more. Something I don't recommend, unless you want to be burned alive."

I gape at him. "Excuse me?"

A scream echoes from upstairs, sending a chill down my spine. I immediately look toward it, the high-pitched cry sounding more childlike than adultlike.

"What—"

"Focus, Sydney. You need to answer four questions to release yourself. Ready?"

"Only four?" I don't understand. Weren't there thirteen?

And what did he mean about being burned alive?

Another shriek follows, this one making my blood run cold. Only for a blast of heat to warm me right up. Because holy shit, he wasn't kidding. There's a fire blazing in the living area. "Oh God..." I gasp as a gauzy white curtain blows into the nearby fireplace, the fabric going up in flames.

It all happens in a blink.

Yet it feels purposeful.

I can smell the gasoline.

I can hear cruel laughter.

And the screams...

"Why did you major in computer science?" the voice asks me.

"What?" I glance back at the black-masked male. "Why are you…? The house is on fire!"

"Answer the question," he demands. "Why did you major in computer science?"

He can't be serious. The house is burning! There's a child screaming upstairs!

"*Sydney,*" the voice echoes all around me. "You need to answer the questions to free yourself."

"I…" I blink. *This isn't real,* I remind myself. *But fuck, it feels so damn real!* The heat is growing in intensity, the screams… the screams are making my heart ache.

I close my eyes and swallow.

This isn't real. This isn't real. This isn't real.

I chant the phrase over and over again, telling myself that I'm still in that black room, strapped to a chair. *Virtual reality. They injected me with something. There are sensors. This isn't real.*

"Tick-tock, Sydney Evans," the voice taunts. "Why did you major in computer science?"

"Because…" I search for words, search for sanity, search for some glimpse of reality. But it's all so *hot*.

Computer science.

Why did I major in computer science?

"Because I like solving puzzles," I whisper. "I… I like troubleshooting code. It's fun to find the error and fix it."

Silence.

My heart races as I open my eyes again. *"Fuck."* How could they even bother with a polygraph in this environment? It makes no sense. I'm the complete opposite of calm here!

The bracket around my ankle releases as a round of applause reverberates around the room. All those faces are back, and everyone is dressed in formalwear.

There is no more fire.

It's an elegant affair now.

Music. Champagne. Dancing.

Ballroom, I marvel, glancing around. *When did I enter the ballroom?*

It… it's the same size as the theater hall.

It's dark, too.

But rather than a screen, it's a rich, red curtain with golden fringes, framing a stage with a string quartet playing a familiar tune.

I swallow, my skin clammy with sweat. Because I can still feel the heat.

"What do you want to do with your degree, Sydney?" the voice whispers in my ear. "Where do you want to work?"

"I don't know," I reply honestly. "I… I came here… I went with Becca… To think. To decide."

"Do you want to work for Covington Industries?"

"Fuck no," I say, belatedly realizing that's probably the wrong response in this scenario. But it's the goddamn truth. "I want nothing to do with your fucking company or any of you." And I'm pretty sure that was more than three questions, unless I'm counting wrong.

Oh, who cares? I need to get the hell out of here!

A cackle of laughter follows as the dark-haired woman with the spray tan appears. "Oh, darling, you do look marvelous tonight. And this party is to *die* for."

"Yes, look at how cute everything is," another woman marvels, this one with blonde hair and bright blue eyes. "And have you seen the princes? So adorable."

"Like little gentlemen!" the brunette says.

More laughter follows and I blink at them, not understanding a single damn thing they just said.

And suddenly I'm engulfed in blistering heat again. But both my ankles are free.

"You're doing so good," the voice praises as the screams grow louder upstairs. "Now tell us your ideal job. Where would you like to work?"

"Right now? For a legal company that will sue

the fuck out of all of you," I snarl, wincing at the flames growing in the living area.

I realize it's in slow motion, that the room should be burning around me entirely by now. Fires spread so much faster than movies give them credit for. But this simulation is slowing it down, ensuring I feel the heat and giving me time to answer.

The voice tsks. "Now, now, Sydney. None of that. Tell us your ideal job. Tell us what you dream of doing."

"I don't know. That's why I came here," I reiterate. "I… I'm not interested in corporate life. I would rather do something positive. I just don't know what that is."

"And corporate life isn't *positive*?"

"If Covington Industries is anything to go by, then no," I snap.

"Hmm," the voice hums. "Perhaps you don't know the real company, then."

I gesture around me, only then realizing they've freed one of my hands. "This all seems pretty fucking real to me."

"I see," the voice replies. "Well then, final question, Ms. Evans. How did your mother die?"

My veins flood with ice despite the hot air swarming around me.

This… this isn't something I want to discuss.

But it's also public knowledge. Which means

they know the truth.

I just don't know why someone in the room would ask this. It makes no sense. How do any of them even know about my mom?

Did Becca tell them I was a foster kid?

If that's the case, then why ask about my mother specifically? Why not ask about my father?

"I..." I have to clear my throat, the smoke making it hard for me to breathe and to think. The fire is raging now. And I'm still trapped against this chair, frozen in a state of shock from a simple question.

Why not answer?

Why not tell them?

They all already know, right?

"She went on a hike," I manage in a whisper. "And jumped... off a cliff."

That's what the authorities told me, anyway. As she had a history of depression, it wasn't a contested theory.

Especially since her last words to me before she left that day were, "You're old enough to take care of yourself now, baby. Be a good girl for Momma, okay? And stay here." She hugged me tight, her arms thin and cracking from the effort. She didn't eat much. Because it took effort. Everything in life... took her too much effort. "I'll be there in your dreams, baby girl," she whispered.

And then she left.

The next person to walk through the door was a cop.

I can still remember the woman's face, her eyes brimming with so much pity that it made me feel ill.

Even at eight years old, I knew that look wasn't one I liked.

"Sydney," the voice says, awakening me to my surroundings and the inferno blazing around the foyer.

My wrists are free.

My ankles, too.

I'm free.

A clear path is lit up before me, heading straight outside.

But that screaming… I can still hear it. The children. Upstairs.

I stand, uncertain of which way to go. One way is a route to obvious freedom. The other… will probably burn me alive.

"I can't leave them," I whisper, glancing up the stairs. "I… I can't leave the kids."

The voice says something to me in response, but I ignore it, running as fast as I can for the grand staircase and ignoring the heat licking at my skin.

It's not real. It's not real. It's not real.

So why am I going upstairs instead of outside?

I don't know.

But on the off chance this is founded in some sort of reality, I have to try. I have to reach them. I have to *save* them.

The stairs are slick beneath my bare feet, my shoes seeming to have melted in my wake.

I don't care.

I keep pushing, keep running, keep searching for that sound.

The scream beckons me. The pain. The agony. The *fear*.

I find the door.

And shove through it.

To see three boys tied to a bed.

With crowns on their heads.

I dart toward them, ready to help, as the scene dissolves into smoke. "No!" I shout. "But the kids!"

Everything turns black.

My skin goes cold.

And the sensation of hands on my skin follows.

Removing the sensors.

Removing the cord beneath my breasts.

Slipping my shoes back on—which makes me wonder when they were removed.

Everything happens so quickly, my reality settling around me. *None of it was real. The boys… the boys weren't real.*

But what kind of sick fuck creates a simulation like that?

I'm shaking by the time the last of the sensors is removed from my skin. I want to punch someone. *Scream.*

I suddenly understand why everyone else was trembling when they returned. Except they all kept reiterating to us the importance of telling the truth.

I don't feel that way at all.

I want to rant and rave at the creators of this fucked-up program and demand to know why I just watched a palace burn with three little boys inside!

The helmet buzzes as it's removed. My hands and ankles are suddenly free.

I shoot upright, only to fall back down in the chair as a wave of dizziness hits me. "*Fuck!*" I shout, furious with the world. Livid with the people in this lodge.

Angry with Becca for inflicting all this bullshit on me.

Mad as fuck at Kage for tricking me into this room.

Except I know it's not him. He didn't do this. It's just his job.

But hell if I don't still hate him for doing this to me.

I can sense him in the room with me now, his woodsy scent unmistakable. "I fucking hate you," I tell him.

"I know," he replies, his voice whisper-soft. "I would apologize, but I wouldn't mean it."

"Of course you wouldn't," I mutter. "None of you would. But kids? Dying like that? Are you for fucking real?"

"Sometimes the truth hurts. Sometimes the past isn't what it seems, either."

"How cryptic of you," I say, done with everything. Done with him. Done with this game. Just fucking done with… with *this*.

I stand again, this time grabbing the arm of the chair for balance.

Kage doesn't try to touch me. Nor does he try to stop me as I leave the room.

No one tells me to go back to the theater, and for that, I'm fucking grateful. Instead, I go straight up to the room Kage put me in last night.

The stars are out. I have no idea when that happened or how long I was in that theater room today. Or how long the virtual reality lasted.

I don't even really care.

I just want the moon and the stars tonight.

I just want to remember what it feels like to be free.

Because after today, I know that's not going to happen.

This is my new reality now. And if I don't

embrace it, I'm going to end up in a fire.

Just like those innocent little boys.

Fifteen
KAGE

I STUDY SYDNEY'S FACE BENEATH THE MOONLIGHT, MY heart skipping a beat.

She's so fucking beautiful.

So goddamn perfect.

Everything she did tonight, every reaction, every word, made me fall just a little bit more for her.

Judge actually looked at me with pity toward the end because he knew there was no way I would be letting this girl go now. Not after the way she reacted in that simulation.

Two others underwent a similar experience, except not with all the historical theatrics my brother threw in for Sydney.

The other two were just strapped to a chair in

a room that went up in flames while their peers ridiculed them and demanded they answer question after question in order to be freed.

Afterward, each of them was warned not to share their experiences. They were only allowed to comment on how important truth is in this game. "We don't want to spoil the experience for the others," the voice told everyone else. "We need them to feel the realness of the situation, just as you did, in order for this to be fair."

The same was said to Griffin just before he reentered the theater.

And everyone reacted similarly by saying that it wouldn't be a problem, because they wanted the others to suffer just like they had.

We didn't bother having the simulation say those words to Sydney.

Mostly because the experience was unique to her.

The fire simulation is one we intend to use to punish those who killed our parents. To make them experience the pain of being burned alive while cuffed to a chair.

And the agony of hearing their children scream from above.

I didn't put Sydney through this to punish her, though. I wanted her to understand. To experience the pain of our loss. To comprehend our need for revenge.

She wasn't ready to hear the reasoning yet. That much was evident by her agony after the simulation ended. Rather than grab her and force her to hear me, I gave her space.

Only to find her curled in a ball on her balcony, shivering beneath the stars.

The exertion of the mental exercise must have knocked her out because she somehow fell asleep like this. "Poor little dove," I whisper, bending to pick her up. She immediately curls into my chest, seeking my warmth. But her eyes don't open.

She's exhausted.

And still wearing her clothes from today.

I carry her inside and to her room, then I strip her while she sleeps.

She doesn't react at all.

Just continues to shiver.

I take off my dress shirt and wrap it around her. She immediately snuggles into the warm fabric and sighs, making my lips twitch.

"One night together and you're already addicted," I say, amused by her instinctual reactions to me. I slide into the bed beside her and pull her into my arms. "It's okay," I whisper against her ear. "I'm just as addicted to you, sweet girl."

She nuzzles my chest and cuddles into me like she did the pillow earlier.

I run my fingers through her hair and hold her, allowing her to absorb my warmth.

It's almost three o'clock in the morning, and I'm exhausted from barely sleeping last night. And then working all damn day.

We have to do it all again tomorrow. But at least Sydney can relax.

The other six will have their turns with the virtual reality simulator tomorrow.

And the following day, the real opening ceremony will begin.

"I can't wait for you to see our endgame," I tell Sydney. "Just a few more days." Because the opening ceremony is just the end of phase one.

Phase two is where the real fireworks will go off.

But by then, it'll be too late for all those involved.

Not Sydney, though.

Something tells me this is just the beginning for her. For us. For a future I never knew I desired. For a future I hope she'll accept.

I kiss her temple as her shivering begins to abate. I'll hold her like this for a while longer. Just until I'm sure she can truly dream again.

I end up falling asleep beside Sydney and wake

as the sun is climbing over the mountains.

It's a beautiful sight.

As is the woman in my arms.

There's only one problem—she's staring at me. And it's not the sexy kind of stare that says she wants me to kiss her. It's the kind of look a woman wears when she wants to kill a man.

Which, of course, makes me hard.

Because just the thought of sparring with her in such a way turns me on.

"Good morning," I murmur, my fingers tracing up her spine to the back of her neck. "I found you sleeping outside. Your bed seemed more comfortable."

She narrows her gaze. "Is that why I'm naked under your shirt?"

"I assumed that would be more comfortable than your jeans, boots, and turtleneck." My focus goes to her throat, the marks I left there showing signs of healing. I lean forward and kiss her throat, pleased.

Goose bumps pebble in the wake of my touch, making me grin as I kiss a path up to her ear. "Did you sleep okay?" I ask her.

"Tell me it wasn't real," she demands instead, the lack of grogginess in her voice indicating that she's been awake for a while now and likely thinking through everything from yesterday. "Tell me those boys did not die like that."

"Those boys did not die like that," I promise her. *Because I'm one of them.*

"So it was just a fucked-up simulation?" She presses her palm to my chest and gives it a little shove. "Who the fuck comes up with an idea like that?"

"Someone who lived it," I admit, even though I probably shouldn't.

"Wh-what?" she stammers, rearing back like I'm the one who just shoved at her and not the other way around. "So it's real?"

"Parts of it," I tell her, my palm cupping her cheek. *All of it, really. But you didn't see how it ends.* "You'll understand everything soon, Sydney. I promise." *When I let you see the real truth.*

"I'm not sure I want to understand," she whispers. "I don't want to be here at all."

I trace the hollow beneath her eye with my thumb, debating how to respond. I don't blame her for wanting to run. The problem is, there's nowhere for her to go.

And her expression tells me she knows it, too.

"Today will be an easier day," I promise her. "The other six have their simulations and that's it. If you want, we can try for a normal night."

"And what? Act like this insanity isn't real? Act

like I wasn't put through hell last night?"

"What alternative would you recommend?" I ask, curious. "Because we both know you can't leave. So what would you like, Sydney? Tell me what you need and I'll give it to you."

"Except for my freedom."

"We already covered that I can't—"

"*Won't,*" she corrects.

"Yes, we've already covered that I *won't* help you escape. And soon, you'll understand why," I promise her. "But I can't tell you yet."

"Can't or won't?" she demands.

"On that, I mean I can't, Sydney. I cannot tell you everything yet." Because I can't risk her mentioning it to anyone else. I don't fully trust her yet. So far, she's proven admirable every step of the way, but her freak-out right now is exactly why I can't tell her everything.

She needs to understand first.

Then I'll be able to elaborate.

She blows out a breath and shakes her head. "I think I hate you."

I nod, accepting her hatred. "I think you also like me, though."

Her eyes narrow. "Why? Because you're a good fuck?"

My lips twitch. "Am I good a fuck?"

She scoffs at that. "Such a male way to react."

"You said it, sweetheart, not me."

"And of course that's now going to be the only thing you remember from this conversation," she says, rolling her eyes.

"That you hate me, yet like me because I'm a good fuck?" I summarize. "Yeah, likely."

She tries to shove away from me again, but it's less forceful than before. I cover her hand with mine, my opposite one going to the back of her neck.

"Do you need me to fuck the hatred out of you, Sydney?" I ask her.

"Jesus, you would say that, wouldn't you?"

"*Kage*," I correct her.

"Kage. Kage. Kage." She utters my name like it's a curse. "Why do you work here? What part are you really playing in all this?"

Two very important questions.

Neither of which I can truly answer.

But I can give her at least a little bit. "My family, Sydney. I work here because of my family."

"Because you used to live nearby?"

I used to live here, I think. *Before those assholes burned down my parents' house.* But I don't say that out loud. "There's a lot of history here. History I can't yet explain. But what you need to understand is that I would do anything for my family. And I very much value the truth. So I work here because I have to, because it's the only way the truth will come out."

"What truth?" she asks.

"That's the nature of the game, isn't it?" I study her. "Truth or Kill. What will you choose?"

"To run," she whispers. "I would choose to run."

"And yet you haven't truly tried to escape yet. Why?" I give her hand a little squeeze against my chest. "Because you know you can't. You know there's nowhere to go. Nowhere to hide. No one to save you except for yourself. So you keep playing the game until you find an opportunity. Keep playing the game until you find your worth. Keep playing the game until you finally discover… the truth."

She stares at me and says nothing.

Because deep down she knows I'm right.

The only way for her to survive this now is to see it through to the end.

"You can survive this," I promise her. "I know it's cruel. I know it's dark. I know it's a game you never wanted to play. But when it ends, it will be worth the fight, Sydney."

"How do you know that?"

"Because I know how it's going to end." It's something I shouldn't admit, but I do anyway. Who is she going to tell? Landon? Preston? Gretchen?

I'm the only one who has been an ally to her here, and she knows it.

"You're asking me to trust you," she says.

It's not what I said at all, but she's also not wrong in assuming that. "I'm asking you to see it through. There's an end to all this madness coming. It's just not the end you're expecting." Yet another thing I shouldn't say, but I can't seem to help myself with her.

I want her to stay.

I want her to survive.

I want her to be mine.

Rather than say the words out loud, I say them to her with my mouth.

By kissing her.

By demanding with my tongue that she listen to me.

Her nails bite into my bare skin, her little claws sharp enough to make me bleed. I press into her touch, daring her to do it. Giving her permission to scratch me. Hit me. Bite me. *Fight* me.

Whatever she needs. Whatever she desires. I'll give it to her.

Just not her freedom.

I didn't drag her into this mess. Rebecca Edington did.

But I'm the one who can help Sydney extract herself from it eventually. Which is something else I tell her with my tongue.

Something she seems to accept because she lets me push my shirt from her shoulders, leaving her naked against me.

Which is when she starts kissing me back.

It's a biting kiss underlined with anger, fueled by fear, and driven by *need*.

Her nails claw up my chest as she drags her touch upward. Her arms encircle my neck in the next breath, her breasts pressing up against me in beautiful invitation.

I roll her to her back, my thigh sliding between her legs, as I continue to devour her with my mouth. She moans and presses against me, her pussy wet against my bare thigh.

Yeah, this isn't going to be slow like the other night.

This will be ferocious.

Savage.

Vicious.

She claws at my hair, her fingers threading through the strands and tightening. "I still hate you," she pants against my mouth as she arches into me again.

"Mmm," I hum. "You certainly have a fun way of showing that hatred, beautiful." I take her lower lip between my teeth and bite her. *Hard.*

She screams for me in response, making me grin.

I lave away the hurt with my tongue, watching as her pupils dilate in unadulterated hunger.

This is a mark everyone will see.

Because she can't hide it with a damn turtleneck.

"You're mine now, sweetheart," I tell her.

She rakes her nails down my back, sharp and ferocious and alluringly carnal. "Fuck you, Kage."

I tsk, my lips going to her ear. "I believe the words you're looking for are, *Fuck me, Kage.*" I move my mouth to her raging pulse. "Unless you want me to stop."

"Don't you fucking dare," she growls, grabbing my shoulders and holding on rather than pushing me away. "Help me escape again. Please."

"Now that I can do," I say, drawing my mouth back to hers. "That I can *always* do."

My brothers would just have to wait.

This girl needs me, and I'm a slave to those needs.

Sixteen
KAGE

All I have on is a pair of boxers, something she's already removing for me with her eager hands. She doesn't ask me about a condom this time, perhaps because she's too lost to the sensations and the need awakening in her system.

I should stop this and ask her if she wants one.

A gentleman would, anyway.

But I'm not a gentleman.

I'm Kage. I'm *hers*.

And I want to take her bare.

She's on the pill. I'm clean. Hopefully, she is, too. If not, it's a risk I'm willing to take to feel her.

Impulsive, yes.

But that's who I am.

That's who she is. I can feel it in every embrace,

taste it on her tongue, sense it in the way she seems to master me with her touch.

This woman is meant to be here. Right now. Beneath me. With my cock lodged so far inside her that she feels me for days.

So that's exactly what I give her.

My boxers are around my knees, thanks to her wandering hands, and I kick them the rest of the way off. Then I palm her thighs, spread her, and enter her without warning.

She screams, and it's the most delicious sound. I let it vibrate my mouth as I pull almost all of the way out of her just to drive in again.

And again.

And again.

She's shaking beneath me, both from shock and pleasure.

She likes the pain. Because of course she does. She's perfect. She's mine. And together, we're going to explore her limits in full.

I grab her hips and roll to my back while pulling her with me, ensuring my cock never leaves her sweet heat.

She clamps down around me as though to hold on, then shudders at the sensation of having me so deep inside her.

It's amazing.

Perfect.

The most erotic sensation imaginable.

And I need more.

I sit up, my hand around the back of her neck, my opposite palm braced on the bed. "Wrap your legs around me, Sydney," I tell her. "Then ride me."

It's an intimate position, one that puts her in control of the pace.

And she doesn't disappoint me.

She proves her flexibility by moving gracefully on my lap, her ankles crossing behind my back as she grabs my shoulders with both hands.

Then she begins to fuck me.

Truly. Completely. Without a care in the world.

It's fucking amazing.

She just lets go and lets me have it, and I take every move, countering it with a thrust of my own.

Her head falls back, her lips parting as she gives me everything she has.

I'm so stunned that all I can do is watch her. She's magnificent. Her tits bouncing, her rosy nipples stiff and begging for my touch, her pussy claiming me with tight pulses that go straight to my balls.

"Fuck, beautiful," I breathe, giving back in kind, driving upward to meet her wild motions.

I think I'm falling in love, I marvel, utterly lost to this woman.

I still have my palm around the back of her neck, holding her as she arches and grinds and *fucks*.

My lips go to her throat, my nose skimming the bruises on my way down to her breasts.

I can't resist those little rosy tips. I take one between my teeth and nibble, loving the way she groans in response. Then I lick and suck and watch her cheeks flush in response.

She's so damn stunning I nearly come from her expression alone.

But I refuse to go there without her.

I want her so fucking wet and so tight that when she finally explodes, she'll scream loud enough for the whole fucking lodge to hear her.

She's soaking my shaft, but it's not enough. I want more.

I release her nape and draw my hand down her exquisite form to her clit. It's swollen and needy, just the way I like it. I circle it with my thumb while I suck on her nipple, my eyes on her expression as I do it.

She loses some of her finesse, her desire overwhelming her own movements.

She's fucking me faster now.

Panting. Vibrating. Ready to scream.

So I pull back and grab her hips, forcing her to stop. She curses, her eyes flying open. "What are you doing?" she demands.

"Enjoying the view," I admit, my gaze dancing over her flushed skin, along pretty tits, and down to where our bodies are joined. "You're fucking beautiful, Sydney."

"Fuck me," she demands. "Fuck me right now. I was close!"

"Not close enough," I tell her, driving upward once just to make her tremble. She tries to shift, but my grip on her hips tightens, forcing her to remain still. "No, gorgeous. It's my turn to fuck you now. And I want to go slower." I lift her partially off of me, then yank her back down as I shoot my hips upward.

She jolts and moans in response, her head falling to my shoulder. "*Fuck.*"

"That's what I'm doing," I whisper back to her, my lips near her ear again as I repeat the action. "*Fucking* you."

She makes a little noise, the kind that tells me she wants to cry almost as much as she wants to come.

So close, I think. *So very, very close.*

Just a few more slow, intense punches of my hips will take her exactly where I want her.

She's clawing at my shoulders again, leaving marks on me that I'll wear proudly for days.

This little wildcat is mine.

And I'm so fucking glad she's accepting that fact. At least with her body.

Her inner walls clench down around me as she groans again, the sound bordering on a mewl.

"That's it," I praise her. "Feel that tension growing, that ball of need tightening your muscles, taking you so close to the edge without letting you fall over it." My lips are still at her ear. "Is it making you hot, sweetheart?"

"Yes," she hisses, trying to move again.

But I don't let her.

I *won't* let her.

This is my show now. She had her fun. And now it's my turn to have my own fun with her. By prolonging the torture. By making sure she explodes so hard she can't stop shaking for hours. By ensuring she can never replace me with anyone else.

Mine, I tell her with my hips. *You. Are. Mine.*

And the way she cries for me tells me she knows it, too.

Time doesn't matter.

Not between us.

This is a dark dance of fate.

One I'm fully indulging.

And the way she sobs against me now indicates that she is, too.

I'm destroying her. But it's only fair because she's destroying me.

Two destructive souls destined to dance in life and in hell.

I fist my hand in her hair and kiss her, my body coming alive beneath her, no longer capable of holding back the fierceness of my need. Of my desire. Of my impending devotion.

This is insanity. But I embrace it. I force her to embrace it, too.

This is who we're meant to be, and I don't care what anyone else thinks or what they say. This moment is ours. It may not last. It may end with my blade in her heart. But we'll always have this memory.

Till death do us part.

"Kage," she says, her luscious body tightening against mine. "Oh, Kage!"

"Now, sweetheart," I tell her. "Come for me right fucking now." I piston my hips into her so hard that she can't deny my demand.

And that scream.

Oh, *fuck*, that scream.

It's so damn beautiful. So goddamn perfect. That I can't help but follow her over the edge.

I don't know who sent me this girl, but I will forever thank the Almighty for her. Because she's obviously a gift. Perhaps payment for all the hardships. A way to *breathe* in this new future.

Except I forget how to breathe now as the rapture takes both of us under, vibrating between us, setting our veins on fire while cooling our blood at the same time.

It's an eruption of insanity.

Bordering on blissful goodness.

Taking us to heaven and back.

And grounding us in the hell of our reality.

She collapses against me, and I take her down to the bed, holding her as I continue to pump in and out of her, my seed filling her in a forbidden sort of way. Claiming her insides. Making her mine. And I want my cum to stay inside her for as long as she'll allow.

To own her.

To make her truly mine.

It's so fucked up. So wrong. So undeniably mad.

And yet I keep doing it.

I keep fucking her, needing her to be mine.

I'm obsessed. I've lost my goddamn mind for her.

She's kissing me in a manner that suggests she's lost herself to me, too.

Like we're both under some sort of lustful spell that owns us both.

And somehow, some way, she starts coming again. Her sweet little cunt is milking my cock even while she cries from the intensity of our union.

I lick away her tears, loving this embrace and never wanting it to end.

It's a dangerous desire.

One I punctuate with my hips as I just keep fucking her.

This girl is an enigma. Some sort of powerful entity sent here to test my faith in life itself.

I kiss her.

I fuck her.

I kiss her some more.

Until finally I come again with her pussy clamped down so tightly around me, her own orgasm making her scream in agony rather than pleasure.

It's intense. It's… it's something I didn't even know could exist.

But it does. With her.

With Sydney Evans.

This beautiful goddess of a girl.

Mine.

I pull out of her and reach between us to stroke my fingers through her cum-drenched sex, then shove some of it back inside her. She winces, clearly sore. But I don't care. I do it again, needing to ensure she feels and understands my claim.

Then I lift my fingers to her mouth and paint her lips with our arousal. "Lick," I demand.

And she does.

Of course she does.

Because she's Sydney. Because she's perfect.

Because she's meant for me.

I give her more by slipping my fingers into her mouth, and she sucks each digit clean. "Fuck, Sydney," I breathe. "You're absolutely killing me."

I kiss her rather than explain what I mean.

I tell her with my mouth how gone I am for her.

And only when she's panting against me do I stop.

Her eyes are two dark pools swirling with questions and concerns. She understands, but she doesn't.

Soon, I promise her with a look. *Soon.*

Then I kiss her again, this time softly, and press my forehead to hers. "Please show up today, Sydney," I whisper. "I really don't want to have to chase you, okay?"

Her nostrils flare. "What'll you do when you catch me?"

"Fuck you," I admit. "Fuck you until you understand that you can never outrun me."

"That's not a good reason for me to stay put, then." Her voice is a little hoarse from all the screaming.

But that's not why I smile.

I smile because she's flirting with her words. "Don't make me punish you, sweetheart. I can do a lot more than delay your gratification." I pull back just a little so she can see the seriousness in my expression. "We haven't even started playing with knives yet. And I don't think you want our first experience with that to be because you provoked me into hunting you down."

She shivers. "Still not a good reason not to run," she whispers.

I nip her bottom lip on the same spot I bit her earlier, making her wince. "Careful, Sydney." I lave the wound. "You don't want to explore those limits with me yet."

Rather than elaborate, I pull her off the bed and take her into the shower with me.

Where I kiss her senseless.

Worship her with my hands.

And bathe her the way a man should bathe a woman after a bout of rough sex.

By the time we're done, she's staring up at me with eyes that are not hateful at all. They're a bit dreamy instead.

Just the way I want her.

"See you later," I say after dressing in last night's clothes. My shirt now smells like her.

Which means I'll probably end up wearing it all day.

Along with her residual battle wounds.

Maybe she'll give me more later.

After today's session.

Duty first, I remind myself. *Then we can play.*

Seventeen
SYDNEY

KAGE WAS RIGHT—THE NEXT SESSION WASN'T AS BAD. At least not for me. For the six people who went through the simulation experience? Yeah, it probably sucked for them.

But I didn't feel bad about it.

Because their families were the ones running the show. If they wanted to torture their kids, that was on them.

I left the moment they dismissed us, going straight up to my room. I barely touched my dinner, my stomach in knots as I considered what tonight would bring.

Kage mentioned doing something "normal," and I'm wondering what his definition of "normal" is. Because he certainly doesn't fuck like a normal man. Nor does he act like one.

Nothing in this place is "normal."

I collapse on the couch and wait.

When a half hour passes without word from him, I go out on my balcony to stare at the stars. They're not as pretty here as they are from the field, mostly because of the exterior lights impacting my view. But the lights are not too bright, so I can still see a lot.

I'm in the middle of looking for a constellation when Kage lets himself into my room. He doesn't knock. And while that should bother me, I really don't care.

There's something about our connection, this spontaneous relationship, that puts me completely at ease with him. Even when I want to hate him, I really can't.

He walks up behind me and presses his chest to my back, his hands covering mine on the balcony railing as his lips go to my ear. "How was today?"

"You tell me," I murmur. "You watched it all, didn't you?'

"I didn't," he says, surprising me. "I had a lot of work to do that kept me from observing."

"Work?" I echo, curious as to what that means. I know he's the reception manager, but something in his sentence makes me think he's not talking about that job.

"Hmm," he hums. "And that work is partly why I'm late. The other part is because my brothers want you to come watch a movie with them."

I frown. "Wait, what?"

"My brothers want—"

"No, I heard that. Your brothers are here?" I glance over my shoulder to meet his gaze. "Who are your brothers?"

He studies me for a moment. "Do you want to meet them?"

I don't even have to think about it. "Yes." I want to know everything about Kage. Why he's here. What family ties are forcing him to do all this. Why he's participating so openly in all this madness. *Who* he really is. Every single detail.

He falls silent and then slowly nods. "All right. I promised you some normalcy tonight, and I suppose meeting family falls into that category. I'll introduce you to them." He kisses my neck. "But first tell me how today went."

"It was boring," I admit. "All we did was watch people sit in a chair."

"Tomorrow will be more eventful," he says, and it sounds more like a warning than a casual comment. "But tonight is for normalcy."

"Whatever that means here," I murmur.

He chuckles. "Come with me and find out." He runs his palms up my arms to my shoulders and then down along my sides to my hips.

I shiver, his touch doing things to me.

Things I shouldn't like.

The way he fucked me this morning was so possessive and primal. He didn't even use a condom, something I belatedly realized. I want to ask him if he's clean. If I should worry. But I just don't.

There's this weird sort of understanding between us that's borderline insane. I've never felt this way about anyone before. So innately trusting. Like we're meant to fit together.

I'm starting to understand what people mean when they say, "When you meet your person, you just know."

Because that's how I feel now.

When Kage touches me, it just feels right.

Perhaps it's a result of this situation and the fact that I may not survive the week. But I've always been the type to seize the moment. And so I do.

I turn in his arms and kiss him because I want to. Because I can. He's taller than me by a good six inches, but it doesn't matter. The minute I go up onto my toes, he bends his head, and our lips touch. Lightning strikes through my veins, causing my heart to thunder in my chest.

It's magical.

Enchanting.

Sensually pleasing.

He takes his time with me, his tongue parting my lips and gently stroking inside. I lean into him, my hands roaming up his strong arms to his shoulders. I want to explore every inch of him. To be in charge of the tasting and the licking.

He's all masculine perfection and alluring lines. His tattoos spread across his chest, but his abdomen is all muscle. The ink continues onto his arms, going all the way down to his hands.

They're not full sleeves so much as designs that spiral along his skin. I studied them earlier while he slept, enjoying the way they accented his muscles. He clearly takes good care of himself, which doesn't surprise me. Living out here, he has access to hundreds of hiking trails.

I draw my fingers along his arms and down over his torso, exploring him through the fabric. He doesn't stop me, his mouth engaging mine in a continued whirl of sensuality and sin.

"If you don't stop, I'll be taking you to bed instead," he whispers against my mouth. "So pick now, Sydney. A night of normalcy or a night of fucking?"

"We can't have both?" I ask him seriously. "A night of normalcy that ends in fucking?"

His forest-green eyes glitter as he stares down at me. "I think I may be falling in love with you, beautiful girl."

I grin. "You hardly know me."

"I think we both know that's not true," he returns. "But I also think it's time for you to get to know me a little better." He pulls back a bit and lifts his hand between us.

I accept his nonverbal invitation by pressing my palm to his.

"I'll begin by introducing you to my brothers." He starts to lead me back through my room but pauses in the foyer. "Do you have siblings?"

"Just foster brothers and sisters," I tell him. "We don't really keep in touch."

He nods. "So no real family."

"None." I look at him. "I suppose that makes me expendable." Something I imagine he's already inferred. The smart thing would be to tell him someone would come looking for me. But that would be a lie, and I don't feel like lying to him.

"It does," he agrees, his gaze going to my mouth before lifting again to my eyes. "But I think you're worth a lot more alive than dead, Ms. Evans."

"I'm not sure if that's a compliment or an ominous statement, Mister…" I trail off. "I don't know your last name."

He smiles. "No, you don't."

"You're not going to tell me, are you?"

"Not tonight," he admits. "But perhaps soon."

"Maybe your brothers will tell me."

He shakes his head and pulls me toward the door again. "They won't. We're loyal to each other. It's been that way ever since our parents died."

"Is that why you all work here?" I ask as we enter the hallway.

"Everything we do is for our family, yes," he replies, giving my hand a squeeze as the door to my room closes. Rather than head toward the staircase, he takes me to the end of the hall. It's at the complete opposite end of where I stayed with Becca.

He inserts a key into the door there, which leads us into a hallway of sorts.

And to a second door that requires his thumbprint for entry.

I arch a brow at him. "Trying to ensure none of the guests find your room?"

He grins. "Trying to ensure none of the guests are able to access this wing," he corrects, guiding me through the threshold into a stunning entryway. There are stairs that lead upward and downward, the inside far larger than a standard suite.

This is like a palatial *home*.

There's a living room downstairs, on the same floor as reception, with glass windows that stretch up four stories. We're on a platform of sorts that leads to a walkway that overlooks the entertaining area below.

"These are the staff quarters?" I ask, marveling

at all the wooden fixtures and gold ornaments. "It's like a completely separate hotel."

He chuckles and gives my hand a squeeze as he leads me out onto the walkway. It continues over to another hallway. "Our rooms are all this way," he says, taking me to the very end, where he opens a door to reveal a suite. "This area is mine."

He gives me a quick tour, which includes a small sitting area, a kitchenette, and eventually his bedroom. His shower is twice the size of the one back in my room, making me frown. "We should have showered here earlier."

"Maybe we'll shower there tomorrow," he suggests, giving me a soft smile.

His bedroom has skylights overhead and a balcony that wraps around his room. With the way everything is angled, I wonder if he can see my balcony from here. But I don't ask. Instead, I just follow along as he takes me back across the walkway and down the stairs to the massive living area. He explains that it's a reserved area for those who live and work here.

We see a few other people as we walk. They all nod at Kage while eyeing me curiously. He doesn't introduce me, so I assume these people are not his brothers.

He leads me down another hall, this one on the ground floor, and pauses beside a door to listen. A large crash sounds, causing his lips to curl. "As I thought." He pushes through the threshold, taking me into a theater of sorts.

But it's not like the one I've spent most of my week in.

This is a proper movie theater with a big screen and rows of lounge chairs.

The scent of popcorn is thick in the air, making my mouth water. I've not eaten much the last two days, my stomach not capable of it.

However, I love a good bucket of buttery popcorn.

Two dark heads pop up at our entry, both of them grinning widely at seeing me with Kage. "You brought her!" one of them exclaims, jumping up to do something with the screen. The movie pauses in a blink, and the other man stands.

I recognize him immediately as the general manager.

The other is one I don't think I've met. Although, he may have been the other valet that day because he's vaguely familiar.

"We literally just started," the vaguely familiar one says. "The popcorn isn't even done yet." He points to a machine in the corner, making my stomach growl.

Because yeah, I want some of that.

"What movie did you decide on?" Kage asks.

"The remake," the general manager says, his eyes on me. "Hello, Ms. Evans. Did my baby brother get you that canoe?"

I frown. "No. No, he didn't." I look at Kage. "You still owe me a canoe."

"I'm not the baby brother," Kage corrects, ignoring me. "L is."

"You're both *my* baby brothers," the general manager says, smiling.

So I guess my assumption the other day that he may be related to Kage was right. *Brothers. These are his brothers.*

And I presume the one who mentioned the popcorn is *L*. I imagine that's short for something.

Which leaves me wondering what the general manager's name is. "You manage the whole property?" I ask him.

Kage grunts beside me. "Is that what you told her?"

"It's my title, so yes," he says. "I'm in charge here."

L chuckles and releases a low whistle. "You're just asking for a beating, J."

"As if K can do any real damage," *J* says. "And I told Mr. Matterhorn I was the manager to save his ass from K."

"He's still not saved," Kage says, a threat in his

tone. "Not by a long shot."

"L, J, K," I repeat, interrupting their little whatever this is. "K for Kage?" I guess, glancing at the male in question.

He startles like he forgot I'm here and squeezes my hand a little, maybe to ensure that I'm real. "K for Kage," he confirms.

"J for Judge," the general manager, who may or may not be the actual general manager, says.

"L for Loki," the other one informs me. And somehow, I find that name appropriate. He has *trickster* written all over that sly smile on his face. "Do you prefer 'Sydney' or 'Ms. Evans'?"

Because of course they know my name.

They're all involved in this madness somehow.

But Kage promised me a normal night. So I'm going to proceed accordingly and not think about what's happening in this place.

A mental escape, I realize. *He's offering me yet another mental escape.*

This one is a little less intense than the other *escape* he provided me with.

I clear my throat and push away my thoughts. "Sydney, please."

"Sydney it is," Loki says. "Want to join us for a movie?"

I consider it for a second and glance at Kage again

before nodding. "That sounds normal enough."

He smirks. "Normal until you find out that my brothers have chosen a slasher flick."

My eyebrows lift. Although, I'm not sure why I'm surprised. It certainly seems appropriate to watch a deadly movie in this place. "You mentioned it was a remake, right? A remake of what?"

"It's not really a remake. It's just a movie based on an urban legend," Loki explains.

"What urban legend?"

"Killswitch," he says.

I frown. "Isn't that a game?" I've heard it mentioned by a few classmates before. But I've never really looked into it. Mostly because I was too busy focusing on school and sports to have time for playing a video game.

"Is it?" Loki asks, arching a brow. "Because the legend implies that it never really existed. There's no evidence of it at all."

"Loki loves urban legends," Kage tells me, rolling his eyes. "He's been this way since he was a kid."

"Come on, it's fascinating," Loki argues. "The game went out to, like, five thousand people, but they could only play it once. When the player died, all traces of the game were erased from the system."

"Sounds like a good way to hack someone," I comment. "Place something temporarily on their computer, distract them with a game while you work." I shrug. "Definitely a hack."

Loki grins. "But it wasn't a hack, just a game that existed temporarily and disappeared. Or that's what the legend says. And that's what this movie is about."

I consider the concept for a moment. "All right, I'm intrigued." It's been a while since I saw a movie. Which is probably why I haven't heard of this one. "Who is in it?"

"A bunch of Korean actors," he tells me. "It's a foreign film with subtitles."

"Ah, then it's going to be good," I decide. "I love a good foreign flick. Especially horror."

Loki covers his heart and looks at Kage. "I'm in love. Can I have her?"

Kage wraps his arm around my waist and pulls me into him. "No."

Judge just chuckles and goes to check on the popcorn. Then he starts passing out buckets to everyone. I eagerly accept mine, something Kage seems to notice. He takes one for himself, then says, "Pick a seat, gorgeous."

I choose the middle row—there are three—while Loki and Judge take the seats closest to the screen.

"Start it over, L," Judge says as I find the right setting for my chair. The recliner is leather and comfy and much better than the couches in the theater hall.

Not thinking about that right now, I remind myself as I settle a little deeper into my seat. *Focus on the popcorn and the movie.*

It ends up being an easy task, as the film is riveting. And bloody. Not really a slasher flick like Kage warned, but more of a suspenseful movie filled with tension and darkness.

Rather than make it a fun gamer movie, it's a tense flick about a group of people invited to play a game with real-life consequences.

Some of them die.

And at the end, all evidence of the game disappears without a trace.

"That was really good," I say as soon as it ends. "I can't believe they didn't reveal who was behind it, but it also seems so fitting because it makes you wonder if it ever really existed. Was it in their heads? Was it even real?"

Kage is thoughtful as he stares at the screen while the end credits roll. "I think it was real. And that a lot of them deserved their fates."

That I agree with. "They weren't good people." Just a bunch of criminals hoping to gain an edge in the game to win a bunch of money.

Yet they all lost in the end.

"I suppose there's a lesson in that," I muse, thinking out loud. "Greed has consequences. And whenever something is too good to be true, it probably is."

"Always," Kage agrees, glancing at me with a weird sort of glint in his gaze.

"I enjoyed it," Loki says, interrupting the moment by turning on the lights and standing to switch off the projector. "I'll add it to my rewatch collection."

"I expected more blood," Judge comments.

Loki snorts at him. "Of course you did." He looks at me. "Both of my brothers prefer the killing shit over a suspenseful plot."

"I like movies that make me think," I admit. "And that one did it for me."

Kage considers me for another moment, then takes the bucket from my lap and leaves his chair to discard it.

Judge stretches his arms over his head, his physique similar to both of his brothers'. Although, he does appear to be the largest of the three. Slightly taller and wider, but equally as fit.

Now that the lights are all the way on, I can really see how much they look like one another. Dark hair, tall, athletic builds. But Judge and Loki don't appear to have the tats like Kage does. At least, they're not visible. But like Kage, they're all wearing black slacks and dress shirts with the sleeves rolled to their elbows.

Why do men always do that? Do they inherently

know how sexy it is? I've always been a forearm girl. But the ink on Kage's skin definitely appeals to me the most. They're all muscular and fit, though. They probably hike a lot together.

Since it seems they're very close.

And do everything for their family.

I suppose I would be that way as well if I had a brother or a sister.

Kage appears beside me, his hand palm-up. "Want some dessert?" he asks me.

"Is that a metaphor?" I wonder aloud as I accept his help out of my chair.

He grins. "It can be, if that's the kind of dessert you want. But I was going to offer to make you a sundae since we're doing *normal* tonight."

I laugh. "A sundae would be nice."

He winks.

"I'll take one, too," Loki says.

"I'm out," Judge informs us all. "I'm fucking beat, and tomorrow is… a big day." He looks at Kage while he says those words.

Kage nods. "I'll see you when I see you," he tells his brother.

Judge holds his gaze for a minute longer, then grabs Loki's arm. "You're coming with me."

"No, I'm getting a sundae," Loki corrects him.

"I don't think you were invited, L." Judge pulls him out of the room while Kage chuckles and shakes his head.

"I think my little brother might be in love with you already," Kage muses, his thumb stroking over the back of my hand. "But I don't share."

A tingle goes down my spine. "You don't?" Because a twisted part of me likes the sound of his possession.

"I don't." He pulls me into him, his free hand going to the back of my neck. "He can admire from afar, but I claimed you first."

"Why did you claim me, Kage?"

"Because you're too good to be true," he whispers, making me think of what I said about the movie. "And so far, I haven't found anything to prove otherwise."

"You're still getting to know me," I point out.

"I am," he agrees, his lips grazing mine. "And you're still getting to know me. So, dessert?"

I nod. "Yes, please."

This almost feels like a regular date.

Movie. Popcorn. Ice cream.

All of it with an underlying sense of sexual tension.

Because we both know what's coming.

We can't seem to help ourselves.

However, I let him lead me to the kitchen—which is an industrial-size one with multiple ovens, fridges, and stoves. But there's no one else here. Just us.

So he picks me up, sets me on the counter, and spreads my legs.

I don't understand until he puts a bowl between my thighs.

And begins making a sundae for us to share.

It's erotic and causes electricity to dance along my arms and legs.

I'm thankful for my jeans, or the chill would dispel some of the hunger brewing inside me.

Or maybe it would heighten it. I'm really not sure. Kage undoes something in me. He makes me question reason. Forget reality. Stop caring about everything and everyone else.

All I can focus on is him and the sundae he's creating.

Vanilla ice cream. Chocolate. Nuts. Whipped cream. And a cherry.

"Open," he whispers, bringing the spoon to my mouth. "Don't swallow."

I'm not sure what he means, so I let the flavor sit on my tongue. Then I groan as he starts to kiss me, his own taste adding to the decadence in my mouth. I swallow on a tremble that goes all the way to my toes.

This man is an enigma.

I don't understand him at all. Yet I feel as though I've known him my whole life.

He's a puzzle I long to solve. A puzzle… I think I know all too well.

It's an intoxicating conundrum that leaves me breathless as we share the sundae. We barely speak, our tongues doing all the talking for us.

And when he takes me back up to his room, I don't even question it.

I let him strip me.

I let him fuck me.

I let him hold me as we sleep.

Because it feels right. It feels normal. It feels like *us*.

Eighteen
SYDNEY

I DREAM ABOUT *KILLSWITCH*.

Only, it applies to the game I'm currently playing here in this lodge.

And in the end, everything dissolves because nothing is real.

Except it's very real, something that becomes apparent as I sit in the theater hall once again, watching the videos created from our time in the virtual reality chambers.

The confessions revealed make me shiver.

My own video is tame in comparison to the others.

"She's only here to fuck Landon," Gretchen says in a clip during my video montage. It seems to be a collection of moments from this week, all coupled with things I said while inside that helmet.

"I'm sorry, what?" my voice replies, making it sound like I'm speaking to Gretchen when I know I wasn't. "I didn't agree to come on this trip with Becca just to be a piece of meat for a billionaire heir to play with while bored."

That's my statement from the other day, during one of the Truth or Kill rounds.

"I think she's here to get a job," someone else says. A male. I can't place his voice.

But then the screen shows Brayden saying, "I'll give her a job."

"I want nothing to do with your fucking company or any of you," my voice says as the video continues.

There are more whispers about why I'm here, accusations of me being a plant, me being the killer, as my voice continues to address random statements. Except everything is out of context.

The only thing I gather by the time it finishes is that we're being constantly recorded because half the video is composed of commentary captured outside of the virtual reality helmet.

Which suggests the same for everyone else's videos.

Landon confesses to feeling that Brayden is a weak link in the organization during his own video. "He should be removed. He's too reliant on his parents to clean up his own messes and doesn't know how to handle himself appropriately."

"Fuck you, Matterhorn," Brayden snaps from across the room.

"Shut up," Landon retorts. "Focus on the videos. That's why we're here today."

But it becomes apparent quickly that all these reveals are stirring chaos in the room. Everyone is pissed at someone for something, which is making me wonder if that's the point of this exercise.

It's about more than just blackmail.

It's about revealing all their truths to one another, to prove that none of them are actually allies. They're here because of a similar venture—they're heirs to the various branches of Covington Industries.

What I can't figure out is why their parents would wish to destroy all their friendships. Isn't the point to make them work together, not against each other?

By the end of the movie session—which lasts a good three hours—everyone is furious.

Arguing ensues while I watch from the couch.

However, it dawns on me that no one commented on gun control.

It's like my question wasn't asked at all. *How are we supposed to determine the killer if we can't ask vital questions about the weapon?*

Unless the point isn't to determine the killer at all.

There's something about this game that isn't quite right.

Something I'm missing.

I mention this to Kage when he enters my room later that night, long after the chaos of the day is complete, and he just shrugs. "Perhaps you'll find out more tomorrow."

"Or you could tell me," I hedge. "Because you clearly know the endgame."

"It's not time for the reveal yet," he tells me as he pulls his shirt off over his head.

I remove my shirt as well, drawing his attention to my bare breasts. I went without a bra today, and he seems to approve.

His pants go next.

Then mine.

Until we're both standing naked in my room, staring at one another. "Did you see all the videos?"

"Yes," he confirms. "I'm very familiar with them."

"If any of those were released..." I twist my lips. "They're damning."

"Indeed." He cocks his head. "Are you thinking of trying to find copies for yourself? To try to blackmail them into letting you live?"

I snort. "That's a move that'll just get me killed, not saved. I'm no one to these people. But I still don't understand why they're insisting on me playing."

"Maybe they're trying to figure you out, determine your motives."

"My only motive is to survive," I tell him honestly as I kneel on my bed. "I don't want to be here."

His gaze goes to my chest as he joins me on the mattress. "Your nipples certainly suggest otherwise." He reaches between my legs, his fingers gliding through my dampness. "As does your cunt."

"Wanting you and wanting to be here are two entirely different concepts," I tell him, arching into his touch as he spears me with his fingers.

This man doesn't play.

He takes.

And I love it.

"I want to explore you," I say. "I want you to tell me about your tats."

"There's nothing to tell." He curls his fingers inside me, making me squirm. "I see designs I like, I have them put on my skin. Easy as that."

"So they don't hold sentimental value?"

"Only the crown over my heart," he says, drawing my focus to his chest and the familiar logo. I can't believe I didn't notice it before.

"It's like the Covington Industries icon." It even

has *K.C.* etched into it.

"It's a symbol of ownership," he tells me.

"Because the company owns you?" I guess. "Like you're a slave to it?"

He falls silent for a moment. "I'm a slave to my family legacy," he finally replies. "So in a sense, yes. I suppose that's accurate."

I cover his heart. "Does that mean you can never leave this place?"

"If I said yes, would you join me here?" he asks, his fingers still playing inside me. "Would you stay with me, Sydney?"

"I..." My thighs clench as he does something delicious with his touch. "I don't know."

"Hmm," he hums. "I suppose I'll need to give you a few good reasons to stay, then." He pushes me down onto the bed with his hand at my throat, his fingers damp with my arousal. His lips hover over mine. "I want to keep you, Sydney. I want to make you mine."

I pant beneath him. "I may not survive another week."

"Then I'd better make this an everlasting claim that we both remember for eternity," he whispers before taking my mouth in a savage embrace.

He undoes me with every kiss.

Every touch.

Every thrust.

It's like he's thrown me headfirst into the darkest depths of the ocean, leaving me to drown while forcing me to rely on him for air at the same time.

I can't tell up from down.

I can't discern fiction from reality.

I can no longer define what's right versus what's wrong.

Everything is about him. About us. About this intense connection.

He stays with me through the night, showers with me in the morning, and pulls me into a hug before he leaves. "I know you don't want to play anymore," he says against my ear. "But sometimes games have to be played."

"What do you mean?" I ask, searching his expression for more, wanting to understand the purpose of all this. *Tell me how this works. Tell me why you're doing this. Tell me why we're really here.*

But he doesn't.

All he says is "Society is all about games."

And then he leaves me to my fate.

Another day in the theater hall.

Everyone is still tense from yesterday, pissed at one another for all the reveals. I'm again confused about the concept of this game.

It was all about unity at first, team bonding,

ensuring they all worked *with* each other.

But now they're all full of hatred.

No one trusts anyone.

Accusations are flying.

They're no longer trying to figure out who the killer is, but determining steps for new alliances. Threatening to oust each other.

It's insane.

What will they do now? Drop something on them that forces them to unite? Is this just a lesson in how to get along even when they truly hate one another?

I wait on the couch—my usual spot—as Landon paces in front of me.

"Sit down," Preston finally snaps at him.

"Fuck off," Landon mutters.

"So we all revealed a few things yesterday about how we really feel. Who the fuck cares?" Preston presses. "That's the point of this, right? To ensure there are no secrets? Well, now you know I think you're not suitable to lead. Brayden knows you feel he's the weak link. Everyone thinks Gretchen is a whore because, let's face it, she is. And—"

"You're one to talk," Gretchen interjects. "Why am I a whore for fucking around, while you and Landon are celebrated for fucking half the student population at Anton University?"

Well, she's not wrong there.

"You're supposed to be a lady of society, not a slut," Preston tells her. "You've always known that. And your reputation reflects on me."

"Oh, is that why you said yesterday that you don't really want to marry me?" she asks. "Maybe I don't want to marry you."

"Princess, please," he replies. "You want my cock and my status. Don't deny it now."

I pinch the bridge of my nose, exhausted from all of this. They're all too lost in their own world to realize how ridiculous they sound.

"Yeah, because you're the almighty Preston Michaels, the one meant to lead them all," Landon deadpans.

"I'm more suited than you for the position, and you know it," Preston bites back.

"Yes, and I'm just the lawyer wannabe who shouldn't be trusted with your money," Griffin sounds off from the back of the room. "Too bad for you, I'll be handling it all anyway. And now that I know what you really think, maybe I'll live up to your expectations and invest poorly."

I release my nose to massage my temples instead. Because ay-ay-ay. I want to crawl into a hole and hide.

The bickering continues all around me for another thirty minutes before finally the speakers come to life and solicit everyone to attention. I never thought I would be so thankful to hear that voice. But it's finally here, beginning today's game, whatever the fuck it'll be.

Nineteen
SYDNEY

"I SEE SOME OF YOU ARE A LITTLE DISGRUNTLED FROM yesterday's movies," the voice says. "Good. You should be. But this is only the beginning. We warned you that this week is all about truths and revealing your secrets. And the biggest is yet to come. Perhaps once we share it, you'll understand why all of this has been necessary."

Doubtful, I think. *But please enlighten us*.

"Please take your seats and bear with us. We'll begin today's program in five minutes." The crowns start spinning on the screen with a loading bar beneath it.

Fortunately, everyone stops bickering and takes their seats.

I sip my water and start counting, something

Landon interrupts as he leans toward me. "Are you all right, Sydney?"

I blink. "What?"

"I imagine this is all… a lot… I just want to make sure you're all right."

"Aren't you the one who told me to sleep outside?" I ask him. "Now you want to know if I'm okay?"

He sighs. "You don't have to be difficult."

Difficult? Is he for fucking real right now?

Fortunately, the room goes black, giving me cause not to respond. Because I don't think I'm capable of being nice. Not when I want to punch him in his arrogant jaw.

This bastard wanted to fuck me. I said no. He told me to sleep outside. Then he manhandled me against a wall and demanded to know where I'd slept. And now… what feels like years later… he's asking if I'm okay?

No. I'm not fucking okay. I'm a mess. But thanks for asking, asshole.

In what world would I be all right with any of this?

His world, apparently.

Jesus.

An image populates the screen of Timothy Covington, the founder of Covington Industries.

He's maybe in his early forties in the image. Dark hair. Green eyes. Smiling.

Beneath the image is his name and the years of life.

"Many of you are familiar with our founder, Mr. Timothy Covington," the voice says by way of introduction. "He was a man of principles, one many considered to be moral to a fault. And he believed in the concept of honesty."

No one comments. They're all focused on the screen, as am I. But I'm studying something I doubt any of them are noticing.

The shade of Mr. Covington's eyes.

Dark green.

Like the forest.

Similar… to Kage's.

It's a bizarre fixation, one that makes me wonder just how obsessed I am with him. Because I seem to be incapable of removing him from my thoughts.

"Truth is a valuable lesson, one we hope you all have learned this week. Because that's the heart of this organization. It's the foundation our union was built upon. There is nothing we hide from one another. Together, we are united. No matter what."

The screen begins to dissolve, the edges of it going up in flames like that first night as another image takes over.

One of a palace with a fire raging around it.

In the middle of the woods.

I frown at it. *Is that…? Is that from the virtual reality simulation?*

"You've spent the last few days sharing all of your truths, learning about each other's most well-kept secrets. So now it's time for us to reveal our own. The dark history that binds us all together."

The house continues to crumble, the smoke and flames bright against the darkness of the sky while the voice continues speaking.

"It's important to understand our beginning. To realize that even though there are aspects about each other that you may despise, there's one thing that ties all of you together—the truth about our ascension."

A chill sweeps over me as the video turns to a live feed. A media report. One detailing the collapse of an empire.

"In breaking news tonight, it seems a devastating event has occurred at Covington Manor. A charity gala gone wrong as the curtains caught fire in the main ballroom." The female reporter's voice echoes through the room.

It's followed by a new video, one of a female I recognize from the simulation—the fake-tan woman.

Her name runs along the bottom of the screen.

Veronica Edington.

I'm guessing that's Becca's mother.

"It all started so quickly," Veronica says, her manicured hand over her heart. She's even wearing the same green dress from the simulation. "I... I don't even know what happened. One minute we're dancing, and the next..."

"It's tragic," another voice says. The redheaded male. *Grant Chastain,* the screen says. "We haven't received word yet about the boys."

My heart sinks. *It's real. The boys being tied up... it... it was real.*

But Kage told me they didn't die.

Why would he lie? After everything we shared? It seemed so wrong of him to *lie.*

How well do I even know him? I think, my heart aching inside. *He wanted to fuck. Of course he lied.*

Just like every other man.

Except... except he's not normal at all.

What if he didn't lie? I think. *There's something else going on here. Something I'm not seeing.*

Something that's so close... I can almost taste it.

"Firefighters are working to control the flames, to ensure it doesn't spread to the surrounding trees. But there is still no word on the fate of the Covington family." This comes from the female broadcaster again.

And eventually shifts to daylight, where they show the remains of the house.

It's utterly destroyed.

"Authorities have yet to confirm the fates of the Covington family, but several others have already expressed sadness over the loss," the female voice says.

The screen cuts to Becca's mom again as she sobs against another man's shoulder. It appears to be her husband, based on the scrawling names. "Emily Covington was my best friend. I'm sorry. I just can't be here. I can't do this right now."

"The boys were so young. Judas just turned ten," another person says. A blonde female. *Rachel Matterhorn*. I'm guessing that's Landon's mom.

Newspaper articles flash across the screen, confirming the deaths of the family.

Emily and Timothy Covington, along with their sons, Judas, Keaton, and Loren, are dead.

More headlines scroll.

More comments from the parents of the heirs in this room.

But I'm distracted by the headlines with the boys' names. I keep thinking about the fire, about hearing them scream, about finding them tied together with little crowns on their heads.

Judas. Keaton. And Loren.

All dead.

J. K. L.

Judge. Kage. Loki.

I frown. *That… that can't be right. Unless it's a tribute?*

But Kage is twenty-eight. Judge is older. By how much?

This happened twenty years ago. Kage would have been eight. Was Judge closer to ten?

The screen goes up in flames, distracting me from my thoughts as the voice says, "That's the history most of you know. The history our company is supposedly founded upon."

An article appears about the thirteen families that came together to form the current branches of Covington Industries.

They're all seen as heroes, taking up the mantle Timothy Covington fought so hard to create.

"This job is too big for one person," Lucas Matterhorn says in a press conference, his name scrolling across the bottom. "Timothy created a dream, and it's one we are blessed to carry out in his name. As a team. Together we are united in our shared loss and blessed by the memory of a dear friend."

"This is the speech that created your futures," the voice says. "The pivotal moment in history that united your families under one single truth. But it's not the one many of you have come to know. Which is why it's time to share the secret that binds you."

More images appear, all of them of people dressed up for a gala.

The night of the fire, I assume. Because it's from the ballroom again, which I recognize from my simulation.

But it's not a rolling video this time, just photos.

People laughing.

People socializing.

The three little boys in tuxedos.

I freeze when I see them. They're standing with Becca's mom. She's telling the tallest among them something.

Judas. Or is that Judge?

I shiver, the pieces to this puzzle dancing in my mind.

"We forced you to oust all your darkest secrets, to share your hidden truths with one another, to show you who you're going into business with. To ensure all your anger is out on the table, all your relationships fully defined. Because this truth we're about to share will cement you together for the rest of your lives. It's a truth that binds your parents. A truth... they'll never forget."

I'm not sure when the voice started saying *they*

instead of *our,* but it's a distinction that piques my interest.

Because I thought this retreat was run by the branch leaders within Covington Industries. Now I'm not so sure.

It could be a trainer they hired, some devious asshole who enjoys torturing corporate partners.

But I'm starting to wonder if the current leadership at Covington Industries has anything to do with this at all.

Do they even know their children are here?

I can't imagine they would be allowed to travel on spring break to a remote location without their parents' knowledge. Landon also mentioned a conference call with his father and Mr. Michaels earlier this week. He called them about Becca's death, too.

Unless...

Unless none of it is real.

Like Killswitch.

I blink, my mind churning over the facts that continue to populate my thoughts. Maybe I'm sleep-deprived. Maybe Kage fucked the brain cells out of my head.

But... but something... there's something...

"Some of you already know what truth we're about to reveal. So before we reveal it, we invite those already inducted into the inner circle to share what they know," the voice asks.

Inner circle? Isn't this *the inner circle?* I wonder, glancing around.

I don't appear to be the only one confused. Brayden and Gaylord are both looking at each other in uncertainty.

Gretchen and Courtney are as well.

But Preston... he's just staring at the screen, his brow furrowing.

"Prove your leadership," the voice says. "Prove your worth. Share the ultimate truth."

Silence falls.

Then Landon clears his throat. "It wasn't an accident."

Preston glances at him. "Correct. Our parents killed them."

Landon nods. "The gala... it was staged."

"What?" Gretchen asks, spinning in her seat to look at Preston and Landon. "What do you mean?"

"Our parents arranged to remove the Covington family after Timothy decided to take the company public," Griffin says. "They didn't feel it was the right move at the time."

"I don't understand." Courtney looks at him blankly. "Covington Industries is a publicly traded company."

"Now, yes," Griffin replies. "But it wasn't then.

Timothy wanted to push it into the public sphere before our parents were ready, and he wouldn't give them the stock percentages they wanted to make it work. So. They removed the problem, reallocated the funds, and went public when they were ready."

My lips part. *This… this is information that will get me killed.*

And the way Landon glances over at me says he knows it, too.

But they still think their parents are behind all this. They still think I'm a captive in this game and thereby under their control.

However, I don't think their parents are behind this at all.

It doesn't make sense.

Sure, they would want to guarantee their children partnered for life, and blackmail is certainly one way to do that.

But all the secrets, the videos, the *game… L, K, J.*

I swallow. *The boys are alive.*

The boys…

They're Loki, Kage, and Judge.

Which explains Kage's insistence on playing this game. He told me that everything is for his family. He told me how he used to live near here.

In a home surrounded by trees.

That burned down.

Because of the parents of the people in this room.

All their sins. All their secrets. Every dirty deed.

They captured it all, made videos, preparing to destroy the families that destroyed their own.

Kage isn't just helping. He's *managing*.

He and his brothers are behind all of this, and they're using technology—technology that is likely from the company their father created—to do it.

Oh my God, I think. *Oh my fucking God.*

That explains the movie, too. Why his brother wanted to watch this remake. As a coincidence? Or was it a hint? A way to tell me what's really happening without technically admitting it?

Everything Kage has said, everything he's done, now possesses a new purpose.

But why me? Why choose me to provide all those answers to? Why not just tell me the truth?

Because it's a test. A fucked-up way to determine my worth. That word creates a spiral of dialogue in my head, all the comments Kage has said, every hint he's given, every word trick he's unleashed upon me over the last week.

"Keep playing the game until you find your worth. Keep playing the game until you finally discover… the truth."

"There's an end to all this madness coming. It's just not the end you're expecting."

"Because I know how it's going to end."

"My family, Sydney. I work here because of my family."

"I work here because I have to, because it's the only way the truth will come out."

It all makes sense. Every single detail. He ensured I knew it all, without outwardly admitting a damn thing.

And the most important piece of it all…

"Those boys did not die like that," he promised me.

"So it was just a fucked-up simulation? Who the fuck comes up with an idea like that?"

"Someone who lived it," he admitted.

That *someone* being him. His brothers. They created all of this.

To avenge their parents.

And I'm not sure if I want to praise them for this madness.

Or kill them.

Twenty
KAGE

SHE KNOWS. I CAN SEE IT IN HER EXPRESSION, IN THE FIRE in those dark eyes. My brilliant little dove has finally put together the puzzle.

And she looks ready to kill.

I'm not sure if it's me she wants to throttle or the bickering bitches in the room.

"Sydney knows," I admit aloud, warning my brothers.

"Then I guess this just turned into a test." Judge folds his arm as he observes the fireworks.

Rather than focus on the fact that their parents are murderers, they're all fighting over why certain members are in the *inner circle* and others are not.

We hadn't actually been sure if that tactic would work. It was a risk, one Loki played off well by leading today's production.

Our backup plan was to show the images and tell the story we know, then capture all their reactions on film. Which would have done almost as much damage as what we're recording now.

But this is gold.

They're not remorseful at all. They're just jealous that they didn't know the story until now.

The only one not participating in the banter is Sydney.

She's staring at the screen, waiting for something. Perhaps the next video.

No, I think. *No, she's looking for the cameras. She's looking for me.*

I smirk. *Hello, sweetheart. What's it going to be?* I want to ask her. *Embrace the truth? Or kill?*

"She looks like she wants to eat you alive, K," Loki comments, clearly reading her expression in a manner similar to the way I am.

"Then I guess we'll be playing with knives later." Something that doesn't disappoint me in the slightest. "Go ahead and play the rest." I need her to see it, to understand, to respect what it is we've accomplished here.

This is a revenge plot over ten years in the making.

We've had a lot of help and support from those

once loyal to my parents. That's how we survived. How we hid. How we thrived.

The video begins to play, showing the wreckage of the home again.

And then another of some of the parents.

It's a candid shot this time, one not taken from a news reporter's camera, but from a high-tech phone. One of the most advanced of its kind at the time and not yet available on the market. But the recording software on it worked well, capturing a conversation about what to do with the remains of our former home.

"A lodge," Lucas Matterhorn suggests. "It'll serve as a tribute to the legacy of the Covington family, while also operating as a private place of business for our personal affairs."

Which is exactly what this place became.

Only, the architect they hired for the build was someone Mr. Walton had recommended.

Someone who happened to be an old friend of our father. And he designed a lodge that matched Matterhorn's expectations, but with a lot of secrets built into the walls. Then he hired the crew using resources he knew would be loyal to my family.

Since Matterhorn couldn't be bothered to oversee the development, it was easy to hide several pertinent details from him.

Such as the cameras installed in every single

room.

Recording devices.

Control over the internet and phone lines.

So many enhancements that should have been checked, but Matterhorn was lazy and relied on the architect.

Upon the completion of The Lodge—which took two years—the planning began.

Mr. Walton oversaw the hiring of the staff, choosing the employees carefully.

All of them were loyal to my family.

All of them wanted revenge for what had been done.

All of them are on *our* payroll.

It didn't matter that we were still children. Our benefactor had access to some private accounts that Mr. Chastain didn't know anything about. Those accounts were used to keep the employees loyal.

Not that it was truly needed.

Because the deaths of our parents were felt by many. My father was very skilled at networking. And most importantly, he had a good heart.

Something the current ownership at Covington Industries cannot proclaim about themselves.

We've been watching them for years now. Plotting every move. Listening. Observing. Taking notes. *Recording*. We've developed every alternative imaginable for this week. Every detail. Every game.

Every fucking word.

This lodge is a safe haven for us, not for Matterhorn and his friends. Of course, he doesn't know that. He assumes we're all on his payroll and will keep quiet.

Technology is fascinating. It makes falsifying identities so incredibly easy.

One step led to another, which led to another, and here we are, *finally* watching the truth unfold.

The video begins to rewind, showing the fire again at a rapid speed, going back to the night of the gala and the photos captured that evening.

Which morph into the stage Loki and his team so beautifully crafted using graphics technology. It's part of the same simulation Sydney underwent, something that's evidenced by the way she flinches now when the group of well-dressed men and women appears.

Their words are re-creations of sounds based on the voices we've recorded countless times within these walls.

It plays like a real-life video.

And since some of them know the truth already, they believe every word.

This is the part we can't air. The video that will self-destruct at the end. But their words, their reactions, their *conversations* now, will be all that we need.

We know who orchestrated everything that night because we could hear it from our rooms. All thanks to Rebecca Edington's mother.

That bitch took us upstairs, saying our parents had asked her to help get us ready for bed. As she used to babysit us, we didn't question her. We *trusted* her.

Then she said she wanted to play a game and tied us to one another before securing us to the bed.

Put crowns on our heads.

And turned on the television to check the security feeds downstairs.

When it showed our parents already tied to a set of dining room chairs, she panicked. "They started without me!"

Those were her final words.

She ran from the room.

Leaving us to *burn*.

A true psychopath.

No remorse. Not even an inkling of consideration about our fates. Merely her own.

We watched as she joined the others.

We heard their words. Every. Single. One.

And then we screamed as the house went up in flames.

My only true regret is that the events of that night weren't actually recorded.

But Loki made his own version. He remembered

most of their comments, despite being only six years old at the time. And whatever he didn't know, Judge and I filled in for him.

We all experienced nightmares about that night for years.

Nightmares that are displaying now on the screen, showing the elite heirs what happened to our family in clear and concise language. It's eerie to watch. I have to move my arms around just to remind myself that I'm free, that this isn't happening in real time.

We survived.

Because I freed us.

My wrists and arms still bear the scars from the rope burns left behind. Just thinking about it makes me sick to stomach.

Sydney asked about my tattoos.

I told her they meant nothing.

It wasn't necessarily a lie—the details don't hold any significance, apart from the one on my chest. But the ink is there to hide my scars. To erase the past. Just in case someone notices.

But no one ever notices the help.

No one in this circle even considers that someone as lowly as a hotel employee could be up to something nefarious.

They're the future kings. The world's top point-oh-one percent.

But so were we. And we learned what faith can do and how easily it can be burned.

I focus on Sydney rather than the video, noting the way her jaw clenches as the children begin to scream. It stirs goose bumps on my arms, that sound one that still haunts me to this day.

The heat coming from the hallway.

The sounds of crackling.

The *stench.*

But I focused on the ropes. I twisted my arms, searching for a way out.

Veronica Edington hadn't tied them right, her skill lacking. However, my father raised all three of us outside. He taught us the importance of the outdoors.

Which meant we knew a few things about knots.

Once my older brother realized what I was doing, he started to help.

And soon, we were free.

Running. Running. Running.

I can still hear the ceiling crashing. See the staircase burning. "The window!" my older brother shouts, pointing to the one near the end of the hall.

It'll be a long fall. It'll hurt. Mom and Dad are still downstairs.

"They're dead," Judas tells me. "We have to go, Keaton. We have to run!"

Loren tugs on my hand, his dark eyes wide.

Judas is right. This is the only way.

A beam smashes to the ground behind us, the smoke making it hard to see.

But Judas has a hold on my tux.

He's pulling me. Dragging me. Our crowns have fallen. The world around us is crashing down.

The window shatters.

I can't breathe. I can't scream. I can't cry. Everything burns. My arms. The ropes. They've left behind open wounds.

"Now, Keaton!" Judas screams, his arm linking through mine. Loren is on my opposite side.

And somehow… we jump.

We land.

Everything aches. I think I've broken my leg. I don't know. I can't comprehend what's happening.

But arms engulf me.

"Shh, they'll hear you," someone whispers in my ear, telling me to silence my cries. I feel so weak. So broken. I'm weeping and I don't know how to stop.

The world is still burning. My parents…

"It's okay," that voice says again.

I glance up, confused. It's someone I know.

Someone I recognize.

Mrs. Walton. She's dragging me into the woods. Mr. Walton has Judas. "Where's Loren?" I demand, panicking. "Where's— "

"Shh," Mrs. Walton hushes. "He's right here." She helps me see him walking along beside us with a limp. He doesn't appear to be very injured, and part of me is relieved. The other part of me is aching. I cough, my lungs burning.

"They need medical attention," Mr. Walton says.

"I know," she whispers. "I tried to get to them, Bruce. I… I tried…"

They start hugging, her words turning into sobs.

I shiver, feeling suddenly cold.

Dots are dancing before my eyes.

"We can't stay, Mag. Someone will see us. We have to go back," Mr. Walton says. "Trust Suzanne. She'll help them."

"I've got this," Ms. Suzanne's voice is soft, her touch even softer.

I'm not sure where we are now. I blacked out, maybe. I just feel so tired.

But a glance to my left allows me to see both

my brothers.

Alive. Breathing. And hugging one another.

They survived.

That's all I need to know.

And that continues to be all I need as I glance at them now, seeing the triumph on their faces as they record the reactions in the room.

Sydney is the only one not speaking. She's observing the others in a way that tells me she's disgusted with everyone. It helps that Gretchen continues to egg them on, demanding to know why the organization only told Preston and Landon.

She's a brilliant actress.

Her parents taught her well.

She knows who we are but hasn't said a word. Because she's loyal to the true royals of Covington Industries, not the imposters on our thrones.

"Why was all this recorded?" Griffin finally asks. "This… if this ever got out…"

"It's mutual blackmail," Brayden tells him. "Who is going to share it? *Everyone* is on that video. It ensures we all stay in line."

"Well, at least we know it looks real," Loki comments, a smile in his voice. "Too bad we can't use it."

"They're giving us more than enough to use," Judge replies. "But let's help them along. Initiate the next sequence."

I fold my arms, my focus on Sydney as the voice begins to speak to the room.

"Knowing the truth is what binds us all together," the game host tells them.

Sydney rolls her eyes, which makes my lips twitch. She's clearly done with this rhetoric.

"But what's important to understand is that no matter what our truths are, we are in this together. For better or for worse. That's the point of all this. We are a *team*. Which is why we're incredibly disappointed in how you've progressed this week."

Silence falls and several of them look at one another.

Sydney merely arches a brow, and I can almost hear her saying, *Disappointed? Seems like an understatement.* Or something else sarcastic in nature.

"We asked you to identify Rebecca Edington's killer. However, rather than recognize the point of the exercise, you all started to suspect each other. You lashed out, spoke accusations, and generally tried to *hurt* one another. When what you should have done was come together as a team and realize that you are *all* the killer."

Sydney's eyebrows fly upward, amusing me.

She's clearly not on board with this at all.

"When one of you makes a decision, it impacts all of you," the voice stresses. "And you're supposed to work as a unit to protect one another. Cover up the crime *together*, not figure out who is to blame. What if Ms. Edington was really dead? How would you proceed then? Would you decide to incriminate one of your teammates? Is that a smart move, considering what each of you knows about one another?"

Sydney doesn't look so surprised now. She looks worried.

And still a bit pissed.

"We want you to take the next forty-eight hours to consider what you would do if Rebecca Edington was truly dead. Come up with a plan on how you would cover it up. How you would have each other's backs. And on the final day of the retreat, we want you to present it to us."

Sydney's jaw clenches, her fingers clasped together in her lap.

I stand instinctively, anticipating her moves.

If she runs, I'll catch her.

And she won't like what happens next.

"If we're satisfied by what you've learned this week, we'll let you leave," the voice says. "If we're not, necessary arrangements within the company will be made."

Sydney doesn't move. But I sense her desire

to run. I can feel it humming beneath my skin as though we're connected by an enchanted string.

"Take the afternoon and evening to relax and refresh. Tomorrow, your new task as a team begins. And we strongly advise you to work together. Forget the past. Focus on the future. Move forward. And unite as one."

Loki presses a button to cause the crowns to appear again and falls back into his chair. "That went well," he says.

But I'm not paying attention to him.

I'm watching Sydney.

She stands, her movements casual. However, her eyes are on the others, observing them. They're too busy talking to each other to notice, though. Something she takes advantage of by slowly moving backward toward the door.

The minute she's through it, I start to move. "Tell me where she goes," I instruct Loki as I grab an earpiece on my way out the door.

It ends up not being needed.

Because she comes right for me, fully aware of what room I would be in.

She takes one look at me as she enters the hallway, her steps certain as she moves toward me.

"Let's go for a hike, *Keaton,*" she says under her breath.

And heads straight for the exit.

Twenty-one
SYDNEY

MY HEART IS BEATING SO FAST I CAN BARELY HEAR myself breathe.

But I keep pushing.

Step after step.

Faster and faster.

Not stopping until I'm in the clearing, in the place I feel is *ours*.

Kage—*Keaton*—is right behind me, his expression giving nothing away. I stare at him. He stares back. It's clear that he's not going to be the first to speak, that I'm going to have to say what I know before he'll either confirm or ignore every word.

I clench my jaw, a growl bubbling inside me. I'm

mad. I'm *furious*. I'm… I'm… I'm so damn relieved those children are okay that I can't fucking think straight.

"This is about revenge," I finally say, beginning to pace in the field. "That video, the fire, it's all real. But you survived. You and your brothers survived."

"Yes." He doesn't elaborate, but that single word alone confirms everything I suspect.

"You're Keaton Covington."

"I go by Kage now, but yes, that's my birth name."

"Judge is Judas and Loki is Loren?"

He nods.

"And this game… it's… it's not the corporation running it. It's *you*."

"*Us*," he corrects. "Loki is the computer whiz. I'm just good with numbers."

Well, at least he's being honest. I stop pacing and stare at him. "Okay, so this *game*. It'll what? It'll self-destruct at the end, just like the one in the movie?"

He studies me for a long moment. "You know, my brothers chose to watch that last night for your benefit. It was their way of deciding to let you know the truth about this situation."

"Okay." Except that doesn't answer my question.

"They like you."

And that doesn't answer my question, either. "Okay," I repeat.

"What would you do in my situation?" he asks me. "Now that you've seen the footage. Now that you know what happened. What would you do?"

"I would get revenge," I answer without a second thought. "Those fuckers deserve to burn. The parents, I mean. Not their kids."

"Everything we've revealed about their characters and lives are true," he says. "They're not good people, Sydney."

"I could argue that you're not a good person either," I point out. "You've been torturing me all week."

"Yes," he agrees. "I've never claimed to be a good person, Sydney."

That's true. He hasn't exactly hidden his proclivities for darkness from me either.

"I'm the villain of your story," he continues, his voice a soft yet lethal reverberation in the air. "I chose the fire simulation for you. I'm the one who won't let you leave. Just as I've known from the very beginning that you were initially brought here to die."

My eyebrows lift. "What?"

"You were supposed to die the first night. That's why Becca brought you here—to kill you."

I take a step backward. "What?" I repeat, my head suddenly spinning. "I… I… *What*?" He moves toward me, and I stumble backward some more. "Tell me what you mean."

"It would be easier to show you," he says. "Sydney."

I'm still moving away from him. I can't decide whether to run… or… or to just… I don't know.

"Just as I've known from the very beginning that you were initially brought here to die."

I was prepared for pretty much everything else he could say.

Except for that.

"She brought me here to kill me?" The words come out on this sort of high-pitched breathy sound. "Like, *really* kill me? Or just the game's version of a death?"

Except…

I freeze, my eyes going to his.

He's only a step away, his expression radiating determination. If I run, he'll catch me. I know he will.

But I ignore that realization and focus on the other one that just ran through my head. "She's really dead, isn't she?"

"Yes," he confirms, causing my knees to buckle.

He catches me with ease, his strength holding

me steady as he lowers us both to the ground.

"You killed her?" I guess.

"No," he says, surprising me yet again. "Not directly, anyway."

"I… I don't understand." I thought I had this all figured out, that it was a game that would eventually disappear like the one in the movie and leave only video footage behind of the heirs all admitting their sins.

Video footage that can be used to blackmail all of them.

And perhaps force the Covington Industries leadership to return the company to Keaton and his brothers.

That seems like the plausible avenue for all of this.

But Becca's dead.

Which complicates everything.

Unless… I frown, considering the new task given to the group by the voice. "You're going to videotape them all covering up her death as a group and use it against them," I whisper. But… but that… that doesn't fully work. "They're just going to frame me. Because I'm not one of them."

It's such an obvious conclusion and exactly what I would do in this situation.

"So I'm not dead yet. I'm the scapegoat." I look at Kage. "I was never meant to survive this game.

You only let me solve it…" I trail off, unable to finish. Because I don't know why he let me solve it. "Why, Kage? Why let me get this far?"

"Because I like you," he says, his fingers brushing through my hair. I'm not sure when the ponytail came out. He probably took it down when I was lost in my mind. "And yes, they're likely going to blame you for her death. But it'll all be recorded, Sydney. Every detail. Just as her actual death is on film, too."

"Who killed her?" I ask.

"To answer that, we need to go back to the invitations." He cups my cheek, his gaze intense. "Are you ready to learn everything? Because once you do, you'll be considered complicit in these events."

"I'm already complicit just by being here," I growl. Something he already knows. Which means I have no choice now but to move forward. To *play* the game. "The game may self-destruct at the end, but I'm still a player, Kage. I'm in those videos."

"You are," he concedes. "You know why this is happening, you know who I am, you know what we want."

"Revenge."

He nods. "We've been planning this for over a decade, perhaps even longer if you consider how it all began—with the building of The Lodge. Lucas

Matterhorn commissioned it to be used for personal affairs, which is fancy speak for top-secret meetings. Things he wanted off the books. Private dealings he didn't want anyone to know about."

He releases me and pulls his phone from his pocket.

"We've recorded everything. But it's not just us. There are others who have helped us along the way." He doesn't elaborate on who, and I don't expect him to. Instead, he says, "One of our inside contacts suggested this retreat idea about five years ago when most of the heirs were finishing up high school. He said it would be a good way for them to bond and that he knew a guy who could run it."

"You and your brothers?"

He smiles. "Not directly. But a figurehead we control. He created a whole regimen that he showed to the board. They approved. Then we destroyed it and replaced it with our own game."

"And they have no idea."

"And they have no idea," he echoes. "We've controlled every communication. Every email. Every phone call. Landon thinks he spoke to his father this week, but it was just a computer program Loki created."

"Similar to the voice," I guess.

"Yes, but in Lucas Matterhorn's tones." He pulls something up on his phone and says, "They've held so many meetings here throughout the years that it was easy to create a digital blueprint for their voices."

He presses a button, and the words are repeated through his phone in another man's voice—a voice I recognize from the simulation.

"That's how you re-created that night," I realize. "But how did you know exactly what they said?"

"Because we watched it happen on the security cam from the television," he says, frowning. "We saw everything."

My lips part. "They forced you to watch?"

"I'm not sure if that was the intent. I think Veronica just forgot to turn off the television in her haste to get downstairs."

Now I'm gaping at him. "Becca's *mom*?"

"She tied us up, put the crowns on our heads, and tucked us in for our deaths," he summarizes, his tone giving nothing away. "Which should explain why we targeted Rebecca Edington first for the game."

"Yes, except her mom is the one who deserves to be punished, not Becca."

"You say that because you still have morals." His tone isn't condescending so much as soft and slightly commending.

But his forest-green eyes give away his true intent. His lingering darkness. The part of him that thrives at the forefront and commands his every move.

He's not a good person.

I've known that from the start.

However, I don't think he's intrinsically bad either. He's… he's somewhere in between. A person who does horrible things but for the right reasons. Yet also not.

A walking paradox.

"I would argue that you're the only one among us who's still innocent," he says. "And I would apologize for being the one to corrupt you, but the theme of the week is truth. So I won't apologize because I wouldn't mean it."

I swallow. His words are ominous. His tone, so quiet and lethal, is even more menacing. Whatever he's about to show me is going to ruin everything. I can feel it. And yet, I can't tell him to stop. I can't tell him *no*.

Because I want to know.

I *need* to know.

"We put Rebecca to the test," he says. "We wanted to see how far she would go for this corporation. And she answered by bringing you."

He starts messing around on his phone, pulling up video feeds and searching for the right one.

I can see everything.

Every file. Every name. Every image. He doesn't

hide anything, obviously deciding it's time for me to know all the details.

Which makes sense—I've solved their little game.

The question is, will I disappear now that I know?

I'm not sure that he's decided my fate yet. Right now, he's focused on answering all my questions.

I suppose we'll see how I react once he finishes explaining.

"This is the part you've seen," he tells me, showing me a copy of the invitation Becca used to register at reception… whenever that was. My concept of time is flawed. My reality is flawed, too.

You're cordially invited to attend this year's spring break retreat at The Lodge.
It's a highly exclusive experience guaranteed to redefine your future.
Assuming you survive.

I read over the invitation on his screen and nod. "Yes."

"And this is the part you haven't seen," he says, doing something with his phone to create a projection of an image before us. It's almost like a screen, but in the air.

My eyebrows lift. "What kind of tech is this?"

"Advanced cellular technology," he tells me. "Not yet available, but we have some inside sources."

"There are still employees at Covington Industries who are loyal to you," I translate.

"Several," he confirms, adjusting the brightness of the screen.

I look around it, shocked by how thick it is.

But then I hear Becca's voice, and I'm immediately drawn to the video instead of the technology.

"Play this video somewhere private," she reads aloud, glancing around her. "You delivered it to my condo where I live alone. Clearly, I'm reading this in private."

The screen is moving while she talks, making me ask, "Is she holding a tablet or something?"

Kage nods. "The invitation came in a thick package with the tablet she's carrying."

"And you sent it, so it's recording her."

"Yes," he replies as the screen continues to move.

She eventually sets it down on what I'm guessing is a dresser because she sits on the bed across from it. "Begin," she says.

I'm assuming the instructions told her to say that somewhere.

"Hello, Ms. Edington," the voice says, sending a chill down my spine.

That voice is going to follow me into my nightmares, I decide.

"We are excited to welcome you to The Lodge experience. The purpose of this video is to provide you with a tutorial before you go, as well as to deliver your first assignment."

"Oh, goody," she deadpans, reminding me a bit of myself.

"The Lodge experience is designed as a team-building exercise to prepare you for the future. You, along with twelve other heirs, will be assigned roles in a game. And yours is the most important of all."

Her eyebrow arches, clearly intrigued.

"You must pick a pawn. Someone insignificant. Someone who won't be missed. And bring that person to The Lodge," the voice tells her.

I glance up to find Kage watching me as I swallow.

But I don't comment, my gaze returning to the screen.

"This is your loyalty test, Rebecca Edington. Are you brave enough to accept it?" the voice asks. "You'll need to choose your pawn wisely. Make sure this person won't be searched for. That's paramount for this exercise to work."

Becca's brow furrows, her gray-blue gaze taking

on a thoughtful gleam.

"Because the pawn will be killed the first night. By your hand."

Her lips part.

"It's a difficult task for some, but we've chosen you because we believe you're the best suited for this task."

She nods in what I assume is agreement.

"If you decide that you cannot go through with it, you will be removed from the game and the team-building exercise," the voice continues. "There are instructions on the next page regarding what to do in this scenario. The prerecording request is mandatory in case you decide against following through on the night in question."

Prerecording, I think. *That must be the video we all saw where she claimed to be alive.* "How did you do the newspaper?" I whispered.

Kage pauses the video to say, "She was told to hold a paper. Loki replaced it with one for the current date."

"Oh."

He waits to see if I have another question, then hits Play again.

"A masked male will come to your room dressed in black to wait for your decision," the voice says. "If you choose to go through with it, say the words, 'I understand the consequences. But I'll do whatever it takes to succeed.' The person will help you accordingly."

She nods again. "I understand."

"Should you choose not to go through with it, say the words, 'I understand the consequences. I can't go ahead with this any longer.' And you will be removed."

"That won't be happening," she says.

But the voice doesn't reply, just simply displays the instructions for her post-death video next. "Grab a pen," he says and pauses while she finds something to write with.

"Everything was scripted," I whisper as the voice begins to read word for word what Becca said regarding her "fake death." Which apparently wasn't fake at all. Because they gave her a script to read *before* she died.

This script.

The one she's currently writing as the voice dictates every statement.

When she's done jotting it all down, she nods.

And the voice says, "This video will self-destruct in thirty seconds. Please upload your recording within twenty-four hours to the link provided in your email."

Becca stares at the screen for a while, then pulls out her phone.

"Hey, Syd. Give me a call when you have a

minute. I want to talk about spring break," she says, then hangs up and goes to find an outfit for her recording.

My stomach sours as I watch. "She didn't even take five minutes to think of me." Because I was the obvious candidate. I have no family. I tend to keep to myself. "She brought me here to kill me."

"She did," Kage confirms, pulling down the video.

"But she didn't go through with it, so you killed her instead?"

He shakes his head. "No. She was going to kill you."

"What? But she didn't. I'm here."

"Yes, because of the fail-safe we put in place." He pulls up another video, this one of Preston entering his room at The Lodge. Or I assume that's where he is because of the familiar surroundings.

He walks past whatever is taping him, then stops to study it. "Another tablet?" I guess.

"Yes," Kage says.

"Hello, Mr. Michaels," the voice greets. "Welcome to The Lodge."

"Uh, thanks," he says back to the tablet.

"We have a special assignment for you," the voice continues. "One that requires the utmost discretion. Your father felt you would be best suited for this task. Would you like to accept?"

He stares down at the tablet for a long moment before saying, "Yes."

"Excellent." Music begins to play, making me side-eye Kage.

"That part was Loki's idea," he tells me.

I'm not surprised by that at all.

"Unfortunately, we've received some startling information regarding Ms. Rebecca Edington. It seems her father has shared some confidential files with her that she is threatening to take public. We have attempted to rectify the issue, and she has until three a.m. to accept."

"What sort of files?" Preston interjects.

"I'm afraid that part is classified, Mr. Michaels. But they are related to financial data that could prove most damning to the organization. We need someone to help us handle this situation should Rebecca choose to proceed with her current plans. Are you willing to assist, or should we ask someone else?"

"No, I can help," Preston says quickly. "What do you need me to do?"

"We will deliver a mask and a gun to you after tonight's opening ceremony. We ask that you put on the mask and take the weapon with you to her room at three a.m. The mask is to help disguise you from her, as we're aware of your... *relationship.*"

Preston snorts. "I've already agreed to marry

Gretchen."

"Yes, well, we would prefer you to remain anonymous in this pursuit," the voice replies. "Rebecca has been instructed to say one of two things to the masked man at three a.m."

"Okay," Preston says. "And then what?"

"If she still intends to release her documents to the public, she will say, 'I understand the consequences. But I'll do whatever it takes to succeed.' In which case, we need you to shoot her."

"Oh my God," I whisper, realizing what's happening.

"If she chooses to do the right thing and not release the documents, she will say, 'I understand the consequences. I can't go ahead with this any longer.' In which case, you are to nod and leave the room."

"I see," Preston says.

"Is this a task you are willing to accept?"

"Yes," he says without pause.

"Excellent. Thank you, Mr. Michaels. This video will self-destruct in thirty seconds."

Kage starts playing with his phone again.

"She was going to kill me, so he shot her," I translate, not needing to see what happens next.

But he pulls up the footage anyway, showing me Becca creeping out of her room at three in the morning in a nightgown. "What was she going to kill me with?" I ask Kage.

"She's expecting this person to assist her," he tells me.

"Oh, right." I swallow. "Jesus."

For once, he doesn't remind me of his name, just lets me watch.

Becca stares boldly at the masked-face Preston and says, "I understand the consequences. But I'll do whatever it takes to succeed."

Preston nods once.

Lifts his hand.

And shoots her right in the head.

No hesitation. Not even a flicker of thought.

"How did I sleep through that?" I ask, stunned. There was a silencer on the gun, but it still made a sound. One I should have heard.

"I knocked you out with a sedative," Kage says. "It was that or use sleeping gas—there are outlets in every room—but we couldn't risk it spreading through the suite."

Sleeping gas, I think. *Right. Why wouldn't there be sleeping gas outlets in the rooms? That's totally normal.*

For a lodge full of psychos, anyway.

"That's why my balcony door was open that morning," I mutter, recalling how cold I was when I woke up.

"I knew the chilly air would help draw you out of the daze from the sedative," he replies.

Right, I think. *That's... that's on par with everything else, I guess.*

Preston is still on the screen, staring down at Becca. It makes me wonder if he actually does feel bad.

But when he removes the mask, I only catch a small flicker of remorse in his expression. "You shouldn't have threatened the organization," he tells her softly. "I'm sorry, Becca."

And then he leaves.

It's all so quick. So anticlimactic. So *cold*.

Even his apology felt robotic. "These people are fucking insane," I whisper.

"You've known that from the start," Kage points out. "But as you can see, you weren't actually meant to die. However, I won't lie to you. We had plans in place in case something went wrong, and simulations that would have shifted from covering up Becca's death to covering up your death."

I don't know what to say.

I can only gape at the area his screen just occupied.

Everything was set up. Becca's invitation was because of this game.

They needed a pawn.

An innocent.

Someone for her to *kill*.

And she chose to do it. She was going to kill me. Even after I tried to console her over Preston.

"Jesus," I repeat, rubbing my hand over my face. "I… I don't know what…"

Didn't I ask him recently why she invited me? Or was that just a thought?

But I knew there was a reason. I knew she brought me here for nefarious purposes. Which explains the last-minute request, the need for secrecy, her questions about my other plans, and if anyone knew where I was going.

It all adds up.

So now what?

I look at Kage. "If I try to run from you right now, what will you do?"

"Catch you," he answers truthfully.

"And kill me?" I guess.

He scrutinizes my features. "Not unless you give me a reason to."

"What if I try to kill you?"

He smiles. "I would consider it foreplay."

"You're psychotic."

"Maybe. But I consider myself realistic. Self-aware. *Truthful*. Similar to you in that way. You don't mince words, Sydney. You're honest and real. More real than anyone I've ever met." He slips his phone into his pocket.

I just stare at him, not knowing what to say or do.

"I know this is a lot. And if you want to run, I'll give you a head start. However, I will catch you, Sydney. These woods are my home. There's nowhere you can hide. Nowhere you can disappear." He looks at me. "But if running will make you feel better, then go. I'll be right behind you."

Twenty-two
KAGE

Sydney's dark irises are hypnotizing. It's almost like I can see every thought in her mind, all because of her intelligent gaze.

She's thinking about running.

But she knows I'll catch her.

Which is brewing into something else. Something hotter.

Her pupils dilate.

Her nostrils flare.

And that beautiful tongue of hers licks a path along her lower lip.

I follow everything with my eyes, studying her intently, like a predator does his prey.

This woman is mine. She'll either accept it or fight it. I'm open to either option. The former grants me free rein to do whatever the fuck I please. The latter provides a challenge and a reason to dominate.

She knows almost everything now.

She understands it, too.

She's just not sure how she feels about it yet.

This is a dark world filled with dark choices. I've chosen to embrace it, to play the game how it's meant to be played.

What will she choose?

Sydney continues to study me, her cheeks tinting pink as her chest rises and falls. She's about to decide.

What'll it be, gorgeous? I wonder. *Are you going to flee? Or are you going—*

She lunges at me.

Not to hit me, but to *kiss* me.

I knot my fingers through her hair, capturing her the way I warned I would, and wrap my opposite arm around her lower back as she straddles my thighs.

This fucking girl is *slaying* me.

All feisty, fiery energy. And she unleashes it on me with her mouth.

Biting. Nipping. Licking. *Owning*.

It's furious. It's hot as fuck. It's destructive.

I kiss her back with just as much ferocity, battling her tongue with mine.

She bites me again, this time drawing blood. "Savage little thing," I accuse, my arm tightening around her lower back.

"I need you to fuck me," she breathes. "Give me an escape. Help me… help me not *think*."

"I can do that, beautiful," I reply, laving her lower lip.

She tries to bite me again.

I move before she can, my mouth going to her throat, where I sink my teeth into her flesh. She yelps, and I kiss away the pain.

But it's not good enough for her.

She wants a fight.

A sensual one.

Her nails are raking over my scalp, digging into my hair and tugging with fury.

She's angry.

But so am I.

I've been angry my entire goddamn life.

She's tempting the beast inside me, taunting my inner soul.

I don't warn her to stop. I don't give her a chance to reconsider.

"All right," I growl, shoving her off of me and onto the ground.

I'm on her in the next beat, catching her wrists and slamming them into the grass above her head. She bucks up into me, trying to knock me off of her. But my thighs easily pin hers, my weight and strength no match for her much smaller form.

She screams.

I silence her with my tongue.

She kisses me back again, both of us ignoring the metallic taste in our mouths. It's a violent dance, fueled by vehement flames and passionate *need*.

She gets me. She understands my history. She *knows* me.

Her fury is a seductive call I can't ignore. It stokes the waves of my own pent-up rage until she's screaming again.

I lift her hands and slam them into the grass again.

Her hips buck up into mine.

And she snarls. Like some sort of crazed animal.

"Fuck, Sydney," I whisper, so utterly lost to her viciousness that I can hardly think.

"I *hate* you," she says. "You put me in that fire."

"I *lived* through that fire," I growl back at her.

"All of this is a setup," she continues, ignoring me. "I'm a pawn."

"Yes," I agree. "And now you're *my* pawn."

She cries out, her arms tensing as she tries to fight me again. Her legs wrap around my waist, squeezing, her pussy pressing up into my hard cock.

We're wearing far too many clothes.

I want to shred them.

Slice them.

Yes.

I capture her wrists with one hand, which only causes her to struggle more, and reach into my back pocket to pull out a knife.

She immediately stills. "Kage..."

"Sydney," I return as I press the blade to her throat.

She swallows and I watch the motion. *So pretty. So delicate.*

I know how prettily she'll bleed.

I can already taste her essence on my tongue.

It's a beacon. A call for more. A craving her fury has awakened with a vengeance.

I press the sharp steel against her skin, threatening her without speaking.

"Do it," she dares. "Kill me, Kage."

I tsk. "Oh, sweetheart, no. I'm nowhere near done playing with you yet."

She moves, the blade slicing into her skin as she tries to force my hand. But I caught the flare in her eyes just before she lunged, and I moved the knife with her.

"Naughty girl," I say, dragging the tip down to the neckline of her sweater. No turtlenecks today. She showed off her healing bruises, my *claim* around her throat.

I want to reward that.

But I also want to punish her for daring to try to hurt herself with my blade.

That's not what this game is about.

"Keep your hands there," I tell her. "And do not fucking move again."

She makes a sound that reminds me of an angry kitten, which causes my lips to curl in amusement.

So feral, I think. I've awoken something inside her, just as she's called forward my inner savagery.

This is why we're perfect together—she's the other half of my fucking soul.

It's depravity at its worst. Utterly primal. And I fucking love it.

I think I may even love *her*.

I knock her legs loose and sit back between her sprawled thighs to evaluate her position before me. She's panting, her eyes wild, her cheeks flushed.

Absolutely aroused.

Needy, even.

On the cusp of falling apart, too.

It's intoxicating to see her in such a feral state.

I twirl my blade between my fingers as I consider what to do next. Slicing through her thick sweater won't be very easy with this knife. It's meant for the outdoors as a protectant.

"Remove your sweater," I tell her, deciding to

save the fabric and my blade.

Her arms shake as she obeys me, her body fueled by an erotic mixture of wrath and lust.

My little sinner, I think, admiring her bare breasts. That's the second time she's gone without a bra this week. I may demand that this become her permanent state.

Fuck, I may just never allow her to wear clothes again.

Because she's officially mine now. She knows too much. That means I get to keep her.

Assuming she doesn't make me kill her first.

I draw my knife down the center of her body, debating whether or not to mark her. Maybe carve my name into her hip. My initials over her heart. Something to make her truly *mine.*

Hmm.

Her nipples are taut and begging for attention. So I drag the sharp tip over one, pressing down hard enough to make it pinch without bleeding.

She hisses in response, then arches upward as I remove the blade, clearly craving more.

"Fuck, you're perfect," I praise her, all thoughts of wanting to punish her fleeing my mind as I bend to suck her stiff peak into my mouth.

She moans, her fingers twining through my hair to hold me in place. I bite down in reprimand. She's not in charge anymore. I am. And she wanted me to take away her ability to think. So I'm going to do exactly that.

I move to her opposite breast as I press my knife to her throat again, holding her down, demanding without words that she remain still while I explore her with my mouth.

And then I start a path downward, my blade trailing my tongue all the way to her jeans.

She shivers as I remove them, her boots and socks disappearing along with her pants, leaving her clad in just a lacy thong.

That I'll use my knife on.

Goose bumps pebble along her legs as I slide the steel beneath the black strap at her hip.

A flick of my wrist causes it to snap.

Her blush spreads from her cheeks to her tits, her plump lips parting on a pant.

My beautiful girl likes this. The threat. The violence. The hint of anticipated pain with a heady amount of pleasure.

I cut the band along her opposite hip, then dip my blade beneath the triangle of fabric covering her pussy and slowly peel it back.

She holds her breath as I work, clearly aware of the weapon near her delicious cunt.

I don't touch her with my hands, only the knife, as I finish guiding the fabric down.

Her pink folds are glistening with expectation. I run the flat of the blade along her slick flesh, coating the metal in her arousal.

She shudders, her eyes falling closed at the sensation, making me smile. "I could fuck you with the hilt," I tell her. "Bite that pretty clit." I drag the blade up to the swollen nub in question. "And force you to come."

"Fuck," she breathes, vibrating with desire.

It's a beautiful sight.

One I want to memorize so I can re-create it.

Over and over again.

I press down, similar to what I did on her nipple, and smile when she jolts. "Careful," I warn her. "I wouldn't want to make you bleed."

A lie.

I absolutely want to make her bleed.

But perhaps not there.

I have a use for that little nub later.

Dragging the blade back through her folds, I continue soaking it with her desire. I don't stop until it's just as wet as she is, and then I bring it up to her mouth. "Lick," I tell her. "Taste yourself on my knife."

Her eyes open, her pupils so enlarged that I can't even see her irises.

She's on the edge of exploding already, my blade having driven her to that point without my hands or tongue having touched her at all.

It's fucking stunning.

And watching her lips part for me now has me nearly coming in my pants.

That alluring mouth of hers does exactly what I told her to do, her tongue tracing the sharp edge without flinching.

Goddamn, this woman is mine.

When she's done, I bend down to kiss her, needing to indulge in her decadent flavor for myself.

Oh, but it's not enough.

I need her to orgasm on my tongue.

And I want to fuck her with my blade.

It's an overwhelming craving that sends me downward, the knife twirling in my fingers as I grab the sharp side and ram the hilt into her cunt.

She screams in response, the metal end a shock to her system.

"You can take it," I tell her, aware that the handle isn't as wide or as long as my cock.

"Kage," she snarls.

I respond by taking her clit into my mouth and sucking her so hard that she shrieks again.

Such beautiful music, I muse, fucking her with the blunt end of my weapon while I focus my tongue on her sweet spot.

My hand is bleeding from gripping the knife

so hard, but I don't fucking care. This woman is worth the pain. She's worth every ounce of strength I possess.

She's going to be my undoing.

Because the plan ceases to matter in her presence. She's all I want. All I desire. And I show her that with my mouth.

"I... I'm close..." she pants, her legs tensing around me. "*Kage,* what are you doing to me?"

"Owning you," I say against her clit.

And fuck if that doesn't make her even wetter.

She begins to writhe, her body responding to my ministrations and falling easily beneath my command.

But she won't come.

Not until I allow it.

Because she's my gorgeous creature to possess. My woman. My *future.*

"Now," I tell her, my voice a snarl against her slick heat. "Soak me, beautiful. Give me everything."

My name falls from her mouth as she arches beneath me, her tits a gorgeous display below the sunlight. Her nipples are so hard they appear pained, her chest flushed more scarlet than pink now.

She's shaking almost savagely, her orgasm slamming into her with a force that seems to steal her breath. Because she freezes in time, just for a moment, her body strung so tight I'm worried she'll break.

And then she's crying out in an exquisite display of carnality, her swollen lips chanting my name as she falls apart entirely.

I don't give her a moment to rest. I pull the weapon out of her and bring the handle up to her mouth. "Suck," I demand, pushing the hilt over her tongue as she continues to climax.

She's crying now, her throat trying to work as she cleans my knife, her body still vibrating with pleasure.

I leave her there with my knife sticking out of her mouth while I undo my pants.

There's no time for anything else. I need to be inside. I need to *fuck* her. To destroy her. To own her. To bring her back to life again.

I position myself between her legs and thrust into her.

She bows, her scream muffled by my knife. Her jaw is tight, telling me she's biting down around the hilt, keeping it from choking her.

I yank it from her mouth and toss it onto the ground beside us. Then I grab her hip with my bloody hand and fuck her.

I fuck her so hard she almost begs me to stop.

But it's primal. It's feral. It's *us*.

She wanted an escape. She wanted to not be able

to think. I'm giving her that in full, etching my name into her mind, ensuring all she can think about is me and my cock and the way I'm damn near raping her.

But it's not rape.

Because she's consenting, my name falling from her tongue on repeat as I drive her toward another climax.

She's falling apart in the best way, her tears soaking her face as I own her entirely.

I run my tongue along the salty flavor, loving that this pain is for me. That I brought her here. That I gave her the violence she yearned for, the distraction she required.

These tears are mine.

Her pain is mine.

Her freedom and mental reverie… those are for her.

A place for her to hide and just feel. An illusion of liberation. A release from our harsh reality.

She's weeping now, clinging to me as she releases all her emotions into our embrace. Her fear. Her anger. Her relief.

She doesn't hold back, and neither do I as I drill into her, forcing her into an oblivion that I know is going to make her fly.

"You're mine," I tell her, my lips against hers. "Mine to fuck. Mine to cherish. Mine to protect."

And I mean it.

She'll survive this, if she wants to survive it. Because I'll be there to push her along.

The next few days will hurt. The endgame may even shatter her.

But I'll pick up the pieces.

I'll glue her back together.

I'll help her soar again.

"Kage," she cries, arching into me as she tries futilely to keep up with my pace.

She sounds so broken. So utterly wrecked.

I love it. I love her. I love this moment. I love *us*.

And I tell her that with my tongue as I force her over the precipice, dragging her into euphoria with me. She continues to sob even while she comes, her orgasm decimating her reality and yanking her into a state of blissful peace.

It's a conundrum her mind struggles to comprehend.

A paradox that leaves her limp and exhausted beneath me as I spill inside her.

It's hot and consuming, my own climax seeming to go on and on as I claim her from the inside out.

I revel in the pleasure, shaking violently above her, while admiring her stricken expression. *So beautifully broken.*

I kiss her, praising her with my tongue, and eventually gather her into my arms after she falls into a catatonic state.

The emotions have crippled her. The intensity has exhausted her. And now it's my job to heal her.

I kiss the top of her head and hold her. "You're so perfect, Sydney," I tell her, not for the first time. "So strong and intelligent. I know this is a lot, but you can do this. *We* can do this."

She says nothing.

But I don't expect her to speak.

Just to listen. Just to feel. Just to float in her dreams and relax.

Tomorrow will be a new day.

Or tonight, she'll finally understand what it means to be mine.

Twenty-three
SYDNEY

I'M LOST IN A DREAM.

Floating. Flying. Soaring.

I'm really not sure.

Vaguely, I'm aware of being in water. Kage is beneath me, his hands running over my body, taking care of me, petting me, worshipping me.

But I can't tell if it's real. I can't define reality anymore.

All of this… everything that's happened… it's left me wondering who I am. Where I am. What fate brought me to this moment.

And yet, I'm not sure there's anywhere else I want to be.

I was already lost prior to coming here, uncertain of what future to pursue. Because nothing felt right.

However, Kage feels right.

Kage… feels like my end.

I'm not sure if that's a good end or a bad end, but he's the one standing in my path, demanding I follow him. And for whatever reason, I am.

He and his brothers have orchestrated all of this. Yet I don't fault him or even hate him for doing it. If anything, I understand him. Hell, I'm even in awe of him.

It's an intense game, one he's destined to win. All in the name of revenge.

Revenge that is well deserved.

Those families hurt his, and from what I've gathered, they're not the least bit remorseful.

When tested, Becca proved to be just like her mother. *She tried to kill me.*

But Kage and his brothers arranged it all in a way that guaranteed my safety.

It makes me wonder what would have happened, though, if she'd decided not to kill me. They clearly had a backup plan.

However, it seems that backup plan would never have mattered.

So do I even need to ask? Becca proved her "loyalty" to the organization the moment she chose me for this trip.

Which means that if killing me was the backup plan, it still would have been partially her fault for inviting me in the first place.

Kage's fingers comb through my wet strands, his lips against my temple. He's just holding me in this bathtub, waiting for me to surface from my thoughts.

I'm not sure where he sent me with his brutality, how he managed to drive me this far into my mind, but I'm thankful for it. He provided me with an escape, just as I'd asked, which led me to this state.

I feel at peace.

No turmoil. No concerns. No pressure to make a decision.

Just a pleasant silence, a place for me to collect my thoughts and sort through my feelings.

I'm no longer angry with him. I'm more angry with the others, their families, the horror they inflicted on his parents and brothers all in the name of greed.

They deserve their fates.

They deserve *worse*.

Kage should lock them all in a house and watch them burn.

Perhaps that's the true endgame for all of this.

I really don't know, and it's not my place to write that ending. But I'll support whatever Kage decides.

Which probably makes me insane. Or maybe just as dark-minded as him.

Life isn't meant to be all sunshine and roses. There are wicked paths, cruel intentions, and deceptive deeds. Some humans are innately selfish, and they'll go to any lengths necessary to destroy everyone around them in pursuit of their own "happiness."

That's what happened to Kage's family.

I can't even begin to understand that kind of pain. But I do comprehend loss.

Many called my mother selfish for killing herself.

However, I've always understood her need to be free. Fate delivered her a rough hand. I was the product of an unwanted encounter, given to her by a savage man who took what he wanted and left her to handle the consequences alone.

And those consequences were just too much for her to bear.

I could wallow in that choice, hate her for leaving me, despair at knowing the cause of my birth. But I chose long ago to survive. To fight. To *exist.*

However, I've never known *why.*

I've never understood my purpose or my path or my true desires in life.

Until Kage.

Something inside him calls to me, makes me feel whole and on the right track.

Perhaps we're just two deranged souls that

deserve one another.

I can live with that. I can live with him. I… I don't mind his claim.

I don't even mind that he keeps fucking me like I'm a toy. Perhaps I'm broken. Perhaps I've gone insane and dreamt all of this up.

But as I open my eyes to see the marble tile around us, I realize that I don't care. This is exactly where I want to be.

With him.

His hand curls around my throat as I glance back over my shoulder at him.

"Hello, little dove," he whispers, the nickname one he's used before, but not quite like this. Not in that gentling tone. It makes me feel cherished for some reason. *Adored*. "How are you feeling?"

I consider his question for a long moment before finally saying, "Whole."

It's a strange response.

But he nods like he understands. Because he probably does.

He uses his thumb on my chin to guide me back into a kiss, his lips soft and gentle against mine. However, the possession is clear in his touch. He's not letting me go.

And I really don't want him to, anyway.

We kiss for what may be hours, yet the tub never cools. The water drains and refills automatically, his high-tech gadgets seeming to apply to every aspect of his life.

His hand stays at my throat, his thumb brushing my pulse as his opposite arm wraps around my middle.

It's intensely sensual, the two of us naked and kissing in this massive tub. My neck is going to ache from the angle later, but this moment is worth the pain. *He* is worth all my pain.

He's endured more in this life than anyone should ever experience. Perhaps I have, too. That may be the truth that ties us together.

Truth, I marvel. *Truth is the platform that bonds us all together.*

How realistic that is—because it seems to connect me to Kage, too.

Our own personal truths. Our losses. Our pain. Our anger. Our intensity.

I've dated before, but so many men can't handle my mindset. They just don't get me.

Not like Kage does.

He sees me for who I am, like he has some sort of superpower to peer right into my very soul. But I see him, too. I feel his pain. I sense his anger. I revel in his need to control everything and everyone around him.

He won't let anyone hurt him or his family

again. He's the protector. The strength. The *enforcer*.

Which tells me he would have been the one to kill me in that alternate scenario where Becca let me live. Assuming that was the plan—to kill an innocent and watch as the rich kids try to cover it up.

I can't even be mad at him for it. He didn't owe me a damn thing. Kage and his brothers may have organized the initial trap, but Becca is the one who selected me as the mouse. Not him.

I tell him with my tongue that I don't blame him.

He does what he has to do for his family.

And something tells me that after today, he'll do what he has to do for me, too.

It's such a unique link between us, fortified by our spirits intertwining and marrying one another without our express permission.

I can feel it, that tug inside me that draws me to his inner flame, begging him to burn me with his lust and his convictions.

At some point unbeknownst to me, I agreed to be his.

I should hate him. I should want to run. But I believe him when he says he'll catch me.

Because I'll *let* him catch me.

I'll present myself to him, strip for him, and just let him do whatever the fuck he wants to me.

Because I trust him to see me through the pain,

to pull me out on the other side, to ensure nothing bad truly happens to me.

This is the kind of man who will kill anyone who tries to harm me.

Just as he'll do the same for his brothers.

It's a heady realization that leaves me breathless against him, my mind and heart succumbing to his seductive pull. "What happens now?" I ask him, my eyes opening to search his smoldering gaze. "What's next?"

He nuzzles my nose and lets me roll on top of him. My chest meets his, my legs automatically straddling his thighs, my lips still hovering against his mouth.

His hand moves to my nape, his arm swathing my lower back to hold me against him.

My neck immediately sighs in relief, but the rest of me begins to burn, this intimate position stirring all sorts of desire-driven thoughts inside my mind.

"We've created a video montage of all the confessions revealed this week, including the details spoken about our parents' murder. We'll be sending all those involved a preview of it tomorrow with a list of our demands."

"Which are?"

"To admit the truth. Or their children will do it for them." He tucks a strand of my hair behind my ear. "Someone will pay for these crimes. If the parents choose to save themselves, then their children will suffer instead. Just as we've suffered on behalf of our own parents."

A fitting end, I decide. "But what if they bring in the authorities?"

"They won't. We know too much, and we have enough leverage ready to be released that if they tried, we would simply ruin them anyway."

"You've been planning this for a long time." Something I already knew from what he's admitted, but it's worth saying again.

"Over a decade," he confirms. "Longer if you consider that this lodge was built about eighteen years ago, all with the intention of uncovering the truth about our parents."

Something about the dedication and focus required to create such a plan makes me like him that much more. He's determined. Ruthless. Knows exactly what he wants. And he's willing to kill to see it all through.

He's dangerous.

He's dark.

He's a villain.

Yet… I still want him to be mine.

"So what about me?" I whisper.

"What about you," he echoes, not as a question so much as a musing statement. "To be determined, I suppose."

A test, I realize.

He wants to see how I'll react to all his information, who I'll tell…

"We'll see, then," I say, determined to play this right.

He's the first thing in my life that makes sense. I'm not going to lose that over this game. And if he needs me to prove myself worthy of his possession, I will.

"Kiss me," I whisper, needing to lose myself in him once more. "Fuck me all night, Kage."

"If I have it my way, I'll be fucking you for the rest of our lives," he replies, his mouth brushing mine. His fingers curl into my hair as he takes charge, giving me exactly what I need.

More intensity. More mindless bliss. More brutal touches followed by sweet kisses.

And when I finally wake again, it's in the guest room, not his bed.

But there's a single black rose on the pillow beside me.

Along with a note that says, *Welcome to the endgame, Sydney.*

Twenty-three
SYDNEY

I REALLY HOPE KAGE MEANS IT WHEN HE SAYS "ENDGAME" because I don't want to spend another minute inside this fucking theater hall.

The alcohol, food, and luxurious seating are just cruel instruments meant to lull the prey into a false sense of comfort. When, in reality, this is a torture chamber.

No one notices, of course. They all consider themselves to be untouchable.

What does that feel like? I wonder. *To live a life without rules, where you don't have to think about anyone other than yourself?*

That's what makes Kage so different from them—he's learned the value of living. He's embraced the torment of this world, explored the darkness, and come out on the other side with a vengeful plan to right the scales.

His determination is intoxicating.

And I know he's about to put me to the test. I just don't know what he has in store. But I have to prove myself to him, to his brothers, to his *legacy*.

Because it can't be as easy as just claiming me for eternity.

He may have told me I'm his; however, now I have to earn that right.

I understand the game. I understand the stakes. And I'm ready to play.

Do your worst, I think, staring at the screen.

The waiter walks by with a tray of champagne. I deny a glass, taking some water instead.

Everyone is just sitting around chatting, as apparently they're all friends again. It's all fake. Their smiles aren't real. There's tension around their eyes. They're stiff, even while they laugh.

But this is what they're taught to do—to be each other's best friends, all for the sake of staying rich.

They're ready to pitch their "cover-up" to the voice.

Apparently, they spent most of yesterday working on it while I played with Kage.

That's fine. I already know what to expect.

They'll blame me. They may even try to kill

me. Perhaps that's part of the presentation they've prepared.

"We're ready," Preston says for the fifth time.

Landon has tried a few times, too.

They seem to think it'll inspire the voice to return to them sooner. Because the presentation isn't actually due until tomorrow.

"Maybe I can try reaching out via the computer?" Landon suggests. "Shoot our fathers a message?"

Preston nods. "Yeah, I don't want to waste an afternoon here if we don't need to."

Landon heads toward the exit while I roll my eyes.

They're so eager to point the blame at me, to throw an innocent under the bus, when Preston *knows* who killed Becca.

I'm not sure if he thinks there were blanks in that gun and actually believes she's alive.

Or if he's known the whole time that she's dead.

Perhaps it's the latter, which would explain how they came up with a plan so quickly yesterday—he was anticipating the need.

Did he admit it to the group? Or does he really not know?

I should have asked Kage, but I failed to think of it until this morning when I saw Preston again. And by then, it was too late. Because—

"It's locked," Landon says, causing my brow to

furrow as I glance over my shoulder at him.

"What?" Preston stands up to join his friend. He goes to twist the handle, like he thinks he'll have a magical touch or something, and frowns. "It is locked."

"That's what I said," Landon replies.

I refrain from rolling my eyes again—something I seem to be doing a lot of today—and sip my water. *So you're going to lock us all in here now, huh?* I think, glancing back at the screen. *Knock us out with some of that sleeping gas, maybe?*

Landon wanders to the back door of the room, the one we all went through for our virtual reality experience. "This is locked as well," he says.

No shit, I think. *Because if they locked one door, they would leave the other unlocked, right?*

Well, they may have done that if they wanted us to go down that hallway again. So I guess it's fair that he checked.

A bang has me looking back at Preston again. "Hey!" he shouts. "Unlock the door! Landon needs to grab his laptop!"

I snort. *Yeah, that's going to work.*

Of course, it doesn't.

Which leads Preston and Landon to try shouldering it open.

"Dude, you have to kick it," Brayden says

intelligently, then proceeds to slam his heel against the door.

Followed by a cry of pain.

Yep. I'm trapped in a torture chamber with a bunch of imbeciles, I think, sipping my water and looking at the screen again. *If you're trying to test my patience, it's working.*

All the men in the room appear to be trying to break the door down now.

"This is a fire hazard," one of them says, making me grunt.

But then my eyes widen as his words fully register. *Wait… He wouldn't… Would he?*

"Guys, chill," Gretchen calls out from the couch. She's lounging across it like a queen, her long legs crossed at the ankles as she uses the arm as a backrest. One slender arm is stretched out along the back, and she has a book in her other hand.

I don't know why her reading surprises me, but it does.

She just hasn't struck me as the type to be into books so much as climbing the society ladder. Not that she needs to since she's betrothed to Preston Michaels.

Except, she's a Walton. She's wealthy in her own right. So why does she even need to marry him for status?

Her blue eyes meet mine as she arches a blonde brow. "Like what you see, Cinderella?"

"Cinderella?" I repeat. "That's original." *And I don't even have blonde hair.*

She grins. "Do you have a preferred nickname?"

"Syd will do."

She shrugs noncommittally and goes back to her book.

It appears to be a romance novel.

Something tells me she'll be reading a lot of those while married to Preston because she'll need the escape those stories provide.

More time passes, my pulse beginning to race. *Have they set the Lodge on fire?* I wonder. *Have they turned this into some sort of escape room? What endgame are we playing at here, Kage?*

I have no doubt he would put my life in jeopardy.

And expect me to find my own freedom.

That's just the sort of test his warped mind would craft. Because he wants me to understand him. To *be* him.

He escaped a burning house.

Why not throw me in one to see what I do?

I finish my water and start analyzing the room, searching for another way out. But the two doors are our only option. Unless there's something behind the scre—

A giggle comes through the speakers, sending a chill down my spine.

Becca.

She's dead. I know she's dead. I watched the video.

Unless Kage… unless he lied.

Unless this was all still part of a test, part of his fucked-up and twisted game.

I know I'm his pawn. I know I'm the one recruited to be here because I'm expendable.

But I trust him.

Perhaps it's a naïve notion. Everything between us has been a complete and utter mindfuck. However, he hasn't done anything to truly hurt me.

Beyond the harsh and demanding sex, anyway.

Although, that's not a pain I mind. I actually rather enjoy it.

Because I'm depraved and sick like him. Lost in this dark world. Seeking my own sort of light.

The giggle grows louder now, and the screen flips on to show Becca's face. I immediately recognize the video—it's the one Kage showed me yesterday. The one where she received her tablet.

Everyone in the room has gone silent.

Several of the men are returning to their seats.

And Becca is talking to the tablet, telling it this is her private condo, so of course she's alone.

Landon joins me on the couch, his brow

furrowing at what he's seeing.

I fidget, already aware of where this is going. Assuming Kage showed me the truth yesterday.

He did, I think. *He hasn't lied to me at all.*

And as the video plays, that statement becomes truer and truer.

"What the fuck?" Landon breathes as Becca starts writing down the words for the recording we all saw on our second day here.

It continues into her actually repeating the words with a paper in her hand.

And ends with her being shot in the head by the man in the mask.

"But who is the killer?" the voice asks. "Who is the one holding the gun?"

"Sydney," someone says.

And the rest of the room echoes the sentiment.

I don't bother to fight them, because I already expected this. There's also nothing I can say to change their minds.

"Wrong answer," the voice informs them all as a new video begins to play, one showing the highlights from yesterday's working session.

My lips curl at the footage because I understand the point—blackmail.

All of them are actively working together to cover up the murder, debating how to pin it on me, who will voice what alibi, and how they'll all spin it as a jealousy killing.

"She wanted Becca's life," Gretchen says. "She told me that in secret."

"Me, too," Courtney echoes. "And after it became known that Preston is marrying Gretchen, she worried Becca would set her sights on Landon."

"She's been in love with me for years," Landon agrees with a nod. "So of course that would set her off."

I snort. "That's believable."

"Shut the fuck up," Landon demands.

I roll my eyes. "Or what? You'll frame me for murder? Oh, wait…"

This is ridiculous.

"It's our word against yours," he hisses, gesturing at the film.

I shrug. He's not wrong. He just doesn't understand how screwed he's about to be.

The voice already said it was the wrong answer, and it's rolling this footage for a reason.

"What's the right answer?" Preston asks, clearly acting as the only intelligent being in the room.

That you did it, I think.

But instead, the voice shocks me by saying, "Ask Sydney."

My eyebrows lift. "Excuse me?"

"Ask her what she knows. Ask her what's truly happening. And perhaps, if she tells you the truth, we'll set you free." The crowns start spinning on the screen as everyone looks at me.

"What do you know?" Landon demands, facing me.

Twenty-five
SYDNEY

*F*UCK. I DID NOT ANTICIPATE THIS.

"Are you fucking kidding me?" I look at the screen. "Really?"

This is how he chooses to test me? To see if I'll actually break?

I shake my head. "You all saw the video. Becca chose to bring me here to die. Clearly, I don't know anything."

"Then why are you so calm?" Preston asks.

"Calm?" I repeat. "You think I'm *calm*?" Because I don't feel calm. I feel *murderous*.

If Kage set me up just to leave me here, I will kill him.

I'll take that blade he used on me earlier and

ram it down his fucking throat.

He's testing you, some inner voice says. *Don't fail him.*

I nearly growl. Because I know it's true. I know this is all a goddamn test to see if I'll fracture under pressure. "I don't know anything," I repeat. "How could I? You're the ones who are the heirs, not me. I'm just a fucking pawn."

"Yet you've played the game all week," Brayden says, leaving his couch to start toward me. "Why?"

"Because I was told I didn't have a choice," I remind him. "Remember?"

"You keep disappearing," Courtney remarks. "Where have you been going?"

"To fuck the reception guy," Gretchen says with a snide smile. "She's sleeping with the staff."

"And they've told you something," Preston presses. "What have they told you?"

That your parents are monsters who attempted to murder their entire family, I want to say. But, of course, they already know this. That was the point of yesterday's lesson.

So what's the point of today's lesson? I wonder. *To see how much Sydney can take before she breaks?*

Because if that's the case, then Kage is about to find out that I can take a lot.

Something he already knows.

"What have they told you?" Preston repeats when I don't immediately answer.

"It's not what they've told me; it's what they've taught me," I say, taunting Kage a little as I glance at the screen. *This is all a big training session, right?*

"And what did they teach you?" Preston asks through his teeth.

I blink at him. "It was a *he,* not a *they*. And he taught me how to fuck." Because all the boys who came before him absolutely do not compare. They were trying to have sex. Kage? Kage didn't have sex. He *fucked.*

And I now know the difference.

Preston pushes off the couch to get in my face. "Do not play with me, Sydney. Or I'll fuck you while everyone else watches, and then I'll give everyone else a turn until you're ready to talk."

"Torture by sex?" I arch a brow. "I'm not sure whether to be amused or horrified." I look him over. "Hmm, yeah, horrified. Because the thought of letting you put your cock in me…" I make a gagging sound, and he slaps me across the face.

Ow. My jaw flexes with the movement, my chin stinging.

Landon has my throat in the next breath, cutting off my airway as he flattens me against the couch beneath him.

It all happens so quickly that I don't even have a minute to process it. "That douchebag is good enough to fuck you, but I'm not?"

I narrow my gaze and mouth, "Yes." Because that *douchebag* is definitely worthy of my body. While this guy? Absolutely fucking not. Landon couldn't hold a torch to Kage's touch. He doesn't even know how to properly strangle a woman.

"You fucking cunt," Landon snaps, squeezing harder. "Tell us what you know or I'm going to *end* you."

I grab his wrists and dig my nails into his skin.

Which only makes him squeeze harder.

I can't fucking talk, idiot, I want to snap.

But he doesn't seem to care.

He's too busy trying to kill me.

I see it then, the determination in his baby-blue eyes. He'll end me, just like this, and find a way to cover it up with his friends.

I'm the outsider, the one they want to frame, the one who's *expendable.*

But am I expendable to Kage?

Can I rely on him to save me?

No, I realize. *No, I can't.*

Because if he's not ready to reveal everything, he'll stay hidden. He'll choose his family over me.

And while part of me wants to hate him for that,

I can't.

It's the right decision.

This lesson is all about self-preservation, learning to save myself, just like he saved himself. I could easily spout his secrets to earn my own freedom, but that's not me.

There has to be another way out of this.

Another way to *survive*.

"Dude, you're killing her," Brayden says.

"She was going to die anyway," Landon replies, his expression intense.

"But we don't know what she knows yet," Preston reminds him. "Stop. We'll tie her up. We'll figure this out. Then you can fuck her and kill her."

How charming, I think. But I'm too tired to roll my eyes.

There's not enough air.

I've wasted too much time beneath him just clawing up his arms. I need to shove him off of me. Knock him onto the floor. *Something.*

My legs kick out—or try to, anyway—but his body easily holds mine.

This isn't like with Kage when I feel hot from him overpowering me.

This is terrifying.

This makes my skin crawl and my blood turn to ice.

"Landon," Preston stresses. "Come on. We need answers first." He grabs Landon by the shoulder and gives him a shove.

Which causes the hand on my throat to grip me tighter.

But it also frees up my torso and upper thighs a little as Landon's body jolts above mine from the push.

I pull one leg up to plant my boot against his abdomen, my final vestiges of strength going to that single limb.

And *push* just as Preston gives him another nudge.

Landon curses, his grip leaving my throat and allowing me some much-needed oxygen.

Only, inhaling makes me dizzy and I lose my momentum.

I immediately cover my face with my arms, trying to protect my neck.

Landon punches me once, not in the face but in the chest, and I wince out an "Oomph."

And then hands start trying to pull me off the couch.

I kick out, fighting for my life, but it's me against a sea of people.

But I'm absolutely wild, clawing and slapping and kicking and generally trying to breathe.

I can't focus on anything other than freeing

myself from their touch.

It's maddening. Someone restrains my arms, so I kick backward.

My throat is utterly raw. I can't swallow. My chest is aching.

And there's a round of applause sounding from the speakers now, vibrating the floor and making my head spin.

I fucking hate you, I think at Kage. Even while thanking him profusely for interrupting this insanity. For somewhat saving me from this fate.

Except it has nothing to do with me.

He's not helping me at all.

No, the applause is coming from some sort of broadcast.

My head is spinning as I try to focus. No one is holding me down now. They've all turned toward the screen.

"What the fuck is this?" Landon demands. "What's going on?"

I cough, my throat on fire.

I'm still near the couch.

Only a foot away.

I grab at the leathery fabric, trying to pull myself toward it, but a hand at my back makes me flinch. I glance back, half expecting to see Landon coming at me again. However, it's Gretchen. She has a concerned look on her face, one that gives me pause just long enough for her to assist me onto the couch. Then she hands me a fresh bottle of water.

No one else seems to notice.

They're all focused on the screen.

She sits beside me before following everyone's attention. Landon is standing next to Preston, both of them gaping at the broadcast.

I frown, noting the headline. *Breaking News: Covington Heirs Are Alive.*

Wait, what? I unscrew the cap and take several swigs of water as Lucas Matterhorn approaches a podium in a perfectly pressed suit.

He clears his throat at the microphone before saying, "Good afternoon. As many of you have likely heard, Judas Covington, Keaton Covington, and Loren Covington are alive."

"What the fuck?" Preston whispers.

"It was the decision of the branch managers of Covington Industries to protect the young heirs from the spotlight these last twenty years. With the deaths of their parents, we were concerned about the media presence in their lives. So we've hidden them from the public eye for the last two decades under false names."

False names? I repeat to myself. *Is that the story you're spinning?*

I can't imagine that faking the deaths of three

boys is legal.

Although, with how these people work, it would probably be easy for them to find an official to corroborate this story.

Unless it's true.

Did they really cover up their lives? Have Kage and his brothers been working with them all along?

No, that can't be right. What would be the point of this game, then?

The Covington boys want revenge for good reason. They wouldn't just work with these people to hurt their kids.

Unless Matterhorn found out and this is his response to it all.

I blink.

Did someone on the inside get word to the parents? Are they doing damage control before Kage and his brothers are able to carry out their plans?

I think of the note on my pillow this morning. *Welcome to the endgame, Sydney.*

No. This must be his endgame.

He told me they were sending videos to the parents today. Maybe they did it overnight. If there was enough footage of everyone trying to frame me for murder—thereby openly admitting they were trying to cover up Becca's assassination—it's possible that the videos went early.

But with Kage, who the fuck really knows?

"However, it's been decided that it's time for the rightful heirs of Covington Industries to take back control of their father's legacy," Lucas Matterhorn continues. "Effective immediately, I will be resigning from my position as lead chairman, and Judas Covington will be assuming my role." Apart from the slight shake of his hand, he appears perfectly at ease as he gestures to the side of the stage. "Judas?"

My lips part as the camera pans over to Judge, Kage, and Loki.

Judas. Keaton. And Loren.

All three of them enter the stage, not just Judas.

And they're all wearing suits.

"Wait..." Landon squints at the screen. "Isn't that the general manager?"

"And Kage," Gretchen puts in helpfully.

All eyes turn to me.

I swallow.

"What the fuck is going on, Sydney?" Landon demands, making me wince as he starts toward me.

But then Judge clearing his throat on the stage has Landon pausing to focus on the video again.

"Hello," Judge—*Judas*—greets everyone with a charming smile. A smile that looks so much like his father's that I can't believe I missed the familial resemblance.

All three of them have the same head of dark

hair.

But Kage is the only one with matching forest-green eyes.

"I'm sure this comes as a shock to a lot of you," Judas says. "But rest assured, Covington Industries is in good hands. It's our father's legacy, after all. And we've spent all our lives preparing for the positions of leadership required of our family."

There's a flurry of flashes, and *Judas* pauses to smile, as do *Keaton* and *Loren*.

"As Lucas mentioned, I'll be taking over as lead chairman," Judas eventually continues. "My brother Keaton will be handling finances. And Loren will be taking over the creative departments."

Voices rise on the screen, questions being fired at the brothers.

But Judas calms them all with a raise of his hand, the motion so practiced and regal that I can see why his brothers decided on him being the *king*.

"As information spreads regarding the last two decades of our lives, we are confident that you will see our merit in these roles and understand why we've chosen these specific leadership positions for ourselves," he says with a charming smile. "More information will be forthcoming, and our shareholders will all receive a formal update within the hour."

Another round of questions is fired at them, but Judas merely grins again.

"That'll be all for today. Just know that we look forward to introducing you all to a new era of Covington Industries." And with that, he steps away from the podium as an array of voices can be heard calling from the crowd.

Questions about the fire.

Questions about their parents.

Questions about how the branch managers hid them for twenty years.

Everything and anything is on the table, the cameras flashing as the three men move off the stage in the same direction that Lucas Matterhorn went.

And the screen goes black.

"What the actual fuck just happened?" Brayden demands.

"I think the Covington princes just reclaimed their thrones," Gretchen says casually, making me glance at her.

She's not surprised at all.

Which leaves me to wonder if this was all some elaborate plan from the inside, one that certain families were already aware of prior to today.

That would explain how Kage and his brothers were able to pull off this retreat.

Did he already detail that part to me? I wonder, trying to remember everything he's said. *Is this the part he left out? The part about how certain families are exempt from their revenge?*

Or did he lie to me about the game? About the revenge?

No. No, he wouldn't do that.

My mind is so busy spinning with questions that I don't notice Landon until it's too late.

His palm slams into my jaw, making my head rattle.

"You fucking bitch. You've known all along, haven't you?" he accuses me.

I duck when he tries to grab me, and roll off the couch to jump away from him. I put my hands up in front of me. "How could I have known?" I ask him. "Becca is the one who invited me."

"Maybe it's not real," Gaylord murmurs, his voice carrying from the back of the room. He hasn't left his couch, his expression thoughtful. "I mean, think about the simulation. None of that was real. Maybe this is fake, too. Another test. They're just using the staff to fuck with us."

Landon blinks and glances back at him. Then he looks at Preston. "Do you think that could be it?"

"At this point, I don't know," Preston answers honestly before focusing on me. "But she might."

Jesus, can't a girl catch a break? "Why would I know anything?" I ask them again. "Becca—"

"Stop with the bullshit," Landon snaps. "You've been fucking that Kage guy. What has he told you?"

"We don't do a lot of talking when we're together," I tell him. Not exactly a lie, right? We do seem to fuck a lot.

He growls, but Preston steps between him and me. "Chill, Matterhorn," he snaps. Then he looks at me and, in a much calmer voice, says, "Has he given you any reason to believe he may be Keaton Covington?"

The whole purpose of this week is to tell the truth. I've followed that mantra every day. Played every single game without once telling a lie.

And I find that today is no different.

I can't lie.

But I also can't tell the truth.

So I just stare at him and stay silent.

"Come on, Sydney. Think. Has he given you any reason to suspect him as being someone else?" His voice is condescending, making me want to roll my eyes for the umpteenth time.

"Who really killed Becca, Preston?" I ask him, canting my head to the side as I willfully change the subject. "Because it wasn't me."

He frowns. "What? We're talking about Kage, not Becca."

"Yet you all are intent on framing me for Becca. So why should I tell you a damn thing?" I inquire, meaning it. "And why on earth would you think a lowly being like me would know shit about any of this?"

"Because it's always the ones you least suspect," Griffin says. He's been mostly quiet, leaning against a nearby wall, watching it all unfold.

"True," Preston agrees, folding his arms.

Everyone is staring at me again.

Some of them with murder in their eyes.

"Even if I did know something, I would never tell you," I finally say, deciding I have nothing to lose.

I promised Kage I would win this game. That I would prove myself to him. That I would remain until the final moment.

I won't sacrifice his secrets. I won't give these people anything. I'll merely be me—a stubborn survivor with a flair for the sarcastic.

These assholes can't break me.

Only Kage can do that. And he has.

Because I'm willing to give up everything for him. Every ounce of my dignity. Every piece of myself.

"I'm not going to say another goddamn word," I conclude. "Because I choose *truth*."

Landon appears ready to slaughter me, which is nothing new. Preston looks disappointed. And the others... the others I don't even glance at.

Because I don't care.

If this final lesson was about understanding what Kage and his family went through, it worked.

I'm the odd woman out. The one being threatened. The one likely about to die.

But I'm going to stand here on my moral high ground and accept it.

Not just for Kage, but for me. For *us*. Because *that* is how the game should be played.

I choose truth, I think, glancing at the crowns spinning on the screen. *Even if everyone else is about to choose kill.*

Landon takes a step forward as a crackling noise echoes from the speakers. It reminds me of a fire, which is appropriate because the edges of the screen are going up in flames. Not real ones, just virtual ones, eating at the video.

Destroying the game, I think. *Killswitch.*

"This is the end of Truth or Kill," the voice says calmly as the last of the screen dissolves into the burning flames. "Thank you for playing. You are now free to go."

And the doors fly open.

Twenty-six
KAGE

THERE'S MY BEAUTIFUL GIRL, I THINK, TAKING THE laptop from Loki as soon as we enter one of Covington Industries' conference rooms.

He's just initiated the final sequence, destroying all evidence of the game, and Sydney is frozen against the wall.

Everyone is shouting.

She seems to be taking the brunt of their hatred, something that makes my heart ache for her. *This is how it has to be,* I tell her. *I need to know that you're truly mine.*

"She hasn't said a word," Loki tells me.

I nod. "I know." I can tell by the way she's pinned against that wall.

And my soul also knew she wouldn't betray us.

My heart, too.

But that didn't stop me from needing this final test. Because while I may trust her, my brothers need more than just my instincts to decide to agree.

They didn't outwardly say that. They also didn't request it. I just know them. I know *us*. And this… this is how we prove our loyalty to each other.

My little dove doesn't disappoint. She remains utterly silent as they yell at her. I rewind a bit of the feed to find out if she's done this the whole time or not.

And then I hear her speaking, knowing her words are for me.

"I'm not going to say another goddamn word," she says. "Because I choose *truth*."

Her eyes go to the screen, a hidden message lurking in their depths. I can almost hear her telling me she chooses truth even if everyone else chooses to kill.

She's choosing *our* truth, the foundation our relationship is built upon, and remaining silent.

For me. For *us*.

"I'm so going to marry this girl," I whisper, fast-forwarding to the present and watching as Landon slams his fist into the wall beside her head.

She doesn't even flinch, just stares him down.

The bruising around her neck confirms that he's already hurt her. I'll have to go back to review the footage later to see how far he took it.

Because there are strict plans in place—if he's truly harming her, my men are to react.

I won't let her die in there.

But she appears to be holding her own.

I'm not surprised. She's so much more than a pawn. She's a goddamn queen.

My queen.

And I'll come for her soon.

I stroke my fingers over the screen as the others begin to disperse, finally going through the doors we've left open for them.

It's utter chaos.

The families will be there soon.

Because we sent them all the footage from the week, including the cover-up scheme Loki recorded yesterday.

He and Judge were busy while I was away playing with Sydney. They put all the tapes together, creating a warped ransom note that essentially said, "How far are you willing to go to save your precious heirs?"

Lucas Matterhorn reached out first thing this morning after Loki unleashed a press release to a certain group of reporters.

The Covington children are alive.

He provided photographic proof.

And then he sent a copy to Matterhorn with a note that said, *Are you ready to talk yet?*

We didn't want to give them time to regroup.

And it worked.

Matterhorn asked for our demands, and we gave him a script to follow for today's press conference. Now he's in a room full of our lawyers working through the details of his resignation.

As are all the others.

Including Walton.

We agreed that it would be better for his family's safety if he resigned as well. But we'll hire his daughter later and give her a leadership role of some kind.

She plays herself off as a society slut, mostly because she knows that's the best way to gain secrets from men—after a good fuck.

She'll be going to law school.

And when she's done, she'll likely come on as our legal counsel.

Assuming Judge allows it. He and Gretchen have always clashed, her fiery personality not meshing well with his need for control.

Alas, I've found that Sydney's fire only stokes my inner flames. So I'll be taking more of that, and soon.

If she forgives me, I think as I watch her remain

strong as the chaos ensues around her.

I told her the purpose was to reveal the truth because I couldn't share with her the true endgame. Not until I knew if I could trust her.

In reality, telling the truth about that day would destroy the company.

Which is why we developed the takeover plan.

It isn't about the money or the fame, but about our father's legacy. He built that company from the ground up, and to watch it burn down because of his tragic death just didn't sit well with any of us.

Nor would it do any good for those who had remained loyal to us all these years.

So I wasn't completely honest when I told Sydney our intention was to have the families release the truth or allow their kids to do it for them.

That was just the threat—that if they didn't do as we asked, we would release the truth and watch them all burn.

But it wouldn't be about that day.

It would be about Rebecca Edington's murder.

And all the other sordid details we gathered over the last week.

In addition to the ones we had captured inside The Lodge's walls during their various visits over the past two decades.

They are all details we will one day release. However, we need to complete this takeover first.

Which means I need to get to work.

The stocks are already taking a hit due to the announcement today, something I anticipated. That's the real reason Loki arranged for a press release to go out early this morning to a select group of reporters.

We wanted the rumors to fly, to make the market volatile.

To freak out the partners about their stocks.

What they don't know is that I've already sold them all.

And repurchased them.

Under our own accounts.

The market will fall today, and likely into next week.

But we own sixty percent of the shares now—twenty percent each. Making us the majority partner.

We also have access to all our former accounts.

Meanwhile, the families who wronged us have nothing. Because I reallocated their investments into companies I know won't recover from our takeover.

Companies that Covington Industries will no longer be working with as of next week.

Matterhorn and his friends made a lot of crude deals, giving their friends various contracts at specific rates, all of which will be null and void with my brothers and me taking over the enterprise again.

The web woven by these miscreants is about to go up in flames.

And I can't fucking wait.

Once their resources are gone, and their friends no longer want to take their calls, the videos will begin to play.

The bribery. The hidden accusations. The legal cover-ups.

All of it.

Every sordid detail will go viral. The assholes will pay. Justice will be served.

We may not have been able to save our parents, but we will protect and preserve their legacy.

I wasn't lying when I told Sydney that we'd thought through every detail. She would now watch our plans unfold, see what mastery we created through Truth or Kill.

And she'll either welcome me into her world with open arms.

Or hate me for a lifetime.

The choice would be hers.

But regardless of that choice, she would be by my side.

"Because you're mine, sweetheart," I tell her as the room finally clears out around her. She's gazing at the screen with an unreadable expression. But I know she's dying a little inside.

All those harsh words.

Accusations.

Hateful statements.

They have to be taking a toll on her emotions right now.

Yet she stands with her back straight, her shoulders squared.

A true regal.

My intended queen.

My little dove.

"Soon," I promise her. "I'll come for you soon."

Twenty-seven
SYDNEY

Five Weeks Later

"THE COVINGTON MEN APPEAR TO BE SETTLING nicely back into society," a suit-clad female reports from my laptop screen. "They were all seen attending the Met Gala last night, but notably without any dates. However, that didn't stop several women from vying for a spot on their arms."

A series of images appears on the screen, each one making my stomach churn.

Especially the one of Kage leaning in to whisper into some woman's ear.

"The three young bachelors could be seen laughing amidst a circle of female celebrities later in the evening, leading many to wonder if the brothers will soon enter the dating scene."

My jaw clenches as I click the X to close the window.

I don't need this.

I don't need *him*.

He never returned for me. If it weren't for Gretchen and her father, I would probably still be stuck at that fucking lodge.

I still don't know why she offered me a ride. Maybe she took pity on me after everyone else told me to burn in hell.

She was the only one who seemed unaffected by the dethroning of the families. I thought perhaps she was part of the scheme, maybe a hidden member of the game.

But then her father lost everything, too.

That came three weeks *after* the game, though, when it was announced that the families were graciously redistributing the stocks back to their rightful owners—the Covington heirs.

I suspect that all played into whatever Kage and his brothers had originally intended.

It's clear that they forced the families out, but the truth about the fire never came to light.

Perhaps they made a deal.

Perhaps Kage lied.

Perhaps I never truly understood the game.

But it seems as though the truth about what

happened to Mr. and Mrs. Covington was never meant to be revealed. Such a scandal would destroy the company, and knowing Kage, he didn't want to spotlight his family in such a negative capacity.

Which confuses me because he told me that was his demand—to reveal the truth.

Yet everything that's happened over the last few weeks has been about taking control of their empire, not revealing the details discovered from the game.

So either he lied to me, or he's not done yet.

I keep hoping it's the latter.

Just like a pining part of me keeps waiting for him to come for me.

But seeing that newscast about the events of last night makes me realize that I'm pining over a man who used me and left me to suffer.

It's toxic and wrong.

Which pretty accurately describes Kage and our fling at The Lodge.

That doesn't stop me from dreaming about him.

Or thinking about him every day, all day.

I still live my life, though. I finish up the semester. I take my exams. And I maintain my high grade-point average.

Yet I can't figure out what to do now.

Graduation is this weekend, and I still haven't accepted my future. I've let job offers expire. I have two acceptances to graduate school, both with full-ride scholarships, if I decide to move forward with a master's in engineering management.

But nothing feels right.

I know it's because I'm waiting for Kage.

It's a stupid obsession. But I believed him when he called me his.

I trusted his claim.

I trusted our *truth.*

Did I not pass the final test? I wonder for the thousandth time. *Was I supposed to do something else during the endgame?*

I open a new browser and visit a page I now know by heart—the contact details for Covington Industries.

My fingers fly across the keyboard as I type out the note I've written every day for five weeks.

K,

Was I supposed to choose kill?

S

I stare at it for a long time.

Then hit the Delete key in a rhythmic motion that matches my heartbeat.

I don't even know if this contact form will reach him. It probably won't. And the word "kill" will probably be flagged. Police will arrive at my apartment. And yeah, that'll be a bad afternoon.

I keep waiting for the police to show up about

Becca.

But they haven't.

And I've been too afraid to search her name on the internet, to see what the news said about her death. Last month, our volleyball coach sent out a notice about her, telling us she died in a tragic car accident.

There was a memorial service.

I only went to see if Kage might show up.

He didn't.

Rebecca's parents weren't there either.

Neither was Landon or Preston or Gretchen.

I feel as though I'm being kept in the dark. Which shouldn't shock me—I was only a pawn, after all.

My eyes narrow at the Covington Industries page, another idea occurring to me.

A way to reach out to Kage in a manner that may just piss him off.

I consider it for a moment, then open up the employment page and search for jobs I qualify for with my degree.

There are a handful of entry-level programmer positions.

"All right, *K*," I say, selecting them all. "What if I lied? What if I do want to work for Covington Industries? Does that mean I broke a rule? Does that taint your precious game?"

I have fun drafting my cover letter, talking about how it's a dream to work for Covington Industries because I've always wanted to join a large corporate empire. Then I sign off with a little personal note about how I'm a "team player."

I'm the girl in the back of the canoe, pushing everyone else upstream and ensuring we all reach our destination, I type in closing. *Because I believe in open collaboration and helping others achieve their goals. You can trust me because I'm a team player. I value truth and honesty. And I am a firm believer in Covington Industries' founding principles.*

I smirk as I run through the document for any typos, then I upload it with my resume and click Submit.

"Let's see if that gets your attention, K," I say, closing my laptop and heading to my kitchen for a much-needed glass of wine.

I have another week to decide on my future.

After graduation, I tell myself. *Then I'll pick a path.*

I don't end up attending my graduation.

Instead, I picked up my diploma and left.

Graduations are for family celebrations, where

parents rejoice in the fact that they no longer have to pay tuition bills and that their children are finally growing up to be little adults.

As I don't have a family, I don't see the point.

And my school was paid for through scholarships.

"All for a piece of paper," I muse aloud, staring down at the cardstock with my name on it.

It's in an elegant script. Anton University's logo is pretty, too.

But the diploma feels meaningless.

I went into computer science because I enjoy puzzles. But I solved the biggest one of all over spring break, only to be left more alone than ever.

It makes me wonder how I was living before everything happened.

Because the experience made me feel more alive than ever.

And now... now... I look down at my drink. *Now I'm just becoming an alcoholic.*

Not really true. I've been drinking out of the same bottle all week. My grocery money is minimal with the scholarship, so I have to be frugal with my expenses.

Perhaps I should have taken some home with me from The Lodge.

But I was so focused on leaving at the time that I didn't really consider taking anything with—

A knock on my door interrupts my depressive musings, making me frown. The pizza I ordered is already on the table, mostly untouched.

I'm not expecting anyone else.

So I ignore the door and just focus on my wine instead. Besides, it's probably a wrong address or something. Or a neighbor wanting to borrow something.

I'm not home, I think at whoever it is and go back to my thoughts.

Except the person knocks again.

I glare at the door. Obviously, I'm not in the mood to answer it.

"There's no one here," I shout, fully aware that I just gave myself away and not caring at all. Whoever it is wasn't invited over. So he or she can fuck right off.

The person responds by sliding a key into the lock and twisting it, causing my blood to go cold.

"Oh, shit…" I set my glass down and dart into the kitchen to grab a knife from the butcher block.

But someone is on me before I can use it. I kick backward, then stab wildly as I try to hit whoever the fuck is grabbing me.

Strong hands ensnare my wrists as I'm spun around and pinned against my foyer wall.

The knife clatters to the floor as a pair of dark green eyes smolder down at me. "Well, hello to you, too, gorgeous."

My heart leaps into my throat. "K-Kage?"

"Mmm, I've missed that name," he whispers, his nose running along my cheekbone. "'Keaton' is so fucking formal."

Oh God. He's here. Kage is finally here.

I can't decide if I want to punch him or kiss him.

But he takes the decision away from me by capturing my mouth with his in a bruising embrace meant to make me bleed.

He's punishing me.

Because of my job application? I wonder.

Except.

Hold on.

Shouldn't I be the one punishing him?

Yes. Yes, I should be the one punishing him.

I growl and bite his lip. *Hard.*

And he fucking chuckles in response.

Because of course he likes that. He's a goddamn psychopath.

He releases my wrists to grab my hips and hoists me up against the wall, forcing me to wrap my legs around his waist.

Then he presses his impressive erection into me, showing me how much I've turned him on with that little bite.

"I fucking hate you," I breathe against his

mouth. "You left me."

"I didn't."

"You did," I snap, furious all over again. "And then ran off to a fucking gala to flirt with celebrities and whatever the fuck else you've been doing."

He huffs a laugh as he pulls back to stare at me. "You've been checking up on me, little dove?"

I glower at him. "You left me there, Kage. You left me in that damn lodge with no way home."

"Oh?" He arches a brow. "Then how did you get back here?"

"Because Gretchen offered me a ride."

He nods. "Yes. And who asked her to do that?"

"No one. She just... she just randomly..." I trail off, his words starting to register as my earlier curiosity about her comes back. "So she did know."

"A bit," he concedes. "Her parents are the ones who got us to safety that night. After we jumped out the window."

I gape at him. "*What?*"

"Put your arms around me, gorgeous," he says, pulling me away from the wall so that I have to comply. "I asked Gretchen's father to bring you back here. Because I couldn't do it myself. And yes, she knew the whole time."

"But you bankrupted them."

"Because no one can know that they're involved."

"Yet you just told me," I whisper as he carries me into my bedroom.

"Because you're mine," he replies while lowering my feet to the floor. "And as you're a *firm believer in Covington Industries' founding principles,* you'll understand me when I tell you never to breathe a word of this to anyone else. Only me."

Oh, shit. "You saw my application."

"Of course I fucking saw your application. I watched you type the damn thing."

I blink at him. "What?"

He smiles. "Come on, Sydney. You don't think I've missed you, too?" He tugs on my shirt. "Arms up."

I'm not sure why I comply, but I automatically do.

He drags the T-shirt up and over my head, his gaze immediately falling to my chest. "No bra again. Good. That'll be your forever state going forward."

"Excuse me?"

He pulls my yoga pants down and goes to his knees to remove them completely from my legs. His forest-green eyes glitter up at me. "Consider yourself hired, beautiful," he says. "But I'll be the one in the back of the canoe, not you."

I gape at him. "Wh-what?"

"Pushing *you* upstream, guiding *you* toward

your goals," he murmurs, reciting parts of my cover letter while removing my underwear. "Goal number one." He presses a kiss directly to my clit. "Making you scream."

"Kage."

"Yes, sweet girl, just like that," he praises, his hands grabbing my hips. When I start to squirm away, he stands and knocks me back onto the bed. "Grab your headboard for me, gorgeous."

"I haven't seen you in, like, six weeks," I tell him. "Maybe I don't want this anymore."

He snorts as he yanks off his shirt and lets it fall to the floor. "Don't insult me, Sydney. You love me."

"I do not."

"Yes, sweetheart, you do." He pulls off his belt.

I try to scramble backward on the bed, to sit up, to do *something* other than lie here and take it.

But he grabs my ankle and yanks me back down. "Don't, Sydney. Don't you dare taint this now."

"You left me for almost six weeks!" I exclaim. "You can't just come in here and expect everything to be normal between us."

He kicks off his shoes but leaves his pants on as he places one knee on the bed.

His palms go to my thighs as he spreads them and pins my legs to the bed.

"Kage," I snap.

"Shh," he hushes, crawling over me and caging me beneath his exquisite form. "I think you've forgotten that nothing has ever been normal between us, sweetheart," he says right against my ear.

He laves the shell of it, then presses an open-mouthed kiss to my now raging pulse.

My thighs clench in response.

My body going up in flames.

God damn it, why can't I fight him off?

Because I don't want to.

Oh God, because I don't want to at all…

"Don't worry, little dove," he whispers darkly. "I'll remind you of who we are together. And when I'm done, you'll remember that you're mine."

Twenty-eight
KAGE

Sydney's midnight irises glower up at me, her fiery spirit coming to life right before my eyes. "*No,*" she says.

"No?" I repeat, my eyebrows arching.

That's a word she's never said to me before.

And it's just enough of a shock to give me pause.

I go to my knees between her sprawled legs and stare at her beautiful form. She's naked. She's wet. She's obviously aroused. Her chest is pink, her cheeks are flushed, and her pussy is glistening.

"You want me," I tell her. "Why are you telling me no?"

"Because you… you *lied* to me, too. And then you never came for me."

"I'm here now."

"Six weeks later."

"Yes. Because I needed to ensure our takeover went as planned and to guarantee the safety of my family. And you needed to graduate."

Some sort of armor melts from her expression, my feisty little dove revealing a glimmer of pain.

Pain that I feel deep inside my very soul.

Pain… that I worry I somehow caused.

"I thought I failed," she finally says, her dark irises turning into liquid obsidian. "I… When you didn't come… I thought… I thought I failed the final test."

I stare at her, stunned by her admission. "Sydney, you could never fail me." Something I know because of the game. Because of all the tests. Because of the way she handled each and every lesson.

I know her.

I know she's meant to be mine.

But I'm now realizing that I failed her. I gave her space to finish school while I worked on securing everything at Covington Industries.

However, there wasn't a single moment when I wasn't with her. When I wasn't *watching* her.

But she didn't know that.

She didn't realize I've been here the whole time.

How did I miss these obvious clues? Her pain? Her sadness? Her loneliness?

I can see it now in the way her lower lip wobbles. She thought I disgraced her. That I lied and left her to resume life without me.

"Oh, sweetheart, no." I climb over her again, this time to cage her in beneath my body, to ensure she feels me protecting her, *claiming* her. "I never left you at all. I've been with you the whole time, watching you study, ensuring your safety, waiting for you to finally send that note about choosing kill."

Something I now realize I misunderstood.

She was asking me if she should have chosen kill instead of truth.

Because she thought she played the game wrong.

"Fuck, Sydney. I'm sorry. I only gave you space to finish school. That's why I'm here now. You're done. Your lease is up in a few weeks. And now it's time for *us*."

"But you're back on your throne."

"Yes, and I'm missing my queen," I tell her, my hand cupping her face. "I meant it when I claimed you, Sydney. I meant every fucking word." I brush my lips against hers. "None of it was a lie."

"But you never revealed the truth," she whispers.

Okay, so one thing was a lie. "Revealing the truth would tarnish the family legacy. Reclaiming our kingdom mattered more. But those assholes will burn, Sydney. I vow it."

"How?" she asks, searching my gaze. "How will they burn?"

"When we release the truth about Rebecca Edington," he replies. "Along with a myriad of other shit. They'll be buried alive in legal troubles without anyone around to dig them out."

"All of them?"

"All of them except the Waltons," I confirm. "Everyone else will pay for their sins." I consider that for a moment. "Actually, we may also exclude Gaylord Pompkins. We can't find much about him because he seems to be a pretty good guy. Loki's still digging. If his history proves accurate, we may consider hiring him."

Because from what we've gathered, he's not very close to his parents.

And while we believe in punishing those who hurt our families, we don't believe in harming innocents.

"Gaylord may be spared," I reiterate. "Gretchen will definitely be spared and may eventually come to work with us when she finishes law school. But the others… they'll pay."

"Will you release the video of Preston killing Becca?" she asks.

I shake my head. "No. He was never supposed to remove the mask. The point was to frame them all for covering up her murder, not to pin it on one person specifically. It was a group effort. And they all deserve to burn for what they did."

"So you're keeping some anonymity. Like in the movie."

"Yes, I suppose. And like the movie, all evidence of the game has disappeared entirely."

I'm only openly discussing this here because I know Sydney's apartment is clean—I swept it myself six weeks ago before installing a security system for her.

She has no idea.

Obviously.

Because I never told her.

Something I now realize was a mistake.

"I'll tell you anything you want to know," I say. "You're mine, Sydney. But I'm just as much yours."

"Is that why you went to the gala earlier this week and played with celebrities?"

I snort. "Appearances, little dove. Would you like to attend the next one with me?"

Her eyebrows lift. "What? *No*."

I laugh. "That's something we may need to negotiate, Sydney. I want the world to know you're mine, and that requires being seen together."

"That's not why I brought it up."

"No?" I tease, brushing my lips against hers again. Because fuck, I missed this woman. So damn much. "You were jealous?"

"No," she answers too quickly.

"You were jealous," I echo, smiling. "You have no reason to be jealous, gorgeous. You're the only woman I've been with since we met. And the only woman I'll be with for the rest of our lives."

Her eyebrows hit her hairline. "That's one hell of a declaration, Kage."

"I'm all about truth, sweetheart. You know that. And besides, we're in love, aren't we?"

She narrows her gaze again. But she doesn't refute it this time. "You lied about the demands."

"Yes. Because I needed to know you wouldn't tell anyone," I admit. "And you didn't. You *passed*."

"Maybe I want to test you," she says, causing me to grin again. "It's not funny, Kage."

"I'm amused by the thought of being tested. What would you like to test me on, sweet girl? I'll do whatever you ask."

"Oh?" She considers me for a moment. "Maybe I want Landon dead for *attacking* me while you watched."

"I wasn't watching," I tell her, my amusement dying. "And if you want him dead, I'll deliver his head on a fucking platter to you." I ensure she can hear how serious I am via both my tone and the look I level at her. "Just say the words, Sydney."

Some of her ire flees her expression, her dark

eyes searching mine. "You'll kill for me."

I don't hesitate. "Absolutely."

"Without even blinking."

"Yes." I run my thumb across her cheekbone. "Or I'll hand you the gun and let you do it yourself while I hold him."

Her thighs tense around me, her body seeming to vibrate in response to my words.

My little dove likes that, I think, my gaze falling to her lips. *She likes the idea of us killing.*

But of course she does. She's my perfect woman. My dark-haired beauty driven by instincts and truth, and understanding my need for blood.

"I love you," I whisper. "I think I fell for you the moment you approached me at that desk and asked about canoes."

Her brow furrows. "You never did get me a canoe."

"On the contrary, sweetheart, I bought you several. They're back at The Lodge. And I'll order more whenever we pick our future home."

"Future home?" she echoes.

"Unless you prefer to live at The Lodge indefinitely?"

"Fuck no," she says, making me grin.

"I thought that might be the case," I admit. "But it's really not a bad place to live."

"Several of those rooms will need to be gutted,

including the *theater hall.*"

I chuckle. "Noted. But we don't have to live there. We can go wherever you like." I kiss her again. "And you don't have to decide now."

She studies me again, her eyes filling with more emotions than I can keep up with. "You're really serious about this."

"Of course I am, Sydney. Why else would I be here right now?"

"For a booty call?" she suggests.

"If I wanted that, I could have had that at the gala," I point out.

Her eyes narrow. "Get the fuck off of me."

I chuckle, amused by her jealousy. "Sweetheart, I don't want anyone other than you." Which I've already said, but apparently she needs to hear it again. "I'm here because it's time for you to be mine. It's as simple as that."

"It's not that simple."

"It *is* that simple," I correct her. "Sydney, we're not normal. We're not a fairy tale. We're not traditional or vanilla or anything else that society expects of us. We're *real*. We're *us*. We're fucked up and twisted and absolutely meant for each other. And if you would let me fuck you, you would know that it's true."

"Not everything is about sex, Kage."

"What we have is so much deeper than just sex,

Sydney," I counter. "We're *connected*. You're mine, little dove. Whether you accept it or not, you're still mine."

I can tell she wants to argue.

So I kiss her and let our tongues do the talking instead.

She bites me.

And I bite her back.

It's brutal. It's savage. It's *perfect.*

She wants to fight me and I welcome it. *Hit me. Scratch me. Make me bleed.*

Because that's us. That's how we fuck. That's how we coexist. That's how we *breathe.*

"I've missed you so damn much," I tell her, my hands cradling her face. "Fuck, Sydney. You have no idea how many nights I've dreamt of you. Of *this*. I can't go another day without you."

"You're the one who left me," she says, arching into me. "Not the other way around."

"Technically, you left The Lodge, sweetheart." I kiss her again. "And why do you think I have keys to your place?"

She stills.

"Yeah," I whisper, my lips going to her ear. "I wasn't lying about being with you the entire time. There's never been a single moment where you weren't protected by me and my resources. I only gave you freedom to finish school. But you've never once stopped being mine. Just as I've never once stopped being yours."

"Why didn't you just tell me?" she asks.

"Because I wanted everything to be ready for you, Sydney. I'm not lying when I say we can live wherever you want. The company takeover is complete. The world is ours. And I am *yours*."

She stares up at me with a look of awe in her gaze. "You're serious."

"I believe we've already covered that, sweetheart," I reply with a small smile. "Fuck tradition. Fuck normal. Fuck propriety. Be mine, Sydney. And let me be yours."

"You love me," she whispers.

"I love you," I echo, aware that it's not conventional and not giving two shits about what's expected of us now. I lead with my heart. I lead with my instincts. I lead with my goddamn soul.

And this woman is it for me.

Just as I know I'm it for her, too.

"I was waiting for you," she says after a beat. "I couldn't make a decision on what to do… because all I wanted was you."

"Is that why you sent in that application?" I ask her.

"No. I wanted to piss you off."

"You wanted my attention," I translate, grinning.

"Well, you have it now, little dove. So what are you going to do about it?"

She studies me for a long moment, her dark gaze brimming with intelligence. "I'm going to keep you," she finally says.

My lips curl once more. "Yeah?"

"Yeah," she echoes. "Because I love you, too."

Now I'm full-blown smiling. "You love me."

She rolls her eyes. "That's what I just said, Kage."

"I know. I just wanted you to admit it again." Because it's music to my ears. A song that caresses my heart. Words that burn inside my soul. "You're mine, Sydney Evans."

"And you're mine, Keaton Covington."

"Call me Kage," I tell her.

"Then you'll call me Sydney."

"Sydney… Covington," I say, considering the name.

Her eyes go wide. "Oh my God, are you proposing now?"

"Well, not anymore since you keep forgetting my name," I tease her.

"*Kage.*"

"That's better." I reward her with a kiss. "And no, sweetheart. That's not a proposal. But we both know it'll happen someday." I lower a palm to her belly. "When we're ready."

"And now you're talking about kids? I'm on the pill."

"I'm aware." I lower my lips to her ear. "But one day, you won't be. And yes, I want kids."

"You're insane."

"I'm realistic," I correct her. "Yet another conversation I believe we've already had." I consider her for a moment. "You clearly need to be fucked, Sydney. Six weeks has disrupted your memory of us."

She appears ready to argue, but something stops her from proceeding down that route.

"You know what, Kage? I think you're right. How about you show me just how not-normal we are." She wraps her arms around my neck. "Remind me that I'm yours."

"It would be my pleasure, Sydney," I reply, kissing her soundly. "Now grab the headboard. And remember my name."

"Kage, Kage, Kage," she chants.

"Beautiful, sweetheart," I say, removing my pants. "Now I'm going to make sure you never forget it again."

Epilogue
KAGE

Six Months Later

"Hello, Ms. Evans. I need you to pick a box."

Sydney glances up at me from her desk. "What?" Her eyes are a bit dazed from her work. Loki—he's chosen to go by that name instead of Loren—has her working on some new program for a gaming system.

I don't know all the details.

But Sydney is enjoying it, and that's all that matters to me.

"I need you to pick a box," I repeat, holding up a projection screen from my phone.

Her expression shutters. "Kage..."

"Pick a box, Ms. Evans."

She narrows her dark gaze. "Sixty-nine."

"Sixty-nine is not a valid number, but it's duly noted for later," I tell her. "Now pick a real box."

"I don't want to play this game."

"You say that like you have a choice," I reply. "Pick a box, Ms. Evans."

"Seriously, Kage?"

I arch a brow, ensuring she knows just how *serious* I am.

She growls, and the sound goes straight to my groin. I knew this would piss her off. It's exactly why I created this little game.

Or rather, I asked my brother to create it. He's the computer whiz in the family.

"Fine." She shuts her laptop with a little too much force. "Box one."

"An excellent choice, Ms. Evans," I say, selecting the box for her. "Now remember, this is a game of truth. So please answer honestly."

"I'll consider it," she deadpans.

"There will be consequences if you lie," I warn.

"I'm terrified."

"You should be, Ms. Evans. This is a very serious game."

She rolls her eyes. "Ask your question, Kage."

I enlarge the text on the screen and read the question aloud. "Would you rather me fuck you on the desk, or kneel between your legs and eat your pussy?"

"Right now? I choose you on your knees and apologizing for making me play this game."

"That's not what the question asks, Ms. Evans. Would you like me to fuck you on the desk—"

"Kneel between my legs and eat my pussy," she says.

"Excellent," I murmur. "Now pick a second box."

"What?"

"The instructions said nothing about doing it now," I tell her. "So pick a second box, Ms. Evans."

She releases another rumble, causing my balls to tighten in anticipation. "The one with a number two on it."

"Beautiful. Now remember, Ms. Evans, if there is someone you wish to remove from the room before answering, all you need to do is shoot him."

"Give me a gun and I'll comply," she retorts, making me grin.

"But perhaps you want to hear the question first?" I suggest.

She waves her hand. "Fine. But then I want a gun."

"Of course, Ms. Evans." I click the second box. "Would you prefer going to the lake this weekend to play with your new canoe, or going to the islands and testing out the beds at our new home on the beach?"

She considers for a moment. "The canoes."

I nod, expecting that response. "There's one final box, Ms. Evans. May I select it now?"

"Yes," she replies, her expression giving nothing away.

I select box number three and enlarge the screen again. "Would you be entirely opposed to becoming Mrs. Covington soon? Yes or no."

She blinks at me. "Are you proposing to me with a game that's going to self-destruct as soon as I finish answering?"

"That depends on how you respond to the question, Ms. Evans." I cock my head a little. "And we did meet because of this game. So some may call it fitting."

"Some may call it morbid and wrong," she argues.

I shrug. "Or romantic in a fucked-up way."

She laughs and shakes her head.

"Is that a no, then, Ms. Evans? Or are you still searching for that gun?"

"I think I would prefer a blade," she tells me.

I smile. "There's one in my back pocket."

She stands and walks toward me, her tight jeans and tank top making me want to drop my phone, strip her, and fuck her on the desk… after satisfying her between her thighs, of course.

Sydney reaches around me to slip her fingers into my back pocket, then pulls out the knife in question.

"Are you going to kill me, Ms. Evans?" I ask her softly.

She considers me for a moment, the blade twirling between her fingers. "No, Mr. Covington. I think I'll choose truth." The metallic edge stills. "No, I'm not entirely opposed to becoming Mrs. Covington. But don't you dare propose to me with this stupid game."

"I wouldn't dream of it," I tell her, smiling as the game goes up in flames on my phone, all traces of it disappearing after she voices her final answer.

I wasn't actually proposing.

I was just testing the waters.

Because I do have a proposal planned for this weekend.

It'll happen in her new canoe, as I knew that was what she would choose.

So that's where I'll ask her to become my queen.

There will be no more games between us.

Because this is our life now. Our truth. Our abnormal version of a happily-ever-after.

"I love you, little dove," I whisper.

"I love you, too," she replies, leading me backward to the desk. "And I changed my mind."

"Yeah?"

"I want you to fuck me on the desk instead."

"That's not how the game is played, sweetheart," I say, pushing her into her chair instead. "Now give me back that knife and take off your jeans. I have a pussy to eat."

The End

If you enjoyed the dark and suspenseful undertones of *Truth or Kill,* consider checking out the Kinsley Elite Series, where not all dreams have a happy ending. This is something Emma Adrian learns the hard way after she's recruited into a secret society and told that she must qualify for the Olympics in five swimming events. Or die.

USA Today Bestselling Author A.C. Kramer is the New Adult & Contemporary Romance pseudonym for Lexi C. Foss. New Adult Romance is her guilty pleasure, coffee is her addiction, and swimming is her escape.

For details about current and future works, check out her website below:

https://www.authorackramer.com/

Also by THE AUTHOR

Standalone Novels:

Truth or Kill

Kinsley Elite Series

Colton's Secret
Colton's Legacy

Mershano Empire Series - Lexi C. Foss writing as A.C. Kramer

Book One: The Prince's Game
Book Two: The Charmer's Gambit
Book Three: The Rebel's Redemption